*There's nowhere hotter than the South, especially with three men who know how to make the good times roll. But one of the Bayou Bachelors is about to meet his match...*

New York City stylist Poppy Kaminsky knows that image is everything, which is why she's so devastated when hers is trashed on social media—after a very public meltdown over her cheating fiancé. Her best friend's New Orleans society wedding gives her the chance hide out and lick her wounds...

Brandon Boudreaux is in no mood to party. His multi-million dollar sailboat business is in danger of sinking thanks to his partner's sudden disappearance—with the company's funds. And when he rolls up to his estranged brother's pre-wedding bash in an airboat, a cold-as-ice friend of the bride looks at him like he's so much swamp trash.

The last person Poppy should get involved with is the bad boy of the Boudreaux family. But they have more in common than she could ever imagine—and the steamy, sultry New Orleans nights are about to show her how fun letting loose can be...

# FULLY DRESSED

*A Bayou Bachelors Romance*

## Geri Krotow

**LYRICAL CARESS**
Kensington Publishing Corp.
www.kensingtonbooks.com

# Chapter 1

"Poppy!"

Poppy Amberlin Kaminsky had never been so happy to hear her *real* name, no matter that she'd spent the last eight hours and had taken a taxi, train, and plane to do so. All to get to a place she swore she'd never come back to after a spring break visit almost a decade ago.

It was hard to tell whether the New Orleans' bayou air or her best friend's cloud of Kate Spade *Live Colorfully* perfume embraced her first, but once crushed against the familiar curvaceous figure of Sonja Brisco, her college bestie, it didn't matter. Poppy meant to give the bride-to-be a reassuring, "glad to see you" hug, but instead ended up holding on for dear life. Tears shoved past her carefully made-up eyes, threatening to drip off her lash extensions. They were the only part of her previous life that she'd kept.

Sonja pulled back and stared. "Let me get a good look at you. What the hell did you do to your hair?"

Sonja's expression reflected the shock Poppy had also experienced at her first glance of her new do. Gone was her—or rather, *Amber's*—signature sleek brunette bob. Her wild waves were back, as was her honey-blond ombré, albeit with a little more brass. She self-consciously reached for her bleached locks. "It's part of my getaway disguise." As was the huge pair of sunglasses she'd worn from New York City to Louisiana, which had worked since she'd garnered minimal attention on her flight. An unusual event for Poppy after being publicly dumped and Twitter-shamed by her ex-boyfriend. "Ex" as in *I want to draw an X across his face every time I see it*. "It's my real color, so at least the roots will grow out with no issue."

"Aw, boo." Sonja lifted the shades from Poppy's nose as she uttered the Cajun endearment and Poppy wanted to weep with the relief of having the one person who really *knew* her—who got who she was, who she'd been, how far she'd come—look into her eyes and smile with no judgment. "That rat-ass did a number on you, didn't he?"

Poppy shrugged. "Screw him. That's history, baby. Two months and twelve hundred miles away. I'm here, and you're getting married!" They both squealed and hugged, hopping around as if they were still college roommates with big dreams in front of them. Intact dreams that weren't shattered in skin-piercing shards about their feet, as were Poppy's.

"I can't wait for you to meet Henry." Sonja gushed as she opened the hatch of her BMW SUV and reached for Poppy's tote. "And he can't wait to meet you."

Poppy put her sunglasses back on and took in the upgraded Sonja. Gone was the straightened shoulder-length hair of their college days, replaced with a sexy soft afro. Lustrous pearl drop earrings glistened in Sonja's ears. No more flip-flops but designer wedge sandals. Sandals that matched her thousand-dollar bag.

"What?" Sonja didn't miss a beat. "Oh, these old things?" She posed like the magazine model she resembled but after a split second bent over in laughter, her smile flashing as honest and warm as it had ever been. "Poppy, you look like you can't believe it. A nice paycheck and fancy clothes aren't exclusive to New York City."

"Did I ever say they were?"

"You don't have to. Hell, I've been trying to get you here for years and I had to go and get knocked up and married before you showed."

Poppy's stomach flipped. "You're pregnant?"

"Surprise!" Sonja threw her arms up in a big *V*, joy radiating from every inch of her curvy frame. Which was about to grow rounder. "But it's going to have to be our secret. It's super early, but I have all the signs and symptoms. I'm waiting until our wedding night to tell Henry. That man is always surprising me, spoiling me, and I want to be able to do it for him, just once." Sonja's eyes sparkled the way Poppy had once dreamed hers would. Once she was married and having Will's babies.

"How exciting!" Her response sounded so lame even to her own ears. It wasn't Sonja's fault that Poppy had planned to be pregnant with her own baby by now, after having her own spectacular wedding on Will's yacht as it cruised Long Island Sound. She decided on the spot to save her pity party for later. This weekend her wounds had to remain in her room, away from Sonja and the gazillions of Louisianans she was about to meet. She hadn't packed mini-bottles of Maker's Mark and a two-pound bag of Hershey's

Kisses for nothing. Although as the heat was already weighing in on her, she'd be lucky if the chocolate drops weren't all mush.

Brushing her ruminations aside, Poppy leaned forward and gave Sonja a solid kiss on the cheek, seriously happy for her friend. And for herself—it was a relief to close the door on her sad life for the next few days. "We have a lot of catching up to do. I know it's your big weekend, and that we can't do it all now, but I have to tell you I'm so thrilled to be here with you, and happy that you've found your soul mate."

Sonja laughed and gave her another quick hug before she hustled them both into the car and drove away from the New Orleans airport.

"How much of this do you remember from freshman spring break?" Sonja spoke loudly, as she had the sunroof open and the windows halfway down. The tropical air that blew against Poppy's face was a balm after the chill that remained in New York's still-slumbering spring.

"I remember that"—Poppy pointed at the Superdome as they sped by it—"and I remember it being a lot muggier than it is right now."

"It's supposed to get ugly by Saturday, but I'm hoping the rain stays away at least until Sunday. All I'm asking is for the wedding to go off smoothly and for Henry and I to get out of here for our honeymoon."

Poppy nodded, not wanting to share that the weather app on her phone predicted rain in a big way starting tomorrow, early. Before the rehearsal dinner. "The ceremony's all inside, right?"

"Of course. Henry's from a long line of Catholics—they wouldn't be happy with anything but a full-on Mass. They wanted it at Our Lady of the Rosary downtown. It's where Henry's little sister went to school, so they have ties there. But we ended up picking St. Louis Cathedral. We love the history of it."

"Our Lady help of what?" Poppy had been raised in a Polish Catholic enclave of Western New York and her own parish had been Our Lady Help of Christians but she couldn't help teasing Sonja, the professed agnostic.

Sonja laughed. "You haven't changed one bit. Don't even try to tell me that you're not the same girl I met in college."

"Okay, I won't." It wasn't the weekend to tell Sonja that any belief in something greater than herself had sailed away with Will's humiliating betrayal.

"Where do you live again? I know you said it was outside of the city but not far from the French Quarter. Is it near where you grew up?" New Orleans was behind them and they appeared to be following signs for the Lake Pontchartrain Causeway.

"Did you even read the invitation, Poppy?" Sonja softened her sharp query with a wide grin.

"I did." And promptly forgot the details, as her life had been entrenched in trying to put a positive spin on the bad press over her broken engagement. Broken engagement, hell. More like the most obscene, humiliating dump by a man ever. Her entire professional reputation had been sunk by the painful breakup from Will. The Twitter and Instagram shaming had taken off after Poppy's very public Plaza meltdown in front of Will's family. She'd appeared every part the screaming banshee she still felt like.

"Well, I know you're a busy gal. I used to think I was, too, but then I met Henry, and now we're having a baby, and we've been planning the wedding for over a year…." Sonja changed lanes to avoid a trailer hauling what appeared to be a load of empty cages. "Let's just say I didn't know what 'busy' meant." Sonja's profile hadn't changed, nor had her effusive warmth and positive energy. She'd always been the bubbly one in their relationship, while Poppy was more deliberate and definitely less talkative. Sonja always seemed so much more certain of herself. Of life.

Poppy looked out her passenger window. Of course Sonja was grounded and happy. Most twenty-eight-year-olds had a good idea of where they wanted their life to go, right?

Except Poppy. Whoa. *Pity party is later.*

Sonja playfully tapped her thigh. "Listen up. Our new home, where you're going to house-sit, is in the little town of Millersville. It's nothing like where I'm from, closer to the city. My parents are still in a bit of shock that someone from New Orleans society has asked me to marry him, and Henry's parents are, well, coming around. Let's just say this isn't New York City, right?" Sonja tapped her long fingers on the steering wheel. Poppy sensed there was more emotion under Sonja's casual demeanor. "Our house is huge, on the river, and it's spectacular if I do say so myself. Roomy, with a huge deck to enjoy the water view. We even have a small guest cottage. But you'll stay in the main house, of course. You're going to love the greenery after all that concrete." Sonja and Henry were both attorneys for the generations-old Southern law firm owned by Henry's family. It's how they'd met, when Henry's father had hired her.

"So things are still going well with the firm? No conflicts of interest with Henry's family?"

"It's his parents that have issues with our marriage, and they're all calmed down for the time being. By that I mean they haven't requested any more meetings with us, to try to persuade us differently. And they're not totally awful people, if you ignore the 'Henry's marrying a black girl from the bayou' 'tude." Sonja adjusted her sunglasses and pursed her lips. "I hate seeing him so torn up about this. They've given him such a hard time over marrying me. As if I'd sully their good family name. It's the god damn twenty-first century."

"From what you've told me, Henry's family is *very* old school."

"Say it like you mean it, girl. You mean 'bigots with old money' and they sure are careful about anyone who gets close to it! Hiring me was one thing; my résumé speaks for itself. I made them look as if they were diversifying the partners by hiring a black woman who wasn't family, and I wasn't a threat to the family bank account or gene pool. They put me in the New Orleans office, of course, far from where his father runs the offices in Baton Rouge. But having their son fall in love with me? Another thing entirely. This wasn't part of their equal opportunity plan."

"But they've decided to come to the wedding and are supporting you both now, right?"

Sonja stayed silent for several minutes. Poppy waited, knowing that her friend was trying to keep a positive spin on the ugly circumstance. "Let's hope so. It's either that or look like the asses they are. They're often in print in the society pages. I'm betting they'll show, at least for the professional photographs." Sonja's smirk forced a quick laugh from Poppy. *Laughter.* Not something she'd been doing much of.

"Doesn't sound much different than New York. The high society part, I mean." The sun was healing on her nape as the rays reached through the open sunroof.

"Trust me, when it comes to high society, they're all the same. Not the bigoted part, necessarily." Sonja made a lane change and gratitude washed over Poppy in a brilliant wave of nostalgia. Sonja was every bit the open, honest young woman she'd been years ago. "Enough about the wedding drama. I don't want to spend our precious time together talking about Henry's parents. Are you still sure you can stay here for the full two weeks to house-sit?"

"Are you kidding me? You've seen the latest on my Instagram and Twitter accounts, right? Before I shut them down, that is. I can't go back to New York, not yet. You're doing me the favor by giving me a safe place to catch my breath. I have a lot to work on, with the new Attitude by Amber deal." Poppy was excited to have Sonja and Henry's waterfront home to escape to. No paparazzi, no constant stream of Instagram pics of her at her worst moments. Leaving the gym with her consolatory Ben & Jerry's nights displayed prominently in the width of her ass, walking in or out of her apartment with that awful pinched look on her face that she felt down to her toes.

"I am so thrilled for you, Poppy. I read that they're saying you're the new Nate Berkus. This is so incredible! My college roommate, the country's darling stylist. I'm so proud of you for landing this deal with what, every single most successful department store in the country? You're on the brink of being a gazillionaire. You know that, right?"

The money wouldn't be in her accounts until the actual launch of her custom line of clothing, furniture, and home accessories. With her personal stylist business accounts frozen, she was feeling more than vulnerable, financially. But Sonja didn't need to know about Poppy's money woes.

"I'm lucky, yes. But after a while, how much does anyone really need?"

Sonja's smile disappeared and she gave Poppy one of her classic "don't bullshit me" looks. "Let's get real, honey. As in, how are you *really* doing, Poppy? You've sounded better on the phone this past week, but I can't say you're looking your best." Sonja was right; she had felt better this week. Until the last round of tweets from Will. And the threatening private texts from her former assistant, Tori. Nothing she was going to talk to Sonja about now, during Sonja's wedding weekend. No ma'am.

"Thanks a lot! I don't have much makeup on, and I'm a little tired. Things are better. I'm better. Really."

"Is that so?" Sonja frowned. "Remember me, Poppy? The one who knows you better than anyone else?"

"Yes, you do, and you're right—this has been hard. But I'm doing a lot better. Sure, the pyscho tweets and photos suck but it's not about me. I'm not the crazy one here." It was never about her, even when she and Will had been together. That was what probably hurt the most. Not disappointment in herself that she'd broken her own personal ethics code and dated a client, nor that she'd believed what she'd seen too many women fall for: that she'd be the one to change him. That Will Callis, billionaire entrepreneur and famous playboy, would stop whoring around and settle down for one woman. Her.

She'd been partially right. Because Will had changed and settled down, but not with *her*. The new and improved Will was on this very same weekend marrying her former personal assistant, a twenty-one-year-old college intern. Who was five months pregnant with his child.

Will had been screwing around on her for more than half of their engagement, at a minimum.

"So what will you do? When you go back to New York?"

Poppy watched the water that surrounded the causeway, finding the deep shade of blue soothing. "I'll become the goddess of American style. It'll be a full-time job running Attitude by Amber. I never have to style another person again if I don't want to." She ignored the New York City part. Of course she'd go back to New York. It was where she belonged.

"Oh, Poppy. I hope you mean it. I never thought being a personal stylist was the best job for you. You're too smart to just cater to other people. And Will wasn't the guy for you, sugar."

"Sounds like you've been talking to my family again." Poppy's mother and sister had at first resented that she'd made it out of their downtrodden suburb, away from their sorry family drama, and made a name for herself. Until they realized her earnings could be their ticket out, too. Her mother had been vociferous about her suspicions that Poppy had somehow bought her engagement to Will. Why would he want a girl like her, after all?

"I beg your pardon. I'd never sound like them."

"No, you won't, and you don't. I'm sorry, Sonja. It's just that they've always thought Will was crazy to date me, and wondered what he saw in me."

"Poppy Kaminsky. I never want to hear that out of your mouth again. Will is a lying no-good bastard. You deserve better, so much better. And why are you taking any kind of relationship advice from your family?"

Because even though she'd survived her upbringing and against all odds made it into the big-time, a happily-ever-after love wasn't in the cards for Poppy. She was just like her mother and sister, and grandmother and aunt, and all the women in her family. They didn't find true love with the men in their lives. Birds flew, bees buzzed, and men left.

Poppy had outrun the poverty of her childhood, the struggles of a fatherless family. And ran headfirst into the wall that derailed all of the Kaminsky women.

Men liked Poppy; they might even love her at times. But men didn't stick around in her life. Poppy wasn't a woman men gave everything up for.

Which wasn't a problem for her, because Poppy had everything she needed. Good friends, a great paycheck, or well, soon-to-be humongous paycheck, and freedom to do whatever she wanted.

After the haters stopped stalking her and Twitter judging every aspect of her life.

\* \* \* \*

The aroma of spicy gumbo wafted up through the French doors of Poppy's room along with the tinkling laughter of women as the first pre-wedding party began. Casual barbecue and early cocktails were to be followed by the women and men splitting up in New Orleans for a night on the town. All Poppy really wanted to do was hole up in the guest room of Sonja and Henry's fairy-tale riverfront dream home. To her dismay the chocolate had indeed melted. At least the bourbon was intact.

Unlike her pride and reputation.

*No one knows you here.* Even if there were any celebrity-gossip addicts present, she was fairly certain they'd have a hard time recognizing her. She hoped.

Making her way down to the back deck, she noted many of the rooms stood empty. The lack of furniture cast shadows in the rooms and made the new construction home feel older, like it was imbued with Southern history and lore. It was exactly the kind of decor Poppy was drawn to and hoped to make available to her shoppers with Attitude by Amber. Something new and made with quality, but evocative of the history, the ambience of whichever area of the country they lived in.

Quite a crowd was gathered out on what Sonja had described as a deck but in reality functioned as a beautiful terrace. Flowers Poppy had never seen before spilled from oversized terra-cotta pots and she let the blooms cheer her. There weren't any flowering outdoor plants in Manhattan in January. The bright pops of yellow and fuchsia jolted her creativity the way the warm sunshine boosted her vitamin D production, she figured. A mermaid fountain gurgled near where the bar was set up and Poppy wound her way around several groups of young, attractively dressed people to reach it. All were engaged in what appeared to be animated, no-care-in-the-world conversation.

The most delightful part of the evening so far was that not one head turned sharply, followed by "hey, is that...?" No sudden clicks from camera phones that sucked in her image and whose owners sent it out to the world without her permission.

Better yet, it was pure heaven to not hear any mention of her professional name, Amber. Or the other name she dreaded more, Will Callis, followed in short order by Tori. Tori Callis by Saturday, less than forty-eight hours from now. But she wasn't counting and no one here cared about a wedding thirteen hundred miles away.

Maybe there was such a thing as life beyond Manhattan.

Her heeled, beaded gladiator sandals and gauzy sundress were so far off from the tight-fitting style she was famous for she had to keep reminding herself that she was dressed. So used to Spanx and clothing with extra tummy-control to make herself and her clients model-slim, it was at once freeing and disconcerting to let her belly relax in public.

As for her hips and butt, which were always what her trainer in SoHo focused her grueling workout-until-you-puke sessions on, she was beyond caring. So what if her diet wasn't nutritionally perfect? It wasn't as if she needed it to be any longer. She didn't have to put on a perfectly tailored haute couture wedding gown in a month. As she'd planned for the past two years.

Sonja was the one wearing the white gown this weekend. *And Tori.* Anger threatened to tear away her careful composure. Why the hell did that little witch think she could claim Poppy's designs as her own? *Breathe. This weekend is about Sonja.* She smiled to herself as she sipped the cocktail she'd grabbed off the bartender's table. It was going to be fun to be able to relax and enjoy the entire event without either being the stylist or bride. She and Sonja had agreed she wouldn't work Sonja's wedding for this very reason.

Besides, as she looked at what everyone was wearing, her contemporary, take-no-prisoners New York styles were far off from the softer, more casual tastes of this crowd.

"What do you think of your Sazerac?" Sonja appeared next to her, pointing at her cocktail. Sonja was a vision in a simple white halter top and cut-off jeans. Her gold jewelry and flowered sandals made up for the casual wear, so Poppy didn't feel too overdressed.

"It's delicious. Kind of like a Manhattan, but more tart."

"I knew you'd love it! Come here and meet our friends." Sonja dragged her by the hand over to a large group of mostly couples and proceeded to show her off to her friends. Henry smiled at her, as if saying "see what I told you?" When they'd met earlier in the kitchen, he'd been icing down drinks and told her she was amongst friends. Poppy immediately liked him. He was everything Sonja had said. Smart, funny, and sexy. And obviously very in love with his bride-to-be.

Three of which Will hadn't been. Will was always sexy, it was his trademark and what she'd worked with him on for the past two years as his stylist. But smart and funny? Nope. And in love with her? Um, no.

She'd never recognized the signs, though. *You didn't want to.*

"Sonja says you're in fashion in New York? How did you two ever meet?" A pretty blond named Daisy tilted her head, smiling as her boyfriend snaked his arm around her tiny waist.

"Uh, yes, that's right." *Please let this bright smile stop the Q&A.* "We were college roommates, all four years, in New York."

"And when I came back home for law school I couldn't convince Poppy to join me." Sonja kept the conversation going, and Poppy loved her for it.

Daisy wasn't done. Poppy had just enough time to swig back another gulp of her bourbon drink before the gauntlet lowered. "Wait a minute—fashion? You look just like that woman who works for the Kardashians or something."

"You do! I thought you looked familiar. But your hair is way different, right?" Another woman in the group, Marie, spoke up, her smile wide.

Poppy shrugged. "I am a personal stylist, yes. But I've never worked with the Kardashians. Most of my clients are in the business sector." Small lie.

"Didn't you have a television show on TLC?"

"No, that wasn't me hosting, although I've appeared in a few episodes." One in particular that focused on hotshot Wall Street CEOs and their private lives. It had been the night Will proposed to her, on his yacht, with all of Manhattan lit up behind them.

"Poppy's getting ready to launch her design line all across the country. Attitude by Amber." Sonja shot her an "I'm sorry" look as she steered the questions away from the implosion that was currently Poppy's life.

"I thought you looked familiar!"

"Oh. My. God. I just read about you, your, um…"

Humiliation burned raw and sharp, making her skin feel as though it was being rubbed with brambles. The soft touch of Sonja's arm around her shoulders was a lifeline.

"That's all behind Poppy now. She's come here to work on something new while she house-sits for us."

Poppy met her best friend's gaze and smiled through her tears of embarrassment. "I'm here to celebrate your wedding, remember?"

The group laughed, skittishly at first but then the women took Sonja's cue and focused on her new line.

"How cool! What will you feature?"

"Will it be more of that New York contemporary look you're known for, or can those of us south of the Mason Dixon Line use it?"

Poppy was immensely grateful there was no further mention of Will or her disastrous career mistake. "I'm creating both clothing and home decor lines, all based on various regions in the U.S." She could handle this question—it was her job, after all. "The purpose of any kind of decor, whether it's for the home or your everyday work outfit, is to have it express your personal style. Help you enjoy life to the fullest. My focus is on helping you find what fits you, your life, your personality and tastes. As with any other customer-oriented business, style is all about the client."

"So tell us, you make a lot of money doing this, right?" One of the men spoke up. Poppy gulped.

"I have. I did. I'm not as focused on that right now." Oh God, she had to get away from this. Did she really think changing her looks and taking a plane to NOLA would make her problems disappear? No one knew about the whispers that had started right as she left New York. Rumors of the lawsuit type. Rumors that were in fact, true.

"Poppy, let me introduce you to some other friends." Henry was next to her, pulling her away, while Sonja kept chatting up the circle of interested friends. They really were the perfect couple.

Henry took her elbow and led her down to where the steps gave way to a pier. The river flowed past and seemed to make a soft humming noise she didn't recognize.

"Sorry about that. Sonja wondered if she should warn our friends not to bother you."

"No, it's fine, really." She finished her drink and resisted the urge to throw the glass into the river. "That would have been beyond awkward. Like I was the insane relative everyone had to tiptoe around. Besides, what were the chances anyone from here really follows the absurdities of a New York fashion stylist?"

Henry's smile was kind and generous. "Obviously very good. But I think it bodes well for your upcoming launch. People like you as a designer."

"Thanks, Henry. I can see why Sonja fell for you."

He looked out at the water. "Sonja and I have been through the wringer ourselves. It hasn't been all over social media like yours, but we understand the need for privacy and a chance to heal."

"Is your family that tough, Henry?" She assumed that's what he was referring to. Sonja hadn't mentioned any other kind of relationship strain, not that she would this close to the nuptials.

Henry nodded. "Oh, yes. I haven't mentioned it to Sonja but it won't surprise me if they are no-shows for the wedding. They've already called off coming to the rehearsal dinner tomorrow night. At least my mother was polite enough to text me that much."

"Henry, I'm so sorry!" She laid a hand on his forearm. "What about your siblings? You have two, right?" She hoped she remembered it correctly.

"Yes, I have a younger sister, Jena, who can't make it because she's overseas with the military. But my younger brother will be here." His eyes were a bright blue but she saw the shadows of pain and turmoil in them.

"You really love Sonja. And she knows it, you know."

"With all my heart." And he'd be so thrilled when he found out he was about to be a father. Her heart eased the tiniest bit from the hard bindings she'd tied around it. Seeing someone else so in love, so happy, was good for the soul.

The soft humming of the water grew louder and turned into a huge ungodly roar as if it reached up from the depths of the river. Further dialogue was impossible without knowing American Sign Language.

Poppy watched Henry shade his eyes from the late afternoon sun with his hand and followed his gaze.

"What. The. Fuck." She spoke under her breath and besides, no one could hear anything over the engines on the huge metal contraption that was obviously a boat. It had two giant turbo-fan-things on its back part, and the hull was pointed straight at the deck. What the hell was this, *Duck Dynasty*?

Water sloshed up and over the small pier, and Poppy sucked in a breath. Holy crap, it was going to hit the pier and they were going to end up in the water. Poppy turned to run back to the house only to find the entire pre-wedding party at the edge of the deck, blocking her way to safety. They all either grinned, laughed, or nodded in some kind of Cajun understanding. Or was it Creole? Either way, no one appeared as disturbed as she felt.

Poppy turned back toward the boat. Miraculously it hadn't crushed the landing but instead was pulled alongside it. As loud as the engines were, the river was again silent as they powered down without warning. A tall, athletic man in jeans and a white T-shirt hopped off the boat and wound a thick tether line around the single humongous iron cleat she'd missed earlier. Poppy knew a bit about boating from her time in Will's yacht. She'd watched the ship's crew bring them into port dozens of times. But this wasn't a pink sand beach in Bermuda and the ship's crew obviously had a different dress code.

The partygoers behind her applauded as the boat hand swaggered up the dock toward them. Poppy snorted at his stride, because *swagger* was indeed the perfect description. She'd helped countless CEOs, male and female alike, learn to walk with such confidence, minus the shit-eating grin. That a regular workingman naturally had what others had paid her dearly for was comical.

And tragic. She bit back a deep sigh. Later, with her hunk of melted chocolate and mini-bottles of whiskey, she'd indulge. There had to be a hack for carving the strips of aluminum foil wrappers out from the congealed block of chocolate.

"Hey, bro." The hunky ship's mate smiled and only then did she see the blue depths of his eyes, the chiseled chin, the same shade of hair as…

"Gus." Henry took two steps to meet the man who'd called him "bro." This hired hand was Henry's *brother?* Sonja had said he had a brother, but she'd assumed he'd be like Henry, like the gentile Southern family that she assumed the Boudreauxs were.

Not some he-man with shoulders that stretched his optic white cotton T-shirt from seam to seam, tucked into worn button-flys. Who wore their shirts tucked in anymore, by the way? Must be a Southern thing. Or a boat hand who looks like an underwear model on a billboard in Times Square thing.

As the men gave each other a friendly but not overly affectionate hug, Poppy used the few heartbeats to gather her poise. She scanned the crowd from behind her sunglasses. They all looked in awe of Gus.

*Gus?* It had to be a nickname, right?

"Gus! We're so glad you're here. Now the party can start." Sonja had pushed her way through the gawking party and was on her tiptoes to give Gus a big smackaroo on his lips. A tug of awareness in Poppy's gut broke through her observation. As if she wanted to be the one giving him the kiss. *What the hell?* Since Will, her sex hormones had abandoned ship. No way could a good ol' boy driving a tin can on muddy waters be calling them out. She took him in again, finding no fault in his attractiveness. Maybe Gus was some kind of lusty hormone Pied Piper.

"Come meet everyone, brother." Henry looked around and—*please, please, not me, not me*—smiled when his gaze landed on Poppy. *Fuck.*

"Poppy, allow me to introduce you to my younger brother, Gus."

"Poppy?" He had the same lovely drawl as Henry's and the guests she'd met so far, but his voice was deeper. Less cultured, maybe. Definitely not a man who spent his life in courtrooms. He tilted his head slightly as he waited for her to nod in affirmation.

"Yes. Poppy Kaminsky. Nice to meet you." At the awkward pause she shoved her hand forward. Henry's brother met her halfway and grasped it, his fingers wrapping around hers in a firm, warm clasp that she felt to the base of her spine. Double *what the hell?*

"Trust me, the pleasure is all mine. And it's Brandon Boudreaux, by the way. I only let my brother get away with calling me 'Gus.'" His smile had appeared attractive as she watched him greet Henry, but at close range it was deadly. And he knew it, from his sparkling indigo eyes to the incredible six-pack he had to sport to be able to tuck in his goddammed undershirt. "What's that I hear in your voice, a sprinkle of Yankee?" His sexy grin was so practiced she almost giggled. *Giggled.*

As heat that she couldn't blame on the mild Louisiana winter infused her face, Poppy realized that this was the third *what the hell* moment in as many minutes with Brandon Boudreaux.

She forced out her trademark husky laugh, but it sounded more like a bullfrog's mating call from the surrounding marsh. "It's a lot more than a sprinkle. More like a whole handful. I'm from New York." She lifted her chin and mustered her inner vixen. Somewhere deep inside she knew to never reveal her quaking insides to this man.

Because Brandon "Gus" Boudreaux was a triple threat. And her shredded psyche didn't have the energy to deal with him. Her heart beat hard and sure, fighting to shove her ego aside. All the more reason to consider Brandon Boudreaux off-limits. She'd only see him over the next few days, thank all the voodoo spirits in the bayou.

# Chapter 2

Brandon took a pull from the Corona that the bartender had stuffed a lime slice into and made a slow perusal of the crowd. As he took in the party scene it was easy to pick out that it was comprised of couples, save for him and the woman named Poppy. After the initial introductions everyone was back to gripping and grinning with the people they already knew. Except him and the Poppy woman. He'd seen her before he'd pulled up to the dock, before he'd drawn alongside Henry's pier. It was hard to miss her proud posture, the way she held herself so proper and contained. By-products of the Yankee stick up her ass, no doubt.

He took his fill of her now as she fidgeted with her empty cocktail glass, standing aloof and looking ill at ease near the bar. She was everything he registered as a warning flag. Her bleached-blond waves, designer dress that was supposed to look casual but cost more than most people's monthly wages, shoes that would last a nanosecond in the bayou, maybe less in the French Quarter. She hadn't taken her sunglasses off to meet him, either. *Fucking rude.*

"She's been Sonja's closest friend since college." Henry cut in on his observation. Brandon hated when he got caught checking out a woman he couldn't care less about.

"Uh huh."

"Poppy's a stylist to the stars in New York. Sonja was over the moon that she agreed to come down. She's actually pretty famous, but going through a rough time right now. You didn't hear it from me, though." Henry stood next to him, looking a little uncomfortable in a short-sleeve oxford and chino shorts. Henry never looked at ease unless he was in a full-on custom-tailored business suit with a perfectly knotted silk tie.

Like their father.

"Tell me about Sonja." He dragged his gaze off Poppy and focused on his brother. Henry's pale complexion turned ruddy and he started talking. *Babbling* was more like it. Running his mouth like the brook that had run through their backyard growing up. Brandon couldn't quite wrap his mind around it but his older brother appeared to be truly in love. Not that Brandon could relate. Or wanted to.

"You know that Dad hired her two years ago, right? She works in the New Orleans office with me. She was perfect for the firm right from day one. As if she were part of..." Henry trailed off.

"The family?" Brandon couldn't help himself.

"Well, of course not exactly like that, but—"

Brandon slapped Henry on the shoulder. "Chill out, dude. I'm yanking your chain. Let me guess, Mom and Dad aren't over the moon about you marrying an African American? Fuck them."

Henry didn't laugh at Brandon's attempt at humor. Brandon watched his brother as he tried to take the high road, tried to show Brandon yet again that he'd made a mistake by basically disowning his family ten years ago. The moment Henry's shoulders slumped Brandon knew his brother was done pretending.

"No, they're not happy about it. They've threatened to disown me, to fire Sonja, the whole nine yards since we announced our engagement at Christmas." Henry's eyes, the same shade of blue as his own, glittered with frustration. "I've never told Sonja the half of it. Bottom line is that they've agreed to come on Saturday. I don't expect them at the reception but at least they're showing up for the vows."

"Is that good enough for you?"

Henry shook his head. "No, none of it is, but what choice do I have? I'm marrying the woman I want to."

Brandon didn't reply. He'd be happy to tell his sanctimonious, bigoted, holier-than-thou parents to take their racist views and shove them up their tight asses. But Henry wasn't like him, wasn't one to rock the boat. "So you think once you're married and back at work, they'll go on as if it's all okay?"

"No idea. Probably more like as if nothing happened. I'm not expecting invitations to their dinner parties any longer. I can let it all go, but I hate that it hurts Sonja."

Brandon studied his brother's profile as they leaned on the deck railing, backs to the party and facing the river. The setting sun lit the sky and it was probably the last stretch of cool evenings they'd see until next fall.

Henry was a Boudreaux not just in genetics but manner and cocooned beliefs. Brandon almost felt sorry for him. It had to bite to have that protective Boudreaux bubble burst for something that was supposed to be the happiest event of your life.

Henry turned toward him.

"I wish I could be more like you, Gus. You've always known what you wanted and you never took any shit from them. Ever."

"It's not that simple, Henry." And it hadn't been, not for a newly minted college graduate, no matter how solid his engineering degree from Tulane was. Those first years completely on his own had been rough.

And this year, this past week...*fuck*. Not now.

"Look at you, Gus." Brandon didn't tell him to drop the childhood nickname—not that Henry would have. "You're at the top of your game. The *Picayune* said you made fifteen million dollars last year. You certainly didn't need Mom and Dad."

"You still don't get it, Henry." He finished his beer and smiled at the bartender, who handed him a fresh one. "It's not about financial security, it never was. Family isn't supposed to be about the bottom line." He'd made his break to be free of the controlling, arcane nature of his parents. And his financial status was in dire straits, but that wasn't public knowledge. Not yet. None of it was anything he was going to talk to Henry about tonight, two days before his older brother got hitched.

"Easy for you to say, Gus. You're brilliant, getting to do what you love to make your living. The rest of us had to work for our grades."

Brandon let Henry's passive-aggressive statement stand. Not his circus. And tried to convince himself that the slice of shame through his conscience was irrelevant.

"I'm happy for you, Henry, that you've found the woman for you."

Henry's eyes and smile softened in tandem as he dropped the edginess of sibling rivalry. "Yeah, I've done that, bro. She's the only one for me. I still can't believe she said yes."

"Why wouldn't she? You're a catch—you'll be partner soon, right? And from how pussy-whipped you're looking, she's getting a good deal. Two for one."

"Sonja didn't want me to have to fight my, um, our family. She thought she was driving a wedge between us. I told her the only thing worse for me than losing family would be if I lost her." Henry's expression mirrored the emotions they'd all felt when they realized Brandon wasn't going home for any holiday meals, no more Sunday dinners. It'd hurt his older brother when Brandon had made the break he needed.

The squeeze of self-recrimination he thought he'd long buried took ahold of Brandon and shook. Lots of kids made peace with asshole parents, why couldn't he?

Brandon had to choke back his beer around the lump in his throat. *Shit.* "I'm proud of you, bro." He slapped Henry on the back and nodded to where Sonja stood with a group of women, her face radiant with bridal bliss. "Sonja's going to make a fine sister, I can tell already."

"Thanks, Gus. What about you? Anyone in your life?"

"Naw. I'm not a hermit or anything—just not ready to pull the plug on the fun, you know?"

"Your tough talk doesn't fool me. You still stinging over Kelly?"

"Kelly? Hell, no! That was in college, bro. I'm ten years out of that almost-mistake." No, he wasn't stinging over Kelly. Or even Joanie, the gal who'd dumped him a few months ago when, after two years, he made true on his promise that he was in it for the fun, no strings. Commitment always bespoke family to him, and his family wasn't something he ever wanted to emulate.

"You can't want to be single forever, can you?" Henry had caught the whiff of Brandon's angst but attributed it to relationship woes. Not the real reason Brandon was off his game: his company was facing bankruptcy.

"Look, Henry, just because you've been bit, don't think everyone else has." He almost hated himself for being able to portray his Gus persona so well.

"By the way, have you seen Jeb? I thought he'd come in with you."

"Ah, no, he's been incommunicado since he left on a business trip last week." He hated lying to Henry. Especially about Jeb.

"He's practically family. He's coming to the wedding, right?"

"Far as I know." He sure hoped Jeb would show up. And tell Brandon what the hell was going on with their corporate financials. He totally relied on the man who was his best friend and had hung out with their family since they were all teens. Jeb was an ace accountant.

The sickening truth tried to push through Brandon's denial and he shoved it back. This was Henry's weekend.

"Okay, well, maybe he'll show up later tonight downtown." Henry straightened when he saw Sonja wave at him from across the deck, motioning for him to come over. "Looks like I'm being paged."

Brandon called it something else, but whatever. "I don't need to be babysat. And Henry? These are my only two beers for the night. I'm your duty driver for the downtown activities." He gestured with his hand toward the swamp boat. "She's our ride."

"We've hired a couple of limo drivers, Gus. But thanks."

Brandon found himself ignoring the sting that Henry's refusal made. "You can always change your mind, bro."

Henry stared at him. After a few seconds he nodded. "You're right. Let me ask Sonja."

Of course they'd hired drivers. Henry wasn't one to spare any expense. Just like their dad. Water transportation was more fun, as far as Brandon was concerned.

\* \* \* \*

"Okay folks, I need y'all to get on the boat." Henry held up his cocktail as he grinned at his guests. "My brother has offered to get us to New Orleans in a straight line."

Poppy looked from Henry to the "boat" in question. *What. The. F—*

"You're going to love this. It's Poppy, right? I'm not always the best with names." Brandon stood in front of her and she'd bet the last swig of her Cajun cocktail that he was, in fact, excellent with names.

"Sonja told me we were taking limos tonight." She hoped the women still were. Let the guys have this rough ride.

Brandon's lips curled in a half smile she knew had to be practiced. "Obviously she and Henry have seen the light. The only way to traverse the bayou is on water."

"Is that made for passengers?" She sniffed at his floating monstrosity. "What kind of boat is that? I mean, what's its purpose?"

"It's a swamp boat, meant to be able to ride over the marshes without a hitch. It also gets around the Mississippi and her tributaries pretty well."

"Is it a hobby of yours?"

"Hobby?" Why did he look like he was about to choke on his ice water? "Yeah, something like that."

"I can take one of the limos—there won't be enough room in your boat for all of us." Hadn't she been through enough? She'd fled the hot mess of her life less than twelve hours ago. The last thing she needed was any kind of reminder that Will was hosting his prenup party on his yacht right about now. Not that this metal canoe in any way resembled a yacht. She snorted. "We're going to the French Quarter, right? We'll all meet down there."

"Do you have a fear of the water?" Blue-jean-colored eyes crinkled at the sides as he threw out the question like a challenge. A gauntlet.

"No, Brandon, I don't fear the water." Or anything this bayou babe wanted to throw at her. "It's just that I didn't realize we'd be wrangling gators before the festivities. I'm not dressed for it."

He laughed, and from his expression he hadn't expected to. "You've never been down here before, have you?"

"*Au contraire*. I was here to visit Sonja when we were seniors in college." They'd worked on a build site for victims of Katrina but she wasn't about to share that with Mr. Dixie.

"Did you get downtown?"

"To New Orleans? Of course." It had been a mess, most everything closed, but she wasn't going to tell him that.

"It's pronounced 'New Orlinz' down here, Poppy." His intonations made it clear he didn't miss one bit of her judgment, no matter how innocuously she meant it.

"I'm not *from* here, Brandon."

"That, you're not." He made a purposeful perusal of her from head to toe, stopping at her feet, which were getting more and more uncomfortable in the five-inch gladiator sandals. "Nice toes."

It took every ounce of self-control to not wiggle said toes, painted violet and topped with tiny white flowers. Another part of her break from the polished Poppy the world knew as Amber. That woman wouldn't be caught dead with nail art.

Poppy silently shook off any thoughts of who she was before this moment. Time to step into her new life.

"I did them myself." Stupid line. He didn't care.

"I've no doubt." Was he patronizing her?

She gritted her teeth. "Where do we sit?"

\* \* \* \*

"Don't worry about us, Poppy. We'll keep you safe and unseen." Daisy, Sonja's law school friend, shouted over the turbines' roar as they and eight more of the wedding party skimmed the river. Poppy and Daisy were seated side by side in the last row of seats, directly in front of Brandon's place at the helm. He stood behind a large metal wheel, surrounded by a small building with windows on each side. The front window was open so she wasn't sure how much of their conversation he heard.

"I appreciate it." She smiled at Daisy before turning pointedly back to the view. As unlikely as it was that Brandon could hear them, she wasn't about to risk anyone overhearing the details of her catastrophe.

The sun disappeared across the water as they moved toward the city, and the sky was illuminated with intense shades of violet and peach. The colors took Poppy's inner artist's breath away. The hues were so unlike her usual neutral palette, so *vibrant*.

"It must be hard to have something so personal blow up in such a public way. A major crisis that everyone can see." Even in the wind, aboard their odd transportation and with Daisy's appealing Louisiana lilt, there was no mistaking the prying.

"People around the world are starving, surviving wars. My private life is hardly a crisis."

"And then you had that incident at The Plaza. My mother took us there for high tea a few years ago—me, my sisters and grandmother. It was so fancy! And very classy. I imagine the anniversary party for your ex's parents was over-the-top. Had you broken up by then?"

Daisy had read the *People* article, apparently. And then there was that *Huffington Post* piece....

"Has anything you're not proud of ever been made public, Daisy?" She blasted Daisy with what she thought of as her thousand-watt smile, wanting to slap the faux innocence off the Southern belle's face.

"No, not that I can think of. I'm boring that way—I'm the nice girl who never has any fun. Your typical Southern gal."

"Good for you, Daisy." She wondered if Daisy realized that similar to a gently spoken Southern "bless your heart," "good for you" was Yankee-speak for "fuck you."

And then it hit Poppy. The angle Daisy had her body angled toward her wasn't to speak to Poppy but to display her scantily clad breasts most advantageously to their ship's driver. And was that glitter on Daisy's boobs? Poppy looked from Daisy's sparkling cleavage to Brandon's face, and to her shock he wasn't looking anywhere near Daisy or her glitter. He was staring at her, Poppy, blatantly watching for her reaction. He must have seen the desire in her eyes because he commenced a very slow, very deliberate assessment of her, from head to toe, lingering on her breasts and hips.

Hot awareness flushed through her as his obvious interest in her female attributes was reflected in the way his half-lidded eyes perused her curves. Unlike Daisy, whose glittered décolletage indicated a fun streak, Poppy preferred a more understated exposure of her breasts, as evidenced by the peekaboo slit in her sundress, strategically cut over her cleavage. Apparently Brandon liked to play hide-and-seek, as his gaze was riveted on the small opening.

He blinked, his eyes widening as he realized he was caught looking at her. She wasn't sure who was more surprised. He continued to stare at her for a full second. She waited for his gaze to dip, to slide over and check out Daisy's sparkles. Instead, a flash of anger before he looked away, focused forward and steered the boat around a bend. She felt bereft, dismissed as though she hadn't passed his muster.

Poppy angled her body to her side of the boat, her chest exposed to the sunset. She refused to engage either Daisy or Brandon. The scenery was sublime, a true welcome to Dixie, something she shouldn't miss. Besides, Brandon Boudreaux was the last man she wanted looking at her boobs.

* * * *

"Thanks." Poppy nodded at the bartender, took her hurricane in its tall wavy plastic container, and moved to the far edge of the group. She fingered the purple beads partygoers had thrown from the balconies lining Charles Street as the wedding party had strolled down the center of the French Quarter. She wondered how long this crowd would last. They'd been drinking since the deck party, with the only gap the speed-demon ride to the wide, downtown New Orleans pier that Brandon somehow had reserved ahead of time. Getting an open spot on a pier in Manhattan was next to impossible and she didn't think New Orleans was any different.

Sonja and the other girls were up on the stage, dancing and singing with the band. The bachelor party had gone to a different bar and she told herself she was relieved to be without the constant sense of Brandon Boudreaux judging her.

Her head throbbed to the beat of the booming music and she promised herself she'd get a tall glass of water next. She hated that she was making sure she didn't get a hangover. It'd be so nice to loosen up and party like she hadn't just gone through hell.

*You deserve to let your hair down. You've been through so much.*

Her inner whiner needed to shut up. Poppy's idea of letting loose was watching a Hallmark Channel movie and eating organic air-popped popcorn on the nights after she'd had a particularly difficult client.

Clients. She didn't have any left, unless she'd hallucinated her most recent cancelations. But she still had the dream deal with her Attitude by Amber franchise, and by the time her products hit over 4400 outlets in North America alone, the public would have forgotten all about her Plaza meltdown.

A twangy song with a hard rock beat started to rattle the bar and it felt like the whole place moved to it.

"Come on, Poppy!" Sonja screamed from the band's stage, pointing at her.

"Can't!" She shook her head and pointed at her drink, holding Sonja off. No way was she getting on that stage, in front of all these drunk patrons.

"I'll hold that." Brandon's voice was in her ear and he was next to her. She jumped back and stared. He held out his hand for her drink and she spotted the other guys in the wedding party behind him. So much for a girls' night out.

She handed him the glass.

"You can have it. I never drink from a glass I've left unattended." Shoving past him, she wound through the sweaty sea of partygoers and joined the bridal party in a line dance. She could do a Southern shimmy with the best of them. At first she felt good, on the verge of enjoying herself after months of internal badgering. It was almost possible to believe that she was as young and free as she'd been the last time she'd line danced with Sonja. They pivoted in perfect unison, laughing in sheer delight at how in sync they still were. The sandals were killing her feet but she didn't care. Although the next time she danced in New Orleans she vowed to do it with cowboy boots on.

"Welcome to the Boudreaux wedding party!" The singer of the band called out over the rollicking beat and Poppy cheered along with the other women, hands up high as if to keep the ceiling from caving in. This was what a wedding was all about. Pure celebration. It was what she'd wanted at hers, but all the fun, spontaneous ideas she'd come up with had gotten the kibosh from Will. Of course, he'd already been involved with Tori and had no intention of going through with his marriage to Poppy.

The reminder of her shattered heart was all the space her ugly anxiety needed.

*No, no, no. Come on, not now. Not here.*

The room grew too small, her dress too tight. She tried every tool she knew. Deep breaths, tapping her sternum, picturing she was in her happy place. But her happy place—the vision she'd used to short circuit her anxiety for the past two years, her dream wedding with her dream groom—was gone.

Poppy panicked.

\* \* \* \*

Brandon didn't know what possessed him to be nice to the Poppy chick. Jesus, she was a pill. And it wasn't because she wasn't falling over him like he was used to women doing. He could have her eating out of his hand given the right circumstances—there was a palpable sexual chemistry between them. But she'd been standing on the outskirts of the fun, sipping that tourist cocktail, in her fancy New York City clothes, with the saddest eyes. She'd reminded him of how he felt when he tried to be a salesman for his bigger boats, pitching to CEOs or celebrities. Out of place, a catfish not only out of water but far from the mud it was most at home in.

He tried to make it look like he wasn't watching her dance from the corner of his eye, that his focus was on Henry and the other groomsmen. Poppy sure knew how to shake it to all kinds of music, not just the electronic beats from the uppity club scene he remembered from his sojourns to New York. He wasn't only watching her body move, though. It was a delicious package, that bod of hers, but he found himself mesmerized by her face. She carried herself like a woman who'd accept nothing but the very best in life, but her expression screamed "I'm hurting." Did he see her pain because it was the same kind of visceral knife-on-bone pain he was in?

And her breathing—he'd noticed it on Henry's dock, when they'd met. The little hitches of breath that made her ample breasts quiver under the gauzy sundress she wore. The sundress exposed the start of her cleavage, the creamy skin of her chest. Shallow breathing was something he understood well—it was what always preceded the panic attacks that had plagued him through college. They were at their worst right before important exams, and right after his first long-term girlfriend unceremoniously dumped him for a more outgoing, socially fluent rugby player.

As the band pumped on with a throwback millennial hit, Poppy's effortless steps were no longer in line with the other gals' and he watched as she looked like she was going to pass out. And she kept doing this weird thing with her fingers, hitting herself on her sternum and then in the area between her mouth and nose.

"Excuse me. *Move.*" He shoved past the gawkers, drooling as they enjoyed the show. The wedding party women were all beautiful and liquored up to the point of demonstrating their most sensual body movements and had attracted quite the crowd. He reached Poppy, at the end of the line, just as she sank into a squat, her fingers frantically beating out some Morse code on her temples. He touched her shoulder. "I've got you."

She looked up and he knew she didn't see him, not really. He leaned in close. Her pupils were dilated and her mouth was open, but instead of gulping the air her body needed, she was panting and looked like she was on the verge of tears. He hauled her up by her upper arms and pressed her against him, knowing the shock of a practical stranger holding her might shake the panic away, if only for a few moments.

"What, why—wait a minute." Poppy was back, her mouth curled in a shadow of the snarls she'd cast his way all night. "Let me go. I'm fine."

"In a minute. Let's get some air." She didn't argue and in fact leaned against his side when he put his arm around her lower back, his hand covering her hip bone—Jesus, he was going to go to hell for noticing how fucking sexy she was, in the midst of her suffering—and half walked, half carried her out of the bar. Charles Street was crowded with partygoers and he took her hand, made direct eye contact. "You okay? Can you walk?"

Her answering nod was imperceptible except for the way it made a blond lock fall across her eyes. She didn't brush it away and he saw her chest do the shallow breathing routine again. "I've got you, Poppy. Let's take a stroll and find a quieter place. You're all right."

\* \* \* \*

Poppy struggled with her embarrassment and frustration that this stranger—well, okay, not a complete stranger, as she knew it was Brandon and holy fuck he was one sexy dude—was witnessing her at her absolute worst. Her anxiety had been a thing of the past, so she thought, and since it hadn't acted up even when her fairytale wedding and life had blown up, she'd assumed she'd outgrown it.

Wrong.

"Where are we going?"

He held her hand and she grasped his back—if she was going to make a fool out of herself, then she'd earned this one reassurance. Human touch that relayed strength and a sense of compassion she hadn't picked up from the man who'd pulled his swamp boat next to his uptight, socially conscious brother's pier.

Was this Brandon really the same asshole she'd been avoiding all night?

"Not sure. For now, I have a place in mind where you can chill out, take some time to get grounded and come back to yourself."

"And then what, you'll resuscitate me with a night I'll never forget? Let me guess, all the girls tell you that yours is the biggest ever?"

He squeezed her hand but didn't let go. "Nice to have the real Poppy back. Five minutes ago I would have sworn you were on your way to passing out."

Shame she hadn't experienced in years came rushing back. She tried to tug her hand out of his but he wouldn't release it. Relief flooded her senses. "Thank you. You didn't have to take care of me."

"I'm not taking care of you, believe me. Just giving you the space to take care of yourself." He let go of her hand and guided them to a large wrought iron gate that he pushed open. "Follow me."

She walked a step behind him, taking in the overwhelmingly dark, heavily perfumed space of what she guessed was someone's private garden. Huge white blooms the size of dinner plates wound their way up the side of an arbor. "Is there a house in here somewhere?"

His laughter was brief, gone as soon as it reached her ears. He stopped and turned, forcing her to halt. "It's a residential garden, yes. But most folks don't even know it exists. These brick walls make it look like any other colonial building." He patted said wall before he reached out his hand to her. She couldn't see his eyes even in the bright moonlight; the round opal disc hung in a cloudless night over his left shoulder, the dark shape of his head framed by a gazillion stars. But she saw his hand, the way the moonlight reflected off his upturned palm. She shouldn't want to take it again, to accept his offer of strength, maybe even compassion. Men weren't to be trusted and she knew this in the depths of her being. And it wasn't as if she needed his reassurance to keep the anxiety at bay; as quickly as the attack had rushed her it had subsided like a rogue wave that brought her back to shore after sucking her under just long enough to let her know she was in trouble. But she wasn't on a familiar shore or even in a familiar land.

She took his hand again.

# Chapter 3

"We shouldn't be here. This is a private residence, isn't it?" Her voice came out softer than she meant. They walked along a graveled path, through arbors of wisteria and beneath oaks draped with veil after veil of Spanish moss. It was hard to believe that only a brick wall could mute out the blare of the French Quarter. She supposed the lush fauna had something to do with it, too.

Brandon's hand gently squeezed hers, a quick pulse.

"It's okay, trust me. The owners are friends of mine and I happen to know they're out of town this weekend. I've been here plenty of times, night and day, when I needed to get away from the noise." Did he mean for his voice to sound like a caress on the night breeze?

"What do you mean by 'noise'?" All she heard were groans and chirps, but what kind of animal made them she had no idea.

"You know, noise. People talking too much. Internal pressure stuff." He stopped and looked at her. "Do you need quiet to work, or can you solve problems with music?"

Poppy wished she could see his eyes in the dark. Was this man really being nice or mocking her, patronizing the Yankee who'd fallen into her own pile of shit?

"I never thought about it. There always seems to be music in my studio, and at the events I work."

"Henry said you're some kind of fashion director?"

Poppy laughed. His drawl made the question sound as if he were a NASA scientist interviewing an alien. "I'm a personal stylist. I help people get the look they want or need for their special day or for their life—whatever that is for them."

"And you get paid for that?"

"Yes. If you're very good at your job." And she'd been very good. Until the last few months, when she hadn't even known if it was what she wanted anymore.

"Are you? Good at your job?"

"I'm okay." She tugged her hand from his. This was ridiculous. "I'm fine now, Brandon. We can go back." Her stomach twisted at the thought of going back to the crowded bar, but she caught her breath. Calmed down.

"Do you really want to do that, Poppy?" His voice lowered and with their hands no longer connected, he stepped closer, shrinking the space between them to inches.

"Honestly? Hell, no! I want to be in my room, curled up and sleeping like a rock. But this isn't about me, it's about Sonja. And Henry." She wondered if Sonja had told Henry she was pregnant yet. Was she really planning to marry a man before she let him know she was pregnant?

"They aren't going to miss either one of us. The night is getting late and they all have a limo ride back to the house. If you want to go back home now I can make it happen."

"Do you run your business like this? Coming off as the nice guy but really just manipulating everything to your advantage?"

"Why would taking you back to Henry's river house be to my advantage, Poppy?" His voice was impossibly low and as rough as the gravel they stood on. This was a man used to getting his way—she'd dealt with enough of them in New York. Knew the way they never took no for an answer. Knew how easily they threw you aside when a younger, more nubile college intern appeared.

"Let me guess, Brandon. I mean, *Gus.* You think that you have the magic potion in your wand that will make it all better for me?" She motioned to his crotch, figuring he didn't see her hand in the dark.

He grabbed her hand and it wasn't a gesture of comfort this time. She froze, wondering if he was going to put it on the spot she'd referenced. She'd met men who would, who got off on ridiculous banter and a vulnerable woman, casting themselves as a sexual savior.

When instead he lifted her hand to his mouth and kissed her knuckles, she experienced the kind of lightning bolt insta-lust she'd only ever read about or watched in romantic comedies, her version of girl porn.

"I don't do fix-it sex, and I most certainly don't take advantage of jet-lagged, post-almost-panic-attack women." He dropped her hand. "Decide what you want, Poppy."

"I want to go back to the house."

"Done." He fished his phone out of his back pocket and tapped open an app. "We'll have a car outside of the gate we entered in no more than five minutes."

\* \* \* \*

Brandon helped Poppy step down onto the boat from the pier, a small part of him thrilled that she'd accepted his hand as she wobbled in her too-high heels around the French Quarter and garden. And that she trusted him as he helped her onto the deck. He hated that small part that resented that he gave one shit about the welfare of this stranger. Close enough to stranger.

"Next time, you'd be best to wear more practical shoes."

"These work for me." She looked down at her strappy leather concoctions that, while totally impractical, made her legs and feet too attractive. Too sexy. The sandals drew too much attention to her smooth calves, and up her thighs, and made him wonder what was under her sundress at the apex of her legs.

Not that he didn't know. He knew, of course. In fact he considered himself a pussy expert. But he didn't know Poppy's pussy.

*Fuck.* So not the time for this. His life was enough of a mess. He couldn't bring a woman into the picture now, even if it were for just one night or one wedding weekend.

"Do you need any help getting us out of here? No? Then great—I'll be up in that seat if you need anything." She pointed to the chair farthest from the helm, as far distant as she could be from him on the swamp boat. Her humor was tempered by her recent anxiety and yet it warmed him. Something about Poppy spoke to his soul.

"Enjoy the ride." He untied the lines from the pier cleats and neatly wound them onto the boat's deck before sliding behind the wheel and starting the engines. He knew these waters as well as he knew how to build a boat. All through his childhood he'd learned each tributary to the Mississippi, each offshoot of Lake Pontchartrain. So he was able to allow his mind to wander, to meditate, even, as he cruised the boat at an easy speed toward Millersville where Henry had bought his house. It figured Henry had purchased a lot on the water, same as Brandon had. Only Brandon's house was in New Orleans, and Henry's was an hour's drive north, twenty minutes by boat. It was closer to their parents' in the almost exact middle between the New Orleans office and their family's main law office. Brandon was happy for his brother and for the life of him couldn't figure out why he gave two shits about Henry's financial status or apparent ease of life. Sure, Henry hadn't ever faced bankruptcy, had never had to live in a dingy one-room walk-up in downtown New Orleans. But Henry's life had been molded and shaped by their parents, specifically their father, since day one. Brandon had a freedom that Henry never would.

At least, until this week when he found out Jeb had absconded with Boats by Gus's entire financial portfolio. The dead weight that sat in the bottom of his gut was starting to turn rancid, discontent with simply staying silent. The initial denial of the now most certain betrayal by his best friend and practical brother had worn out.

*You're a fucking coward.*

Was he? Yeah, probably. He hadn't mentioned one word to anyone about it yet. Hadn't called in the authorities. Because of the company's current two-week hiatus from direct sales, he was able to focus on the production of boats that had already been ordered. Except he didn't have the funds to pay his employees at the factory and distribution warehouse. As for Jeb, the idea of taking legal action against his best friend and business partner still bothered Brandon. The anger he knew he should be feeling wasn't there yet. As if by waiting and ignoring that his entire life's work and savings was gone he'd somehow figure out that Jeb was playing an elaborate prank. Or needed the money for something grand and worthy, that he'd be back at any time and redeposit the funds.

"It's cold up front." Poppy's voice spooked him. He'd been so deep in his sucky prospects he hadn't noticed she'd moved. She kneeled on the bench near him, her arms wrapped around herself.

"It won't be much warmer here. There's a jacket on the bench there if you want it." A waft of her scent, something to do with jasmine, brushed his nose as she maneuvered behind him to get it. "You don't have to be all Gumby, getting around me. I'm not going to take advantage of you." He needed to call his lawyer in the morning. Take action on the Jeb situation.

"Do I give the impression that I'm worried about it?" Her eyes were steady on his and she had remarkable balance on a flat-bottomed boat that thumped rhythmically across the black water.

"You've been around boats before, I'd guess."

Even in the soft moonlight he saw the immediate change in posture from sassy New Yorker to wary animal, as though she'd had to chew her leg off to get out of a hunter's trap and would never again trust another human being. "Some. But only in a social way."

He made it a point to keep his eyes on his route and not look directly at her. It kept his sexual attraction to her in perspective, made the possibilities of what he would have loved to do with a woman like Poppy only a week ago less real. But not less tempting.

She finally stopped staring at him and looked out at the shore lights that twinkled but were no competition for the almost full moon. "I've been on a lot of frivolous boats. The entertaining kind. You know, like tour boats that go around Manhattan, and yachts. I've styled people to look their best at social functions that are really business meetings. And some fun ones, too, like, like...weddings." She ended on a quieter note.

"Are you the stylist for Henry and Sonja's wedding?" He assumed she was, since Henry had said she was Sonja's best friend.

She shook her head and he hid a smile at how the motion fluffed her hair out, making her look like she had a huge fuzzy halo around her oval face. "No, Sonja didn't want me to do anything but enjoy her wedding. And as it turns out, this is a perfect time for me to stay down here for a while."

That weight in Brandon's stomach kept it from turning over in interest. "What do you mean, 'stay here'?"

"I'm house-sitting for Sonja while they're on their honeymoon. Two weeks. Since I'm launching a new line of home decor and fashion within the next ten days and don't want to go back to New York at the moment, it's worked out better than I could have planned."

"Good for you."

She laughed.

"What's so funny?"

"Don't tell me you don't know. Saying 'good for you' where I'm from is like when you say 'bless your heart.'" Her head was tilted and her lips puffed in a tiny pout. If they'd met at another time, if she wasn't giving off such a prudish air, it'd be the perfect time for a first kiss. Her eyes widened slightly as if maybe she was thinking the same thing. He knew she was getting the same vibe as he when she took a step backward.

He laughed easily. "Aw, come on now, Yankee girl. Tell me what it means."

Her chin tilted up and she crossed her arms over her chest. "It means 'fuck you,' Brandon. Fuck. You."

\* \* \* \*

*Dear sweet baby Jesus, please let me live through this night.* They couldn't be more than ten more minutes to the house, ten more minutes and she'd be rid of Brandon Boudreaux. And his dark looks, the sexy eyes that promised a different kind of southern heat. It tugged at her, she had to admit. The thought of letting loose and letting him put those capable hands on her breasts, her ass. But then she'd wake up, because she always woke up, and she wasn't up for the self-recrimination and low self-esteem that would greet her with the sunrise. If they'd never see each other again, it would be one thing. Two more full days of having to deal with one another at a dress rehearsal and then the wedding, though? No way.

She hadn't meant to be such a bitch but then she couldn't believe he hadn't put the moves on her after being so damned nice in the French Quarter. So gentlemanly. Acting like he understood her panic attack, as if maybe he'd known someone else who had them. The walk-through-the-garden Brandon had disappeared in a New York minute when he'd eyed her minutes ago, looking at her like she was a chump and he was a hungry shark cruising for a substantial snack. She shivered and in the jacket that smelled like him it wasn't from the chill of the breeze off the dark waters. It was from the side of Brandon that had looked like he'd enjoy nothing more than stalling the boat and pulling her against him for some bayou boinking. His look, even his *silence*, had made her knees quake and it wasn't from her high heels.

They pulled up to Henry and Sonja's dock and she shrugged out of the jacket, dropping it back on the bench where she'd found it. "Thanks for the ride, Brandon. See you at the rehearsal tomorrow."

"Hold on, Poppy." He cut the motors and expertly threw the lines to the deck, lassoing one on a cleat and pulling it taut before hopping off the ship to tie the second line. He reached down to give her a boost.

"I don't need your help, Brandon. I'm fine." She focused on making it off the boat and onto the dock without catching her heels in any spaces or, worse, tripping. She stood and faced him, her back to the house. "You didn't have to secure the boat. Thanks again."

"I'm not letting you go into an empty house on your own."

"You're not 'letting' me do anything. Thank you for the ride. Good night." She made what she thought was a graceful exit considering the tumult of the past two hours. At the sound of his steps behind her she stopped at the back patio French doors. Without turning back she spoke to his reflection in the glass. "I'm safe. You can go now." She tried to open the door and close it right behind her, but it wouldn't budge.

"You have to undo the latch up here first." His arm reached over her head and she heard the *click* of whatever fastener he unlocked.

She turned and looked at him. "Thank you." His expression wasn't very readable in the dim light, as clouds had started to play peekaboo with the moon. He said nothing and her old sense of everything being her fault tugged at her. "Do you need to use the, um, facilities before you continue on?"

"As a matter of fact, yes. My house is another twenty to thirty minutes, back toward the city."

"I'm sorry you went so far out of your way." She was glad, really, to be able to be away from the happy crowd they'd left. Happy was a bit elusive to her, too hard to grasp or pretend.

"Like I said, no problem. You have a good night." He reached around her and opened the door. Poppy went in and bolted for the stairs, needing to be alone, yes, but more, needing to be away from Brandon and his manners.

\* \* \* \*

Brandon meant to use the bathroom and then leave, but he'd found himself wandering from room to room downstairs. It was clear Henry and Sonja had lived here together for a while, since the place was comfortably decorated and appeared well lived-in, save for the empty spots that still needed furniture. His attention was initially caught by all the photographs on the grand piano in the expansive family room. He clicked on a small reading lamp and looked at photos of Henry and Sonja, Sonja with what he assumed was her family, Henry with college friends. His gut took a sucker punch at a recent photo of Henry with their parents. God, his father looked every bit the son of a bitch Brandon remembered. He hadn't seen him since two weeks before college graduation, well over ten years ago. His father had issued his ultimatum for Brandon to apply to law school with the promise of joining the family law firm afterward. For the umpteenth and last time, Brandon had refused his father's manipulation.

Hudson Boudreaux looked the same, save for his hair being more on the white side than the glossy silver it had been for decades. His mother, however, looked so much older than Brandon remembered. Gloria Boudreaux posed with Dad, Henry, and their sister Jena in front of a huge poinsettia-laden Christmas tree. His mom's figure looked the same but the lines around her eyes had deepened and the strain in her smile was palpable.

He'd missed a lot. Years he'd never get back.

Muffled sounds came to him as he set the frame back on the black lacquered piano top. He moved to the base of the stairs and the sounds were clearly sobs. So little miss Yankee stylist had needed to come back here not to rest but to cry her heart out. From her conversation with Daisy and what he'd pieced together from the other partygoers, she sure had a lot to weep over. Not that it was any business of his, or that he cared.

He kept up his perusal of Henry's house, telling himself it was to learn more about the brother he'd missed and to gain insight into the woman Henry had fallen for. *Sucker.* When quiet descended over the house like a blanket on a cold night, he chanced a walk upstairs, to make sure Poppy was settled. Then he would go home. Brandon never liked leaving anyone or anything unsettled.

A bedroom door at the top of the stairs was cracked open. With the glow of a cat-shaped night light, he made out a huddled figure under a coverlet on the double bed. A few locks of her bright hair haphazardly poked out from under the blanket. Who slept so far under the covers but a distraught child?

The ticking of a Big Ben alarm clock on the nightstand was the only sound, save for quiet little gasps of what he discerned were Poppy's soft snores. Glancing at his watch to confirm the glowing hands on the bedside clock were accurate, he swallowed a deep yawn. It would be daylight in less than two hours, and he was suddenly, incredibly, exhausted. He could crash on Henry's couch downstairs, but would be woken up when the rest of the folks came home. And have to explain why he'd stayed. He couldn't go into another guest room, because they were all occupied, as Sonja had mentioned the house was "full to the brim."

He stared at the wide window seat that stretched the full length of the bedroom's only window. He might need to bend his knees but he could catch twenty winks there. A couple hour power nap was all he needed. He'd be gone before anyone woke, especially the woman in the bed before him.

He eased onto the cushioned ledge and let out a quiet sigh of relief that he didn't have to go home yet, where reality would crash in and he'd be reminded he might not have his home for much longer. By no means was he crashing here because he gave a rat's ass about a Yankee girl stylist from New York.

\* \* \* \*

Poppy woke from a deep snooze fest and remained still, taking a minute to remember where she was. New Orleans. Louisiana. Sonja. Henry. Henry's brother, Brandon. Brandon. Brandon's boat. Oh God, Brandon's lips on her hand.

What the hell was that noise? Maybe everyone had returned and their drunken movements had awakened her. The clock on her nightstand said it was almost dawn but the house was still, the light barely starting to change.

Shock jolted through her when she saw the figure on the window bench. What the hell was he doing here? In her room? *Son of a bitch.*

She rose to wake him, preferably by choking, but when her bare feet hit the rough pine planks it was as if the house halted her, made her stop and take a breath before reacting. Because wasn't reacting to events in her life what had gotten her to this deep, dark pit that was her current emotional and professional status?

As she stepped closer to the window, Brandon's profile became clearer and for the second time that morning shock stilled her. He was as sexy in repose as he was awake, every taught line on him begging for a woman's touch, promising delights only the most skilled lover can dole out. What was different was his face. While his profile was very similar to Henry's and what she imagined was a Boudreaux genetic stamp, his expression was…vulnerable. The lines of contempt and judgment she'd observed yesterday were softer, yielding to an expression of desperation.

*Yeah, right.* She silenced a snort behind her hand and went to the bathroom down the hall to get a drink of water. Obviously her dramatic life events of the past months had caught up to her, as the Brandon Boudreaux she'd met yesterday barely resembled the man sleeping on her window seat.

When she returned to her room, armed with verbal reprisal and her own scathing expression, he was gone.

# Chapter 4

"I'll have the po'boy, fully dressed, and the seasoned French fries." Poppy gave her order to the waitress, doing her best to ignore the rehearsal dinner guest to her left.

"You know what 'fully dressed' means, right?" Brandon's voice was so close to her ear that his breath blew her hair onto her cheek. The room shrank, her focus on only the two of them. If she thought about it too hard she'd realize that the sense that she somehow knew him, was connected to him, began the minute she'd met his blue-eyed glance.

"Yes, and I like pickles and hot sauce and anything else they want to put on it. It's not my first time here, remember? And there are several great Cajun restaurants in my neck of the woods." Damn but she sounded like a stuck-up Manhattanite. Something she'd usually accept as part of her identity and public persona—it had earned her several spots on reality television, after all, and more importantly, earned her a decent paycheck. But in this moment, in this laid-back restaurant where the Southern hospitality wrapped around her like the hot humid air outside, her words sounded rude. She sighed.

"I'm sorry, Brandon. That didn't come out very nicely, did it?"

"No, but that's what I like about you, Yankee girl. You don't hold back." The innuendo meant only for her let her know that he wasn't just talking about her verbal sarcasm. He'd only kissed her hand yet had her as worked up as if they'd been doing the horizontal zydeco since yesterday.

Brandon Boudreaux had a way of plucking on her tightest strings, starting with when he'd pulled up to Henry and Sonja's deck in that crazy boat.

"What are you having, honey?" The waitress was young with the beautiful glow on her skin to prove it. Poppy wondered if the constant high humidity had something to do with it. It'd be like having a misting treatment during a facial, but constantly and free.

"The same, but skip the fries. Do you have any dirty rice back there?" Of course Mr. Bayou was also a health nut. Don't let any fat gather on those washboard abs. Abs she'd only taken brief note of. No sense wasting time on something she wasn't going to touch.

"Stop staring at me, Yankee girl."

Why did it have to be his voice that was the first male vibration to get her wet since the breakup with Will? Instead of answering, she made a point of visually perusing the laid-back restaurant. And kept a side eye on Brandon.

Brandon was completely at ease in the low country diner, obviously a favorite of his and Henry's since they'd picked it for tonight's celebratory meal. Sonja had been thrilled when she'd told her that Brandon had insisted on helping Henry with tonight's plans, since their parents weren't involved in any of the wedding planning. Poppy was surprised that her detail-oriented bestie had agreed to such a casual venue, but knew from working weddings that the rehearsal dinner was often an area the bride relented on to coax her groom to go along with her wedding day plans.

"You surprise me, Poppy. I thought this might be too down-home for the likes of Park Avenue. Aren't you worried the aroma of the hushpuppies frying in all that grease will pack the pounds on?" He rubbed his chin as if perplexed. "I had you pegged as one of those zero-carb types."

"Back off, Brandon."

"My old friends call me Gus."

"Exactly. I'm not old and we're not friends." She sipped her sweet iced tea, savoring the pucker from the juicy sliced lemons. Even in winter, citrus was fresh and brightly colored in Louisiana.

His half smile took the smirk off her lips, which threatened to match his sort-of smile.

"Careful there, you look like you might laugh at Southern humor. Can't have that from the Queen of New York High Society."

"Save it. I've styled my fair share of Southern belles, and their husbands. A handful of men from the South, too. A portion of my home decor line was inspired by memories of my time here in college, as a matter of fact."

His brow lifted, his eyes never leaving hers. Well, except to look at her lips. Did he know he was a walking sex god?

*Yes.* Like her, Brandon had been around the block several times. Too many, maybe. He appeared to wear it better than she did, as he looked fresh and energized. Two things she'd not felt in months.

"Go on."

"The ins and outs of the fashion industry would bore you. You're used to way more complicated challenges building ships, I'm sure." She shouted the words, her throat sore from talking over the cacophony of conversation, platters being slapped onto tables, all punctuated by the steady stream of Lynyrd Skynyrd through deceptively tiny speakers.

He scooted his chair close enough for one of the worn wooden legs to bump her seat. Tremors of awareness would have run up her spine but never made it past the hot pounding between her legs. He leaned in close and she fought to stand her ground. Holy Cajun grilled shrimp, he wasn't going to try to kiss her, was he?

"Relax. I can't hear your tough Yankee girl voice over the din in here. I want to make sure I don't miss a word." His breath formed words against her ear and she breathed in his clean but tinged with river scent. Very natural, very Brandon. Another side to the man who'd saved her from herself last night. "What you said about the house in New Orleans that you toured—do you remember which house it was?"

"The 1850 House."

He smiled appreciatively when she mentioned the landmark.

"That was right after Katrina."

"Yes." Their eyes met, no longer than the heartbeat it took for another bead of condensation to run down her beverage glass. Enough time to acknowledge that nothing had been the same here since the natural disaster.

"It was so beautiful, so untouched. I felt like I'd caught a ride through a wormhole and landed in antebellum Louisiana."

"That house was part of so many of my grade school field trips." His nostalgic smile gave her a sliver of insight into the boy he'd been. Happy. Content.

She nodded. "It captures the height of middle nineteenth century culture in America, and the kind of home I pictured every kind of woman of Scarlett O'Hara's generation grew up in." She'd created one of her idea journals about it, mostly photos she'd shot while there.

"You know it was only the wealthy who enjoyed the pretty lifestyle, right?"

"Yes, and I know there were slaves there. Which made it more meaningful for me, because I was on the tour with Sonja, and we looked at one another while we were standing in one of the slave's cottages. We realized we wouldn't have been allowed to be friends back then, not even one hundred years later. Not without a lot of effort. Sonja wouldn't have been able to ever go to school as a slave."

"No women did, except for a rare few."

"True, but for a black female slave? Her life was predestined from the moment she was born on the plantation."

"And yet you used the charming, overly decorated style of the main house to inspire styling a Southern couple?" His distaste couldn't be more clear. She didn't think Elvis had a better sneer. She stayed silent, regrouping.

"Let me guess, the bride was a white sorority sister who wanted to have the perfect society 'vintage' wedding."

"No, they were the Calvins." The starting quarterback of the New Orleans Saints and his wife had both gone to LSU and happened to be African American. "I was able to imbue the sense of where their families had come from while keeping the natural beauty of the South in her dress."

"Come again? You turned James Calvin's wedding into a civil justice statement?"

His words cut across the din at the right moment of quiet, when the streamed music was between songs and the majority of guests appeared to be drinking, eating, or watching the large-screen television as LSU fought for the national championship.

"Catering to the rich and famous can be done with civic duty in mind. Unlike slapping a pre-fab boat together and adding whatever gold-plated faucets your most recent tycoon asks for."

He leaned back, his brow near his hairline. "Don't sling mud when you don't know what you're aiming at, Yankee girl. It strikes me that your 'catering' to the rich and famous hasn't worked out so well for you lately."

She couldn't help the gasp that blew out of her mouth. Her stomach felt like it did when she'd been five and fallen off a swing set belly first onto the hard Buffalo dirt. It didn't last long, though, the disorientation, the shock at his well-aimed barb.

"So much for Southern manners, *Gus*."

So it was official. It was to be war.

\* \* \* \*

Her anger was more beautiful than a keel for one of his custom sailboats. He created the sailboats as part of a side business, the workshop in a part of his boat production facility. It allowed him to get away from the constant stress of the higher-end yachts and factory production of the flat-bottomed boats.

He savored the delicious satisfaction that he'd goaded her to this point. Where she was totally fixated on him, her eyes sparkling and her delicious mouth drawn in a straight line, all the while her nipples studded through the thin cotton of her fancy schmancy haute-whatever top. Pure exhilaration fueled his pounding pulse.

Except for the part where he felt like a complete ass. Poppy and her Maker's Mark eyes brought out the brute in him. *Brute.* If only. A brute would use every ounce of seduction he possessed to get Poppy into his bed. Brandon couldn't do that, not now, and probably not ever. Even if the time were right for both of them, they were salt and road rash. Who was the more damaged and who rubbed the salt in was a toss-up.

Although the music had picked back up, the din of conversation at their party's table hadn't. He shot a quick glance around, meeting the gaze of each person he could in the span of three seconds. It gave him the space he needed to figure out how to dig out of this hole. "I didn't mean it like that."

Nothing. She didn't smile, nod, nor blink. Christ she was a ball-buster. "I'm sorry. I was only trying to poke some fun at you for being from New York City. I don't mind Manhattan." Murmurs turned into conversations and the protection of the din allowed him to relax his shoulders. So he wasn't braced for the shove that landed solidly in the center of his right shoulder, making him rock back on the rear legs of his chair.

"How many times have you been to New York, *Gus*?" It was the second time she hadn't called him Brandon and he didn't like it. He didn't hate it, but he liked how his given name sounded with her TV-talk non-accent.

"Too many to count. You'd be surprised who orders custom yachts and then decides they can't deal with the upkeep."

"No, I'm not surprised. Dealing with the mega-rich and celebrities can often be difficult. It sounds like you get twice the fun, though. You build, sell, and help to resell?" Her interest was genuine.

"Something like that." He was so not going to tell Yankee girl that each boat was like a child; he had to let it go to the owner but if the kid was going to be sold Brandon wanted the boat back with him rather than risk it winding up in the hands of someone who wouldn't take care of it. It made him sound like an idiot, or worse, a control freak.

"Wait. Do you actually buy back the boats you've already made a fortune on?"

"Yes. And the boats themselves are the fortune, the investment as far as I'm concerned." Besides his employees, who were his family. "Profit margin is something else."

"Profit on your net can't be that bad. But how good is it for business to buy back your own product?"

"Very, actually. I let my accounts manager take care of it." The response was automatic, what he'd always replied before Jeb had taken off with the company treasure.

At the moment the only boat he had to sell needed at least a month's worth of rehab, and a lot of it included the pricy interior of the sailboat. "The last boat I purchased back had the cabin torn to shreds. The owner used it for a pit-bull tournament."

Horror flashed over Poppy's features, but to her credit she quickly compensated with what he thought of as her professional, high-fashion stylist detachment. "Did you get it back via the police?"

"No, the loser never got caught. I couldn't report him, as it was only hearsay, and my word against his assistant telling me that's what happened."

"A sense of entitlement is my least favorite character trait." Her mouth was set in a grim line. "Remorse would be nice every once in a while."

He laughed. "You do get it, don't you? Something tells me that our clientele have a lot in common."

"Maybe. My work is done with an event or wardrobe purchase. I can't imagine what you've invested in an entire custom boat."

"It's always a piece of my heart, that's for sure."

"How long does it take you?"

"No telling. Depends on the customer, their requests. At least six months, one time almost two years."

She regarded him with what he thought was respect. Maybe they wouldn't be at each other's throats except in the most pleasurable of ways.

Christ he had to stop thinking about sex with her. At least, his dick did.

"So you do mostly sailboats?" Her trademark flush illuminated her creamy skin and he knew she felt it, too.

"With full power and custom luxury fittings, yes. Think of them as yachts with sails. Smaller, but lacking no convenience."

"Do any of your owners actually sail or is it all crew?"

"A fair number want to learn to sail, or at least they act like it when they're touring the production facility. A handful have been lifelong sailors and pick us because of our reputation for quality. Then there are the sailors who save a lifetime for a Gus boat, and maybe they come into money from an inheritance or decide to let go of a retirement fund or two and cash it in for a boat."

"That's pretty dedicated. Giving up your retirement for a boat."

"There's a freedom in sailing under your own skill, in the middle of all that blue ocean. It's a sacred experience, being out where no other boats are in sight."

"Freedom?" She squished her nose. "Sounds like a lot of hard work." He didn't expect her to get it, just like he didn't expect his clients to all share his sailing zen.

He had to make the bottom line to keep Boats by Gus afloat, so he'd sold a boat or two to buyers he knew damned well would never appreciate the beauty of what they'd purchased. But it bothered him that Poppy didn't get it.

Why was he wasting his energy on her, a woman he'd have to spend, what, one more day with? So far from what he'd heard she had major trust issues, or should, by the way she'd been mistreated by her ex. With his own psychic wounds any consideration of involvement with her, no matter how casual, sent up flares of fiery premonition. The warning kind. As in, "this is lethal to your heart, buddy."

He met her gaze and the wariness behind her cool composure reminded him why he couldn't stop talking to her. Why he had to fight an erection at her mere scent or husky voice.

"That reminds me, we need to exchange phone numbers."

"You're kidding." Her deadpan reply threatened to coax a laugh out of him.

"No. With my brother and Sonja keeping the early part of tomorrow traditional, at least you and I should be able to communicate in case one of the limos gets lost or gets a flat."

"It's funny how people can be so modern, so hip, and yet when it comes to weddings, tradition shows up." She sipped her tea and the way her mouth closed around the straw made him want to press closer, force her to either back away or preferably cozy up as snugly to him as his jeans fit across his hard dick.

Jesus.

This woman was *waaaaay* too much work, way too complicated for him, even when he wasn't facing career annihilation while simultaneously feeling the effects of losing his lifetime best friend.

"Okay, I'll phone you. What's your number?"

He told her and watched her slim, adept fingers fly over her phone. No fancy nail polish for Poppy. She left that for her toes. Within seconds his phone rang with a 212 area code.

"Got it, thanks." Did he sound casual enough? She didn't think he wanted her number for anything other than the needs of the wedding service, did she?

"Let's hope we don't need to use our phones tomorrow." She always lectured her wedding parties to forget about the technology for one day. Let the wedding photographer do his or her job and put the phones away.

"It's hard to know." As he spoke he caught a movement up at the head of the large mass of tables that had been shoved together to accommodate their group of a dozen or so.

Two recognizable figures, even after years of dodging family functions, stood next to Henry and Sonja. Hudson and Gloria. His parents.

*Holy hell.*

# Chapter 5

Brandon's face went white under his generous tan and his eyes narrowed on a point somewhere over her head.

"You look a lot more uptight than you did last night, Gus. Sad that your brother is tying the knot?"

He opened his mouth to speak, to tell her to stop using "Gus," but his reply was lost to the sudden blanket of silence over the group. All eyes were toward the head of the table, where an older couple now stood. They appeared more than a little awkward in the low country establishment. The man was tall with the same profile as Henry and Gus, so it was clear this was their dad. The woman was perfectly turned out from her haute label outfit to her blunt-tipped nails, polished to look au natural but too precisely filed. Silver and blond wove together in her perfect bob, and her gaze scoured over the table and landed on the man next to Poppy. The flash of recognition in her blue eyes revealed to Poppy that the woman adored her son and that she was where Henry and Brandon's baby blues had come from.

"Aw, hell." His warmth left her as Brandon rose and walked to greet his parents. Poppy looked for Sonja, to give her a reassuring smile or wink. No need as Sonja was at Henry's side, beaming. Tears threatened under Poppy's lids at the scene. Poppy was happy for Sonja's sake, and Henry's, that his parents were offering this olive branch by showing up for the rehearsal dinner, after all.

But Mrs. Boudreaux's face froze when Sonja stepped up and kissed her cheek, and Mr. Boudreaux turned beet red at the same gesture from his future daughter-in-law. Good for Sonja. She'd teach these racist jerks what graciousness meant. A familiar sense of pride expanded under Poppy's ribcage. Poppy loved it when people became their best selves and let go of petty arguments that threatened otherwise enjoyable gatherings.

She'd certainly seen the former in her work but the more recent blowup at Will's parents' anniversary gala was most fresh in her mind. Where she'd been the one with the inappropriate behavior.

Chairs were pulled up to the table for the latecomers, conversation resumed, and Poppy decided to lose herself in the chatty fray. She wasn't enjoying her conversation with Brandon that much, anyhow.

*Liar.*

\* \* \* \*

Brandon broke ties from his family's business more than a decade ago. In the time since, he'd founded and maintained what was now a global shipbuilding business. He had much-worked-for recognition and the bank account to match. Well, he'd *had* the funds to match the description before Jeb had taken off.

Yet as he faced his parents he was once again the sixteen-year-old who was alternatively spoken to with stern warnings to "get it together" after being caught with his girlfriend, both naked, in his father's study. The boy who'd been iced out for weeks of nonverbal abuse from his miserable parents after he'd thrown a huge party with high school classmates. Or the college co-ed who'd been lectured for refusing to major in something more amenable to the law degree he'd certainly earn after undergrad.

He'd failed in his parents' eyes so many times he couldn't remember all of what they'd expected from him, anyhow.

"Dad." He held out his hand and his father gave it the customary shake followed by an uncomfortable pat on Brandon's shoulder.

"Brandon. We weren't sure we'd see you here. You're always busy these days." A dig at his frequent no-shows to family gatherings.

"I wouldn't miss it for the world." Unlike the mandatory Sunday dinners he'd forgone about the same time he'd started Boats by Gus. He turned toward his mother, who to her credit wasn't dressed over-the-top in one of her charity-function suits but instead in a casual sundress. "Hi, Mom."

"Brandon." She placed both hands on his shoulders to pull him in for a hug as he placed a kiss on her cheek. "I miss you, honey."

"Then it's great we're all together tonight, isn't it?"

"Give it up, son, for one night." Her smile belied the cold tone.

He didn't reply but instead turned to take a good look at Henry and Sonja. Happiness reflected off Henry's expression, but Sonja appeared a bit more subdued. If his brother was happy, that was all that mattered. Brandon had to admit that having his entire family here, save their sister Jena, to celebrate a joyous occasion was nice. A positive change from the more estranged relationship they normally shared.

"If you don't mind, I'll catch up with you both after dinner." Before any arrangements to the contrary could be made, he turned and sought his original seat. When he saw Poppy looking at him with interest, he relaxed. Next to her was where he wanted to be.

*Shit.*

\* \* \* \*

Poppy had a good view of the family reunion from her end of the worn barn-board table. Her heart squeezed with regret at how stilted and awkward the discourse appeared at the head of the table, in front of the large wedding party. Brandon and Henry had both shaken their father's hand. No big bear hugs, no laughing. And their mother—holy gumbo she looked like a piece of work. A woman who'd been pretty, beautiful, even, but hadn't aged quite so well. Poppy had a theory that miserable people could dress themselves up with top-tier fashion, literally "dress for success." But you couldn't fake genuine pleasure, none of which was evident in the exchange between the two generations of Boudreauxs.

From what Sonja and Henry had told her, the couple had raised three biological children and were stuck in the idea that their children were indeed *theirs*. As much as their house, their cars, and of course their family law practice belonged to them.

Poppy's study of the Boudreauxs' dysfunctional family dynamics was interrupted by bright blue eyes as Brandon turned and looked at her. As if searching for an anchor. As he lowered himself to the chair he leaned in and spoke to her privately. The puff of his breath on her ear was from his agitation at seeing his parents, she'd bet. Nothing sexual or flirty meant by it. And yet the sensation was as erotic as if he'd licked her ear with his tongue.

"That's Hudson and Gloria. Our parents in the flesh."

"Aren't you glad they changed their minds?"

"What?" Sharp, intent.

"Um, just wondering." She hadn't meant to appear so judge-y. "Sonja and Henry mentioned they were having a bit of a hard time with the wedding."

"That is the most astute thing you've said, Yankee girl." His drawl drew her eyes to his lips, and just like that the event again shrunk back to a party of two.

# Chapter 6

Sunlight streamed through stained-glass windows and cut through dust motes and the cloud of perfume that vied for attention over the scent of fresh cut gardenias and soft pink roses. Poppy ignored what felt like a lump of too-dry mashed potatoes in her throat as she tended to Sonja, the other bridesmaids chattering across where the bride sat in the center of the large closet that was used for bridal parties at the cathedral. Choir gowns were hung in color-coordinated order, the hues lined up according to the liturgical season. Being January before Lent and more significant to New Orleans, Mardi Gras, Sonja had decided against any colors reflecting either season, opting for more traditional bridal fashion sense.

"You don't like the flowers in my hair." Sonja's brow furrowed and Poppy stopped adjusting the sheer veil's headpiece. The bobby pins were refusing to cooperate with the beaded tiara.

"I love the flowers. Everything is perfect." Except for the lack of bridal joy that Poppy had expected would ooze from Sonja today. "Do you want a sip of water, honey? Or something stronger?" She knew Sonja wasn't a big drinker but her friend looked so forlorn, so anything-but-thrilled to be getting married that she had to try something.

"I'm fine." Sonja swallowed, her jaw set in an uncharacteristically harsh line. "Just make sure this thing is on straight."

"Whoa." Poppy put down the bobby pins in her hand and placed her hands on Sonja's shoulders. "What. Is. Going. On."

Sonja wouldn't meet her eyes. "I'm getting married. Anxiety is part of it, right?"

Sonja might be an accomplished attorney but at the moment she was the same woman Poppy had roomed with. Defensive as a cornered cat, with the claws to match.

"Jitters, yes. Crankiness, not so much. Do you want me to get Henry?" Poppy didn't believe in luck of any kind any longer, good or bad. The right man would be by your side no matter what.

"No, that's the last thing I need." Sonja rubbed her temples, and a sick sense of dread filled Poppy's stomach.

"Honey, what is it?" Her mind flashed to the sight of over four hundred people in the historical sanctuary, the grandly but tastefully decorated venue for the reception to follow, the planned brunch tomorrow morning before Sonja and Henry set off on their decadent honeymoon.

*Stop it. This isn't you, Henry isn't Will.*

"Sonja?"

Sonja remained silent and eerily still. Her face lacked its trademark glow and her eyes were glazed over. Poppy had to do something quickly or she feared Sonja wouldn't make it down the aisle. She'd seen enough last-minute wedding cancelations up close to know a bride on the edge of taking off.

"Sonja, honey, listen to me. Do you need to talk to Henry? We can call him. Yes, let's text him." Poppy turned to get her tiny clutch and Sonja's voice stopped her.

"No. Do not call anyone." Sonja's eyes raced around the room like a trapped raccoon. "I just need some air." She headed for the nearest door, which happened to exit out into a tiny garden that was normally lush with greens but in the winter months more subdued. Just like Sonja.

Sonja sat on a concrete bench, her expression stunned.

"Your dress, Sonja. Are you sure you want to sit on that?" Poppy tried to lift the long skirt and train off the damp ground.

Sonja shook her head, slowly and deliberately. "It's not going to work, Poppy."

"What's not going to work?" She had to ask the question but dreaded Sonja's response.

"Look at me, Boo. I'm a dyed-in-the-wool Baptist, about to walk down the aisle of one of the oldest Roman Catholic churches in America."

"It's not about the religion, hon. You know that and so does Henry. You agree on the big things. Didn't you say it's a way for you to celebrate your vows in community with all of your friends and family?"

"Not all of our family. And it's not about the religion part. It's about the differences in our backgrounds. Not the color, even. The culture, the fact that he grew up with everything money could buy and I never wore anything but hand-me-downs until I had my first job in college. Remember?" Poppy nodded. Of course she remembered. Like Sonja, she'd grown up on hand-me-downs and thrift store finds. It had been a celebratory moment for both of them when they'd gone shopping together in New York City for new outfits. The first of many joyous occasions they'd shared. Poppy would be damned to let this particular joyous event go down the drain.

"Talk to me, Sonja. I don't get it. I thought you'd be thrilled to have Henry's parents show up last night, after all. They looked as I expected, but you and Henry seemed to handle it okay."

"I was excited to see them, at first."

"But?"

Sonja fiddled with the crepe overlay of her long skirt, her cocoa skin perfectly highlighted by the rich pearl hue. "They spoke to me when Henry went to the restroom."

"You didn't mention any of this last night." Poppy regretted that she hadn't stayed with Sonja, insisted on a girls' chat the night before the wedding.

"I couldn't. I can't tell Henry how awful his parents are. I decided to ignore them, to ignore all aspects of it. I'm going to resign from the law firm when we get back..."

"From your honeymoon?"

Sonja shook her head, her braids set off by the waxy leaves of the magnolia tree behind the bench they sat upon. "There won't be a honeymoon." She looked at Poppy with her big round dark green eyes and Poppy knew the intent. Whenever Sonja was certain about any decision, whether in life or law, she got the same determined glint of steel.

"I'm calling Henry." Sweat dripped between Poppy's shoulder blades and her sweaty hands made gripping her plastic-covered phone difficult.

"No, you're not. I will." Sonja's hand covered Poppy's, stilling her fingers. "Give me five more minutes alone. I need to...to say a prayer. Then I'll call Henry and work it out."

Always a sucker for a spiritual moment, Poppy stood up. "All right. Five minutes. But then I'm coming back here and we'll do whatever you want me to." She wasn't going to allow her dearest friend to mess up the best thing that had ever happened to her because of some overbearing racist bigots who happened to be her future in-laws.

Poppy let herself back into the bridal room and found five sets of concerned eyes staring at her.

"Where's Sonja?"

"They've seated her mother!"

"The hostess says we have to start the procession now!"

Poppy held up her hands in the universal sign to shut the freak up. This was her territory, her bailiwick. "Ladies. Sonja is taking a minute to meditate, to calm down before she enjoys the most important event of her life. She needs each one of us to stay grounded." She made a point of making eye contact with each bridesmaid, not relenting until each face let go of concerned lines and puckers. "That's better." She motioned toward the entry to the narthex. "Let's go ahead and start lining up for the procession. Sonja will be back in here before it's my turn to walk." She sent up a silent prayer that this was the case.

The hostess was waiting at the entry to the sacristy when Poppy looked out of the bridal room. She went back in the room and watched as, one after another, each bridesmaid disappeared in a fluff of the palest pink pearl, the tulle skirts echoing the femininity and nod to the past, similar to Sonja's gown.

Poppy had helped dozens of nervous brides and bridegrooms pick out gowns and tuxedoes. Sometimes she was asked to be there on the wedding day, too, as an extra measure of reassurance. Only one or two had bailed. Three if you counted Will, but that was well before their scheduled wedding day.

Poppy resented that any thought of Will materialized at all. She had thirty seconds before it was her turn to walk down the long, centuries-old aisle of St. Louis Cathedral. Her palms sweated and her heart pounded as if *she* were the one getting married.

Before the hostess could come in and start asking about her and the bride, Poppy ran back into the side garden to get Sonja. She'd drag her friend down the aisle if she had to. Henry was the love of Sonja's life and there was no reason for them to not marry. Fuck the Boudreauxs.

"Sonja—" She gasped in horror at the sight of the garden just as her phone buzzed to indicate a text. From Brandon.

*WHERE ARE YOU?*

"Sonja!" she shouted, uncaring of anyone overhearing her frantic cry. The garden she thought was a courtyard actually opened up onto the cemetery, with easy exit to the large parking lot. Her heart thudded like a sailor's feet on the gallows. Shakily, she typed a reply no maid of honor ever wants to make.

*SONJA IS GONE.*

# Chapter 7

"You had one job, Poppy. One job." Brandon chastised her in between shots of bourbon, his tuxedo tie long gone and his shirt open to reveal a very sexy Adam's apple. A body part that had too much use as the bridal party all crowded together at a bar in the French Quarter, where no one batted an eye at the group sans bride and groom.

"You try outwitting Sonja. She's a genius, always has been."

"If she's so smart, why did she let Henry's asswipe parents change her mind?" Daisy spoke up from the other side of the group, her dress crinkled and her glass of Chablis almost gone.

"Yeah, explain that one, Poppy." Brandon's voice was smooth and she didn't hear anger in it, per se, but she couldn't shake the gut instinct that he blamed her for the hot mess that the wedding of the bayou had turned into. Plus he was calling her by her given name, not something he'd done much until now.

"Wait a minute. You're acting like I knew about this. As of last night Sonja was still excited to be getting married today." Well, sort of. She and Henry had been unusually quiet, and Henry left after the rehearsal dinner to stay with Brandon. All in the name of tradition, which right now didn't seem as charming as it had last night. "You're the one who had Henry at your place last night. What did he say that might have tipped you off to Sonja running away today?"

"Nothing. He was as surprised as I was that our parents showed up, and had some concerns about how our father is going to treat Sonja after the wedding. In the office. Which is a moot point since no wedding ergo no issues at work."

"It had to have been your parents. They said something to her last night. What else could it be?"

"Oh, I've no doubt it was my parents. This has Hudson and Gloria stamped all over it."

"Did they…did they ever try something like this with you?"

His eyes pinned her for a heart-stopping moment before he threw his head back and laughed at the tin-tiled ceiling. "Honey, that's all they know how to do."

She let the endearment run over her skin like its moniker. The things that she'd do with honey and Brandon's body…nope. She put her drink down. No more booze—it wasn't a good way to keep her heart safe.

"Well, it's a sure thing that when Henry catches up with her he'll change her mind." Pathetic words even if they were her own.

"Who says he wants to find her?" Brandon pulled at his open collar as if his tie was still there, revealing a smexy sprinkling of chest hair. Which probably indicated the start of a path to between his legs, where no doubt hung a magnificent cock. Because men like Brandon didn't do anything halfway. "See something you like, Yankee?"

*Caught.*

"Not at all. It's the artist in me—I scope out my surroundings."

Heat flared in his eyes and her nipples were pressing against her pink chiffon halter dress as if they'd been imprisoned for years. And it had only been, what, a few months since she'd had sex?

*Try six.* Okay six months since Will stopped the bedroom activity. Three months since she'd had a man as much as run his fingers down her arm, scratch her back. Until Brandon.

A warm hand on hers, pinning it to the smooth oak bar.

"Stay here, Poppy. With me. Forget about whatever happened in New York."

She looked at their hands, and at him. "What do you mean?" Her words came out like a torch, drawing a definite line between them. His hand lifted. They didn't know one another well enough. What was he thinking?

"Just don't want you to have another panic attack. None of this is your fault. I shouldn't have teased you." His puzzled expression underscored her pathetic neediness.

"I thought you meant stay with you. You meant stay here, in the present moment."

His expression sobered. "I'd never tease you about staying with me."

Her stomach flip-flopped. Rubbing her hand over it, she tossed her head and managed a smile. "I can handle teasing. And I'm not about to have a panic attack."

"You drifted there."

She had. And she wasn't sharing why. Hell, he already knew, along with the rest of the world that paid attention to social media and reality television. "I take it you've never followed the rules." She stirred her Manhattan, preferring to stick to what she was used to. Besides, it was her comfort drink.

"I tried to. Until I couldn't." He motioned for the bartender to bring them another round.

"Oh, no, I'll take a soda water." One more Manhattan and she'd never be able to work in the morning.

"You have somewhere to go in the morning?"

"No, but I have work."

"And you expect to still have the house to yourself for the next two weeks?"

Faced with the same two weeks to house-sit, but not knowing if either Sonja, Henry, or both would appear sooner, Poppy planned to work on her home decor line for the following spring, fourteen months out. She'd already turned in the autumn designs for Attitude by Amber and was waiting to hear at any minute which distributors had picked up which designs.

"Sure, why not? For all we know they went on the honeymoon anyway." She doubted it but hoped. Hoped that at least Sonja found true love, a real happily ever after.

"What do you have to work on? Now that your office in New York is, ah, on hiatus?"

"There's more to Designs by Amber than personal stylist and event planning. I'm getting ready for a major launch of a home fashion and decor line. I have plenty to do."

The large home on the banks of the tributary was quiet and the perfect place for her to set up shop. Thank God for the home decor line and associated women's fashion line or she'd be sunk, career kaput. She wanted to sink into her too-familiar world of stewing over why she hadn't been good enough for Will, what she could have done differently. Unfortunately Brandon's annoying intensity wouldn't let her go anywhere but the present.

"What are you staring at?" She used her best New York attitude.

"Come walk with me, Poppy." The warmth of his hand on hers wasn't clammy or suffocating as she wished it was. It would be so much easier if this man was a turnoff in at least one little way. Before she could come up with a protest, she was following him out of the bar, into the misting evening. Brandon's profile under the streetlights was tall, dark, and combined with the heat of his hand holding hers, sexually potent. A little groan escaped Poppy's lips.

"What's that?" He sounded distracted as he led them through the more familiar streets, back toward where they'd been the first night she'd met him. Two nights and a lifetime ago.

"Nothing, where are we going? The others are going to wonder."

"They're halfway drunk by now."

She couldn't argue with that, as she probably was, too. She'd fought to not drink too much, hoping Sonja and Henry would call and the entire nightmare of a day would have a happy ending.

"Have you ever done something that you know is completely out of the norm for you, totally inadvisable?" He spoke as he tugged her along, impatient to get wherever they were headed.

"Sure, I mean, I don't know. Maybe. Wait—we're going back to the garden?" Poppy was all about atmosphere and ambience but what did Brandon have to say in the garden that he couldn't tell her in the bar? "Are you talking about Sonja running away from her own wedding?"

"Sonja and Henry aren't on my radar right now."

Nothing sexier than for the man holding her hand to be determined, confident. Her mind raced with all kinds of sexy encounter ideas. Her stomach tingled at the possibilities and the heat between her legs, which had become a damned glow stick since she'd met him, raged.

"Brandon, wait, it's raining. I don't have a coat." Actually, all she had was a wrap, which was a frothy pile of pink on her abandoned barstool.

They'd reached the private garden and Brandon led them through to a side area they hadn't visited the other night. He smiled at her in the dark, his white teeth promising things her body would gladly beg for.

When they stepped up onto a small gazebo, Brandon took off his coat and placed it around her shoulders. As he drew her up against his hard length, she felt surrounded by him—his musk, his fresh-wood scent, his presence.

"Poppy." He placed his hands on either side of her face and she didn't stop him, couldn't look away as he lowered his lips to hers.

\* \* \* \*

Brandon couldn't let another chance to kiss Poppy Kaminsky go by. After tonight, he'd never see her again and—

Hell, who was he kidding? He wasn't after one kiss from this incredible woman. If they ended up back at his place, that'd be even better. She wasn't a shy debutante or young college grad who'd expect more from him. Poppy was as worldly as he when it came to sex, he was certain. And besides her burning body that he was insane to explore, he sensed they both needed this. Poppy had survived a huge personal loss and so had he. It didn't matter that she had no clue what he was going through. He needed respite and inexplicably felt that she did, too. A healing. Two adults, helping each other. What he needed to do, wanted to do to Poppy, with her, for her, became clear.

Until his lips touched hers. All certainty, all of what he was so sure of, vanished like the millions in his bank account had. Instead of being absconded to God knew where, though, his thoughts formed into a tight, hot, uncontrollable awareness of the woman he held in his arms.

"Poppy." He spoke against her lips, afraid if he broke the intimate contact she'd disappear. Her mouth opened to his and her tongue met his with sinful hot need. When she wrapped her arms around his neck and pressed against him he lifted her a couple of inches off the gazebo deck and turned them around until he had her back up against a smooth white column. He took his time to set her down, allowed her front to run along his, allowed her to feel his erection against her softest parts. Even through layers of clothing his cock felt her heat as he ground into her. She rewarded him with gasps and sharp, short pants. Not anxiety breathing this time but turned-on, let's-keep-it-going gulps for air. Seeing that she wanted him as much as he did her was the biggest turn-on. Ever.

He kissed her throat, licking at the creamy skin, his nape and scalp tingling from being this close to her, finally kissing her the way he'd imagined nonstop for the past forty-eight hours. And he thought he didn't do "tingled."

"Brandon." Her ragged voice told him all he needed. All he wanted.

"Come back to my place, Poppy."

"Not smart." She kept moving her hands over his back, pulled his shirt out of his pants, and pushed her hands under to touch his back. When she moved to his abs the floor under them felt like his boat deck.

"Christ, Poppy, not yet." He grabbed her hands and held them above her head, flush with the gazebo column. It was natural to take full advantage of the position, to kiss her with a need beyond his experience. And he considered himself most experienced with women and raw, unapologetic erotic sex.

He knew in that moment that it wasn't a fluke, or coincidence of a family wedding. Poppy had something no other woman could give him.

* * * *

Poppy wanted to blame her light-headedness on the cocktails, on the long, sad day. Not on the fact that she couldn't catch her breath when Brandon kissed her like this because the way he kissed was knock-it-out-of-the-park good. Expert. Exactly what she needed to escape the heavy. When he lifted his head and broke their kiss she let out a cry of dismay.

"There's more at my place, Yankee girl." He licked her bottom lip, sucked on it gently until she had to totally rely on the gazebo post and Brandon for support. Poppy had experienced intense sexual attraction before, but this was different in ways she wasn't willing to admit. Not tonight, not when her skin was on fire for Brandon.

"I want to, Brandon, I do. But then there's tomorrow and we'll have to face that we did this and..." She stopped talking as he switched his hold on her wrists to one hand and explored her body with his free hand. He touched her so lightly, so provocatively on her face, her throat, the side of her body where the dress perfectly fitted her along her ribcage.

"Brandon, this is torture."

"Patience, Yankee girl." His hand cupped her breast and his gentle squeeze through the chiffon would never be enough, nor would the way his thumb flicked at her hardened nipple.

Her heart pounded against his hand but she was more aware of the velvet heat that pulsated between her legs. Brandon had to feel her need, and not only because she was writhing her hips against his pelvis as if she were a dog in heat.

His chuckle was rough around the edges and betrayed his want. As if his rock-hard cock hadn't. She tugged to release her hands, needing to feel the length of him. "Not yet, Poppy." In one motion his mouth was back on hers and his hand under her silky skirt, his fingers seeking her center. No words were exchanged as he found her, dripping with want for him, and plunged two fingers into her.

Poppy let out a squeak and would have died of mortification if his fingers, his kiss, weren't pushing her to the precipice of what she was certain would be the best orgasm of her life. When Brandon's thumb, that magical thumb, pressed her clit at the same time his mouth sucked on her tongue, Poppy broke apart. Wave after wave of complete sensual release hit her. Brandon let go of her hands and her arms clutched at his shoulders as the climax wrecked her. When she finally floated back to reality, her cheek was on Brandon's shoulder, his arms wrapped around her as he dropped kisses against her hair and murmured sexy talk in her ear.

"That's only a teaser for later." His deep voice vibrated in his throat, his chest, and she was loath to lift her cheek.

"I don't think my heart could take more than that." The words were a no-filter expression of what she felt, but as soon as they came out she realized how he could take them. She pushed back and looked up at him. His eyes reflected the same desire she felt, as well as the same defensiveness. "I don't mean that in an emotional sense. I'm saying that the cardio workout you just gave me was better than any spin class. Not that it wasn't more. God I suck at explaining my emotions!"

"Enough." He leaned in and she allowed the kiss without any hesitation. Instead of the passionate come-on she expected, however, Brandon's lips were sensual in their exploration, his tongue completely claiming her again but without the possessive stamp of earlier. He lifted his head and smiled at her. "There's no need to fret, Yankee girl. Let's call it a night here."

"But you're…you've got to be in discomfort."

"Nothing I can't handle. And trust me, Poppy, the pleasure was all mine." He kissed her on the forehead and wrapped his arm around her waist.

Poppy walked out of the garden with Brandon, and it wasn't until they neared the French Quarter again that she realized she hadn't thought about anyone or anything going on her life since they'd left the bar.

For a blessed hour, Poppy had been totally herself.

\* \* \* \*

Brandon didn't make any attempt to sit near her for the rest of the evening but she felt his gaze on her, the hot caress of his baby blues. Each time she sought to meet his glance he looked away as if to prove his point that whatever they'd shared back in the garden was definitely "no ties."

"I want Sonja to be happy." Daisy chattered away albeit much more sloppily after the pre-dinner cocktails and dinner drinks turned into shots. Poppy enjoyed another cocktail but nothing to get her drunk or even buzzed. It wasn't her scene and she didn't need to justify herself.

Another new feeling since being in New Orleans. She was feeling so good, in fact, that the old Poppy whispered in her ear that something was bound to go to pot at any moment.

"Sonja will be happy, Daisy. And I do think Henry could still be the man for her. They need time and space, I suppose. To work things out."

"I'd like to work things out with him." Daisy leaned drunkenly against Poppy as she pointed at Brandon. The jealous reaction in Poppy's stomach was familiar—hadn't she lived with it these past two months as she watched her assistant and Will plan their life together? The jealousy she experienced now wasn't so sophisticated, though. It wasn't about her career, her aspirations to marry the "perfect" man. It had nothing to do with the sense of possessiveness she'd experienced before, over Will.

It was a more melancholy, primal type of jealousy she wasn't familiar with. And it was laced with deep sadness. As if her heart knew she'd never have the likes of a man like Brandon Boudreaux. A man who could touch her like that but still challenge her mind. And make her laugh.

*Kaminsky women don't do lucky in love.*

As if to prove her point, her phone vibrated and lit up. She'd kept it out on the bar in case Sonja called or texted. Her stomach flipped at the ID. Carolyn. Her agent in New York, the woman who'd brokered the entire Attitude by Amber deal. On a Saturday night when Carolyn knew Poppy had scrammed out of town to escape the social media meltdown and attend her best friend's wedding.

"Hi, Carolyn."

"Poppy. I'm sorry to bother you today, but we need to talk."

"Sure, go ahead."

She had to press the phone to her ear and plug the other.

"Poppy, I know it's your sister's wedding, which I trust went well, but, well, I'm afraid I've got some bad news."

Poppy's skin started to crawl and a flush of heat rose up her throat, her face. "No problem. I'm getting together the designs for the next season's release." The words came out in a rush. As if they could stem the bad news Carolyn was trying to break to her.

"Poppy, there isn't going to be another season."

Poppy laughed, a nervous reaction to what she hoped was a garbled statement. She wasn't hearing well amidst the Saturday night revelers.

"Wait, Carolyn. What did you say? Hang on. I'm in a bar in downtown New Orleans. I'm walking outside now." The bar was noisy and she grabbed her clutch and slid off the barstool. She made a beeline for the door, grateful for the break from the din and Brandon's subversive intensity.

Once on the side street, dark and deserted compared to the main thoroughfare, she spoke. "Okay, go ahead, Carolyn. Sorry about that. It was so loud I didn't make out what you said. I thought you said there wasn't going to be another season!" She smiled, knowing the impossibility of Attitude by Amber being canceled this close to the first season's release. It was too big of a deal for the distributors to back out of.

"That is what I said, Poppy." Carolyn's voice was kind, compassion oozing from each word. Each. God. Damned. Word.

"But we're only weeks—"

"Your brand is too risky, Poppy. There's the public debacle of your breakup with Will, and now the lawsuit from your former executive assistant against your brand has gone public in a big way. You're a liability the buyers are unable to risk. I'm sorry, but with over eighty percent of the retail sites refusing to carry Attitude by Amber, they've decided to cancel your entire line. They're voiding your contract in its entirety. I'm so sorry, Poppy. I know how rough the last few months have been for you." Carolyn had known her since she'd started her personal stylist business and had encouraged Poppy to reach further, to stretch her creative talents beyond catering to rich celebrities. To build something more solid, more independent. Something of her own.

"Carolyn, what the hell am I supposed to do now? There has to be somewhere else to send the designs, the entire concept. What about an online launch?" She heard the desperation in her tone as if she were viewing the scene from high above the weathered pavement.

"You're free to keep the samples you've already received, of course. For your future inspiration. But for the foreseeable future, Poppy, you're out of the design business. Why don't you use the two weeks you were going to spend working on Attitude by Amber to unwind, decompress. Think about what you really want out of your talents."

"I want my own label on decor and fashion, Carolyn. Which apparently you're telling me is not going to happen. Ever."

"I didn't say ever, exactly."

"You've never been one to beat around the facts. Please don't start now." Poppy pressed her palm to her forehead, hoping against all hope that she wouldn't start to panic or get a migraine. Not on top of this.

"You're tired. How was the wedding?"

"About as good as my career. It didn't happen." She briefly filled Carolyn in, still feeling as though she were in someone else's body.

"How can this be happening?" She fought to breathe, fought against the pounding in her ribcage, stomped her foot in her high heels, let the pain in her toes confirm this wasn't a dream, that she wasn't in an alien body.

Carolyn's sigh came from twelve hundred miles away but sounded crystal clear in Poppy's ear. "It's business, Poppy. You have a lot of talent, and you'll eventually land on your feet again. But no one's willing to risk launching your line when your brand has plummeted."

"Attitude by Amber is the new line the retail stores need. You know how much they're struggling, unable to compete with online sales. Please,

talk to them again. Talk to anyone who can help us. Convince them to let
the first season launch. Give me a chance. We can rename it if you want."

"It's not that simple, Poppy. What is clear is that Attitude by Amber is
dead, and you need time for the public to forget your recent mishaps. And
time to come out with a new, commercial game plan."

Accusations she'd hurled at Will for being a fake and imposter roiled
in her mind, the accusations suddenly applying to her. She was a fake.
She wasn't a designer, the one thing she thought was bulletproof in her
arsenal of talent. Nothing could take her talent away. Wrong. Bad timing,
an uneven temper, and unfortunate circumstances with her ex-fiancé had
led to this point. She let out a soft moan.

"Give yourself time to process this. We'll talk after you're back in the
city. Call me in a couple of months." Carolyn ended the connection as
abruptly as ever. Usually Poppy accepted it as the cost of having such a
highly competent agent. Now she realized it was because her agent had
lost faith in Poppy's competence.

The line went dead and Poppy gulped. In a few short weeks her brand
had gone from a potentially multimillion-dollar commodity to zip, nada,
zero. Negative zero.

She was an utter failure, alone in a city she barely knew, and stuck in
a huge empty house while her best friend traipsed the country trying to
find herself.

Worse, Poppy had no idea who she was anymore. What did it say that
the only time she'd felt one hundred percent natural and totally the woman
she was meant to be had been in the arms of a man she'd known for less
than a week?

The music from the bar sounded like a hollow echo in the alley and
she watched a couple stumble out of the exit, laughing and hanging onto
each other. Was that how she'd appeared as she'd gone into the garden
with Brandon?

She'd lost her focus. And now she'd lost all she'd ever worked for.

She had to get out of here before Brandon came looking for her. She
saw the flash of car lights on the cross street a block up and headed for the
main thoroughfare. The anonymity and relative safety of a well-lit street
in the French Quarter oddly calmed her. She'd be back at Sonja's in under
an hour, thanks to her Uber app.

# Chapter 8

Brandon ripped the earbuds out and rested his head on the back of his shipbuilding office's chair. He'd managed to track Jeb to the NOLA airport, but that was it. Forced to hire a PI, all he could do now was wait for more information. Short of reporting Jeb as a criminal, he was fucked. The roar of silence in his ears mocked him, a constant reminder than there were no new custom orders coming in. Hence the quiet shipbuilding facility. When he'd walked the floor of the flat-bottomed boat factory earlier today, every employee had been upbeat, focused on their work. Because they didn't know what was coming down.

Nothing had gone smoothly in the week since Henry's almost-wedding. Not one damn thing. His only respite was working on a custom order for a sailboat that he wasn't sure he'd be able to scrape up the funds to finish. The customer had put down the full payment, in cash, but it had been eaten up by overhead. Brandon spun his chair around and looked at the rivulets of rain webbing down the windowpane. He'd never thought it all could turn on a dime like this. His only option was to file for bankruptcy.

Unless he put a bid in for the San Sofia contract. The small Caribbean island nation had reached out to Boats by Gus about contracting for ten hybrid boats that would allow their national drug defense agency to patrol and apprehend their territorial waters. Brandon wanted the contract so badly he could taste it.

But he wasn't a Foreign Service Officer. He could be diplomatic, sure, but didn't have the *savoir faire* needed to pull off a meeting with foreign country representatives, for God's sake. And he'd be competing against much larger, more experienced shipbuilders. Even if his bank accounts were flush, his former best friend and accountant not a scum-sucking thief, he'd be hard-pressed to land even a portion of what was on the table. His gut churned at the thought of his employees becoming job hunters overnight. His text dinged and he absentmindedly checked it, still holding out hope that Jeb would reach out to him.

It was Henry.

> *Saw storms coming in. Please check on the house for me. Key under flowerpot with gecko decoration on side. Don't let Poppy get stranded in flood. Won't be back until my vacation days run out.*

Brandon hesitated, wondering how much of this was his business, before he texted a reply.

> *How long will you be gone?*

Henry's response was swift.

> *At least two more weeks. Maybe 3. Thanks.*

Henry gave no clue as to where he was, what he was doing with Sonja, *if* he was with Sonja. What the hell? And wasn't he supposed to return from his honeymoon by the end of next week? Brandon wasn't in any place to judge his brother's emotional needs. But he thought it was okay to be annoyed at him for forcing him to deal with the one woman he hadn't been able to forget about. The woman he wanted to believe was back in New York. That she wasn't still this close and hadn't so much as texted. He'd left the next move up to her but deep in the crevices of his betrayed heart a tiny ghost of himself had kept a light lit with the tiny hope she'd been as turned on by him as he was her.

Henry thought Poppy was still house-sitting, but Brandon wasn't so sure. The way she'd left the party at the bar last weekend, disappearing without notice, made him think she'd left NOLA. That was good, if she did. Because she'd crept into his thoughts too many times over the last few days. He hadn't allowed himself to contact her. He'd wondered too often if he'd made a mistake, letting her go like that.

He shook his head and punched in a reply to Henry.

> *Are you sure she's still there? I'll go check either way. Hope you're well.*

He'd bet his last dollar that Poppy had taken the next flight out of Dodge, back to her familiar habitat in New York City. The city reminded Brandon of a gerbil tube. He'd appreciated the museums and being able to have whatever kind of food you wanted, sure. But he'd felt he was inside more than out and if he didn't have claustrophobia that would give it to him. As unsure of his life and future as he was right now, one thing he knew about himself was that he had to be in nature every day, no matter for how long. Office work wasn't his gig.

He didn't have a last dollar to bet on Poppy being gone, though, and tapped on his weather app. There had been some notifications that heavy rains were possible, but since he'd come into the office this morning the advisories had turned to warnings.

"Shit." The weather was nothing to mess with in New Orleans or the surrounding bayou. Flooding happened at the drop of a hat and it was indiscriminate in whether it affected residential areas or not. Henry's place was up on a bit of a rise, but nothing was high enough for the torrential downpours that NOLA was known for. According to the forecast, the rain that was currently a steady drizzle wasn't going to let up for the next five days, with the heaviest bands moving into the area in about an hour and lingering for seventy-two. He was going to have to make sure Poppy was okay. Or rather, check on Henry's place. If she was there, whatever.

"Double shit."

"You okay, boss?" His office administrator poked her head in his door. She knew he talked to himself regularly, but he hadn't realized how loud he'd been.

"Fine, Greta. Have you seen the weather? I think we'd better close up shop so folks can go prep their homes."

"Already done. I've let anyone who asked to leave earlier go, and the rest got ready last night. They'll finish out the workday but I think we'll be stuck at home for a few days."

"Right. Thanks. You'd best go home now, too. I take it they've let school out?"

Greta laughed. "Yeah, my kids have already texted me a grocery list of the snacks they want on hand."

"Stay safe and we'll stay in touch about when to return to work."

He'd been so wrapped up in finding Jeb he'd missed the weather threat until now. Thinking about Poppy's heat for him, and she *had* been hot for him, hadn't helped, either. If she was still here he couldn't see her—it'd only lead to more crazy. Checking the weather and local news again he saw that the airport was still open but expected to shut down within the next several hours.

First, he'd try her cell. If she was still in town he'd have to convince her to get out and fly back to where she came from. Gerbil habitat and all.

* * * *

The Piggly Wiggly grocery cashier didn't bat an eye at Poppy's order as it passed by her on the rubber belt. The well-groomed, if a bit heavy on the blue eye shadow, woman moved her crimson acrylic nails over the register keyboard as she scanned a brick of processed cheese followed by a can of spicy tomatoes. Poppy half expected the cashier to say something about her lack of nutritional food. Hell, she judged her poor choices but still planned to indulge. Cow Tales, Chocolate Kisses, and other junk food joined the array of colorful fruits and veggies she couldn't resist. The Piggly Wiggly's produce section was robust and cheery, a happy place on the overcast day. A bright spot in the perpetual gloom of the depression she'd sunk into. She'd failed to keep her best friend's wedding from being canceled and oh, by the way, lost the biggest deal of her career, probably her life. How was she expected to recover from this without licorice whips? Register five's cashier, "Brandy" according to the embroidered name above her heart, rang up the last item, a half-gallon of Blue Bunny ice cream *Bunny Tracks*, and raised one perfectly drawn red eyebrow at Poppy. "That all, sugar?"

"Yes." Wasn't her sugarfest enough?

"How about a case of water?"

"Water?"

"Storm's hitting tonight. Last time it was this big there was no drinking local water without boiling it first. It lasted for two weeks."

"Okay, two cases of water." Poppy didn't need to be strong or act like a know-it-all. Not to the ageless copper redhead cashing her out.

"Got it. Jimmy!" The petite woman bellowed in a volume to match a pro wrestler's. "Two cases on five!" She turned back to Poppy.

"You visiting, sugar?"

"Yes. Housesitting for a friend." She pushed back her greasy bangs. Showering had been too much of an effort since the wedding. Since that awful phone call from Carolyn.

Since the most incredible sex of her life, and even that had been one-sided. Brandon hadn't wanted her to reciprocate. Add "failed blow job attempt" to her list of reasons to stay depressed.

"Did your friend show you where they keep their canoe?"

"A boat?" An immediate image of Brandon standing in his flat-bottomed boat flashed in her mind. "No, I'm pretty sure they don't have a boat."

"Then you better find out which neighbors do, sugar. There's going to be flooding if the weather guessers are right, and you're going to need a way out of your place, just in case. You might want to try to get a hotel reservation, if there are any left."

"Um, we're up on a hill. I'll be fine. Thanks." She silently begged the chip reader to finish digesting her credit card's code.

Cashier Brandy cackled. "Sweetheart, there are no 'hills' in these parts." Fluorescent purple nails highlighted her air quotes. "Some patches of property are higher than others, but we're all on the tributary around this neighborhood. When you're right at or below sea level it's all the same, trust me."

*Ding.* Finally. She grabbed her card and her cart, filled with three week's worth of self-pity food for her remaining eight days in New Orleans. The bayou, she reminded herself. Not NOLA proper, where she'd had the best kiss of her life and the worst phone call of her life. For a city below sea level NOLA packed a wallop of life's extremes.

"Thanks for the suggestions, Brandy."

She beat feet out of the Piggly Wiggly and threw her goods into the trunk before she scrambled into the luxurious interior of Sonja's car. Blasting the air against the heavy humidity, she drove the short distance through three or so neighborhoods until she reached the turnoff to the river house. It was hard to believe that all of these streets would be under water. It was January, not spring or summer, when she imagined the truly heavy rains came. And hurricane season was over, wasn't it?

As she pulled onto the short gravel driveway she frowned at the strange vehicle in front of the garage. Damn it. If Henry was back then she'd have to leave. And if he'd brought Sonja with him, she'd have to leave now to give the couple space.

Poppy parked the car, got out, and went to the front door. She'd bring the groceries inside in a minute. First she had to determine whether it was the bride, groom, or both who'd returned.

The decorative front door opened to the empty house and she looked around the foyer and living room. "Hello?"

At no response she listened for running water. Maybe Henry or Sonja were in the bathroom. Walking further inside, she checked the kitchen, dining room, and side balcony. No one.

Sighing, she put her purse down on the counter and continued into the family room. And stopped short, fighting a scream at the unexpected man sitting there.

*Brandon.*

Maybe her blues were making her crazy and this was a hallucination. The man had terrorized her dreams and popped into her waking thoughts all day, every day since last Saturday.

"Hello, Yankee girl."

He sat on the sofa, poring over her portfolio albums. It was her personal, safe place to work on her artistic visions while in the house. The invasion was as physical as if he'd broken into her own home and ransacked her most private rooms.

"What the hell are you doing here?"

Only after a long moment did Brandon look up and study her, much as he'd been doing with her design concepts. His eyes widened as he took her in from head to toe, and damn it if her skin didn't feel an electric jolt of heat from his attention.

"What's going on with you? You feel okay?" He nodded at her, as if she'd shown up in her worn terry bathrobe with used tissues in the pockets. She looked down at her pull-on Capri yoga pants and wrinkled T-shirt. The robe might have been a better choice, if it weren't already draped over the sofa.

"I feel fine, thank you, and you didn't answer me. How did you get in here? Wait—Henry keeps a key with you, I suppose. You knew I was here—why didn't you call first?"

"I did try to call and text. Your voicemail is full or your phone is off. I even emailed you through your website. And there's a spare key under the front flowerpot as backup."

She'd shut her phone off Saturday night and refused to go online since holing up here. Or rather, house-sitting. The thought of someone being able to unlock what had been her fortress since the wedding made her shiver. Was anything what it seemed?

"I'm too busy to have outside distractions right now." She crossed her arms over her chest, dreadfully aware of the thin comfort bra she wore under the crumpled top. It wasn't the best presentation of her breasts. Fine for Piggly Wiggly, but not hot-as-sin Brandon Boudreaux.

"Do outside distractions include showering?" His comment was dry but non-accusatory. As if maybe he'd had a bout of no-shower days himself. Although his skin looked freshly scrubbed, his hair damp from the sprinkling rain. His teeth contrasted next to his tan skin screamed fit and healthy. Completely opposite of how she knew she appeared.

"I prefer baths, and my hair needed deep conditioning." What made him an expert on female beauty regimens?

"Stay down here long enough and the humidity is all the moisturizer you need." He snapped her largest journal closed, the one with all of the Southern-inspired designs, and held it up in the air. "You did this?"

"Yes."

"Ever think of interior decorating, design? Instead of being a personal stylist?"

"That's what I was doing with my Attitude by Amber line." Using the past tense hurt her heart.

"I want you to outfit the cabin on a boat I'm building."

"I'm not into boats."

He held up a hand. "I know you're all busy with your brand deal, but I promise I'll pay you well. Your nautical take on furniture in this book lends perfectly to what I need in this boat. I realize you'll have to work around your Attitude by Amber launch. But since you might be stuck here longer with the weather coming in, it'll give you something to fill the hours."

"I...I don't have much to do with that deal right now." He hadn't picked up on her clue that Attitude by Amber was off the table, which was just fine. She didn't have to admit her failure. Not yet. Not to him. Especially not to him.

"It'd be a new area for me. Outfitting boats." She was reluctant to meet his gaze but when she did, his blue eyes assessed her without scorn. His arms looked buff and strong in his T-shirt. She remembered how wonderful it had felt to let go in the most basic, intimate way in those arms. They'd feel good in a hug while she cried on his shoulder, too.

She stood up straight and reminded herself that she didn't need anyone's shoulder.

He cocked his head. "So you'll do it?"

"I didn't say that."

"You've been a stylist for several of my clients. And I know you've been on their boats. So you've already seen what I do."

She nodded. "Yes, I have. I didn't know they were your boats at the time. It seems we've both created businesses that attract the same client demographic." A demographic she wanted to change. She'd learned so much from her high-end clients, as much from the divas as the humble. But it wasn't enough anymore.

He scratched the back of his head, looking a little less comfortable than he had when she'd walked in on him.

"This is a bit off topic, but what do you do for your male clients? As a stylist."

Standing in Sonja's house, in jeans and a T-shirt, he looked every bit the sexy man he was, and it would be too easy to give him an erotic reply. Just for the hell of it. If she was freshly showered, and her hair wasn't plastered to her scalp in her best pity-party style.

"I help them decide on a basic look that they're comfortable in, and riff on that. Take your jeans and T-shirt. You seem to make a uniform out of it, so I'd suggest keeping the jeans but updating them, and maybe putting a collared shirt over your T-shirts."

He looked down at his outfit as if seeing it for the first time. "I spend my days either on a computer or the phone, negotiating deals, and the rest of the time building boats. I don't need fancy. Not usually."

"Do you ever give your clients tours of your facility? You said you've been to Manhattan to deliver your boats. Do you meet your customers dressed like that?"

"I have several suits for when I need them."

"Off the rack, right?" At his shrug she continued. "There's nothing wrong with that, but you're selling million-dollar products. You need to look the part of the successful business owner."

"Maybe in Manhattan but not here. People in the bayou are more laid-back. Visitors expect the local charm."

"Give me a break. Southern style, especially here in New Orleans, takes its cue from the early settlers. The Duke of New Orleans and French culture in general has left an indelible mark here. Just look at all the fleur-de-lis!"

"Someone's been reading her history."

Brandon didn't miss a thing. He must have seen the thick book on New Orleans she'd pulled off Henry's shelf, lying on the wide ottoman. And he mocked her for it. Didn't he realize a trip into the complicated, rich history of this area was the best kind of escape when your life was in shambles?

A bright flash of light startled her but not nearly as much as the immediate crack of thunder. "What is this, the Great Flood? It sounds like Poseidon's right over the house." She shouted at him, needing to be heard over the sudden cloudburst.

Brandon was unmoved by her declaration, his hands on his hips, his face down. As if he were shoring up for a huge battle, calculating his next move. When he looked back up his blue eyes reflected the stormy winds that lashed crepe myrtle branches against the windows.

Awareness, as intense as it was instant, pulsed desire through her veins. It all pooled between her legs and she knew her panties weren't daintily damp but in fact dripping with her want. Her need.

"I didn't come here to talk about business, Poppy."

# Chapter 9

Poppy's eyes were Southern Comfort laced with Cajun spice—the kind that burned your tongue if you got too much of it. Even in her obvious state of depression over what he assumed was her recent breakup, she was a sexy woman. Her wrinkled clothes did nothing to hide the ample roundness of her breasts or the succulent nipples pushing against her top. The pull-on yoga kind of pants, but shorter, revealed more curvy parts that included her sumptuous ass. His fingers itched to run over the round cheeks, to see if they were as ample yet as firm as they had felt in his hands last week. And her bare calves—angels didn't have such beautiful, creamy skin. Angels definitely didn't have red toenails with daisies painted on them.

The daisies pushed him over the edge from the constant awareness he'd had of her since she'd walked into the house to a full-blown, pushing-against-the-crotch of his jeans erection. And she probably hadn't showered in a few days.

"Christ." Another flash, a long rumble of thunder. He couldn't do this. Not with her, not in his brother's house. "I'm here to check on the house, to see if it'll hold up through the rain. You know about the weather reports, right?"

She tugged at the bottom of her shirt. "The grocery cashier mentioned it. I got a couple of cases of water, and—oh, shit!" Her eyes grew round and she turned and ran for the front door.

"Poppy, wait, you can't go running out in this lightning." He followed her, figuring the deluge would stop her. Yankee girl wasn't from these parts and no amount of lightning was going to waylay her, however.

Wind slammed the oak door open and Poppy ran out to her car, slipping and sliding on the wet pebbles. Lightning flashed like a strobe through the sheets of tropical rain. His brain registered that the rain wasn't going to stop for a long time—this was catastrophic, flood-making rain.

Poppy wasn't stopping, either, as she struggled with the handle on the passenger door of what he thought must be Sonja's car. He caught up to her and stopped, watching the rain run in streams down her smooth, flawless neck as she reached into the BMW SUV and pulled a couple of Piggly Wiggly bags off the seat. Her T-shirt was no longer baggy but clung to her. He reached out and touched her shoulder. It would be easy to lie to himself, say it was a concerned contact, a physical way to get through to her in her obvious state of dismay over whatever was inside the vehicle.

All he wanted was for her to do exactly what she did. Close the door, turn around, face him. Look up at him through the torrent, allow him to see how her large nipples were outlined by the soaked fabric, reassuring him that their time on the gazebo hadn't been a dream. Her amber eyes were liquid sex and the heat in them blew away his last shred of resistance.

He pushed his pelvis up against hers, giving her time to change her mind, even as her lips let go of a moan and she tilted her head back against the body of the car. The heat between her legs made his erection painful as it strained through the denim. When Poppy put her hands on his waist and wrapped her leg over his hip, he followed the rain and let go.

A flood of lust, desire, and sexual frustration that had built since he'd seen her last overflowed his mental restraint and he held her face in his hands as he kissed her. It wasn't anything sentimental or romantic—it was pure need, greedy and unapologetic. Need for the most intriguing woman he'd ever laid eyes on. Her tongue was hot and she didn't only match him stroke for stroke but she demanded her take of him, too.

He wanted to worship her, cradle her breasts but he had to have her close to him, part of him, so he wrapped one arm around her waist and one lower, grasping her hard little ass in his hand.

A soft *splat* as the bags hit the ground and Poppy's arms wound around his neck. This time it was Poppy pressing against him, her breasts flattened on his chest.

"Where, Yankee girl? Tell me where you want to do this." He bit her lower lip and she groaned, the vibration from her throat going straight to his cock.

He shifted to have a better hold of her and his foot settled into something soft and messy. Looking down, he saw the half gallon of ice cream he'd squished, its melted contents melding with the rain. A bright box of microwave kettle popcorn was near his big toe.

Chick food. *Sad* chick food.

He looked at Poppy. Her swollen lips matched the half-lidded expression that begged him to keep going, to fuck her senseless right upside the Beemer where anyone who drove by could see them, rain and all. Still holding her, he took a step back and allowed room between them. Room for the raindrops to fall and hit the plastic grocery bag with decided *plop-plop-plops.*

"Fuck, Poppy. We can't do this, babe."

"What?" Clouds of lust cleared from her amber eyes and anger snapped out of their depths. "What. The. Hell." She shoved against his chest and he let his arms drop to his sides.

"Let's go inside and talk." Since when was he the sensitive type? His dick was never going to forgive him. The ache for Poppy was insatiate.

She bent over to grab the groceries and clutched the sodden bag to her chest. "I don't want to talk to you. Stay the hell away from me!" She stalked away from him and he hung his head, let the water drip off his nose, his face. Christ, he was soaked—she had to be, too. Gritting his teeth, he turned around and followed her to the house. Because of his stupid, let-my-dick-do-the-thinking move, it was going to be a lot harder to convince Poppy that she couldn't stay here. And that the only place left to take refuge from the storm was his house.

*Double fuck.*

\* \* \* \*

Poppy shivered under the hot stream of water, thinking she'd take a steaming bath later tonight, too.

It'd been too close of a call out there with Brandon. Thank God for the rain and for an excuse to run into the house like she had. It would have been polite to at least give the dude a towel but he could figure out where the other shower was if he needed it. Hopefully he'd taken his big truck back to what she figured was no doubt some fancy mansion his boat business had paid for. It'd be easier on both of them if they never saw one another again.

She dried off with thick fluffy pink towels that had to be Sonja's and tried to ignore the shame that made her gut wiggle. Brandon had seen her at her absolute worst. Five days into her pity party, the longest she'd gone without dressing up or putting on makeup since starting her stylist business in New York six years ago. And still, he'd kissed her. Shit, she'd almost gotten down on her knees and made up for what he hadn't let her do Saturday night. Cock-blocked again, and he hadn't even pretended it was the rain that stopped him.

*He's better gone.* Although it would have been fun to try to design nautical decor. She put on a clean pair of yoga pants and a loose-fitting lightweight sweatshirt, relishing the crisp clean scent and soothing textures. Yup, a shower had been what she'd needed. No wonder she'd let him kiss her like that—she'd been half crazed from her mopefest.

*You kissed him back.*

Yes, she had. Making her way downstairs to the kitchen she let out a yelp at the sight of Brandon sitting at the expansive island. "I told you to leave. Did the rain make mush of your brains?"

"Sorry, no can do. Not until you agree to let me get you to the airport."

He was kicking her out?

"I can't leave. I'm house-sitting for Sonja and Henry." She looked around the kitchen for candles and grabbed a glass jar filled with one from the counter. "Look. Emergency lighting, and it smells like cottage roses."

"Poppy, when the power goes out so will the sump pumps. At this rate of rain we've got about another twenty minutes to drive out."

"Because they'll block the roads?"

He placed his hands on his hips. "No, because the Mississippi is overflowing its banks and this tributary is next."

"I can't leave the house to the weather."

"Henry asked me to come check on you. It's my assessment that you're no longer safe here. You've got fifteen minutes to pack and then we're out of here. I'll find you a flight while you pack, if you want." He was serious.

"You're still wet."

"Poppy."

"Fine!" She ran back upstairs and did as he asked, throwing her clothes into her luggage in five minutes flat. Once back downstairs she loaded her portfolio, laptop, and art journals into her backpack and turned to face him with satisfaction.

"Done. But you don't have to take me. I'll follow you out of the neighborhood to the main road. I can get to the airport on my own in Sonja's car. We'd already planned for me to leave the car there for her and Henry when they get back. When they were going to get back. You know what I mean." When there was going to be a honeymoon, before the wedding had been ruined.

Brandon shook his head. His T-shirt still clung to his chest. He had to be freezing, but not an iota of shiver emanated from him. "No can do, Poppy. Sonja's car will never make it through the water. It's rising too quickly. My pickup's the only choice."

She wavered between deciding to stay put regardless of his opinion or to ignore him and drive herself out of here anyway. She'd driven through the residential roads less than an hour before. It wasn't raining that hard.

A flash followed by an immediate growl of thunder made her decision.

"Let's go. I'll move up my flight while we drive. If there are still flights going, that is."

"The airport's not due to shut down for another two hours. It's a half hour away in good weather, so if we're lucky we'll get you there with an hour to spare. Check in online, obviously."

"I always do."

He nodded. It was impossible to tell if he was relieved she'd agreed or had thought he'd already made the decision and was waiting for her to figure it out. She'd never allowed a man to make decisions for her. Even with Will the choices had been all her own. That should have been her first of many clues that Will wasn't invested in their relationship. In her.

Within two minutes her bags were on the backseat of the truck's cab and Brandon was maneuvering around and through the shallowest parts of the flood water, nearly all of the road covered. He swore softly under his breath as he concentrated, and Poppy tried to get a signal on her phone. Brandon had the radio tuned to an AM station. The broadcast was static and continuous emergency weather information.

"I can't get a signal." Her phone wasn't responding to her efforts to launch her airline app, much less make a call.

"Cloud cover's too dense, and with the lightning there's a good chance one or more of the towers are out."

Her shoulders tensed when the truck seemed to groan as it crept through the water that rapidly approached the level of her door's window.

Brandon stopped the truck and rapped his fingers on the wheel, staring out at the rain and wind.

"Why did you stop?"

He took in a breath, shifted the car into reverse, and placed his hand on the back of the seat so that he could turn enough to look out the rear window.

"We're going back." The strain of maneuvering the vehicle was evident in his taut throat. Damn her lips for wanting to kiss it nonetheless.

"Why? You said we have to get out of here now. There's one other way out, if you turn left back over there." She hadn't wanted to come out of the safe, dark hole she'd burrowed under since the wedding but now that it was clear that New Orleans wasn't going to help her feel better she wanted to be anywhere *but* NOLA. She wouldn't go back to the city, not yet, but she could get a flight to Western New York and stay with her mother or sister for the time being.

First, she had to get to the airport.

"You'll still be able to get me out, right? To the airport?"

As if he heard her, the AM radio deejay declared: "New Orleans airport has been closed. Repeat, New Orleans airport is closed. Shelter in place or safely move to a community shelter. Do so as soon as possible."

Poppy's stomach flipped.

"I can stay at the house, really. I'll stay on the top floor." Did she sound as frightened as she felt?

"We're going to have to boat out of here, Poppy." He'd turned the truck back around and she was relieved to see hard road again.

"I don't understand how the water is so high back there when the house is right on the river and we can still get to the driveway just fine."

"We're on top of the bayou, Yankee girl. Henry had the house built on the highest point of land, but also on a significantly raised foundation. Few folks around here can afford to do that. But even with all the safeguards, Henry's house is probably going to flood, at least the first level."

"That's awful! All of their furniture will be ruined."

His eyes flashed over her face and she saw a definite twinkle there. "It'll be fine. We'll move everything to the second floor. Then we'll go to my place."

"I'm not staying with you! And how do you know your house isn't in just as bad of shape?"

"You don't have a choice, Poppy." His hands held the wheel firmly, his confidence in being able to navigate the treacherous waters evident. But his knuckles grew white and his mouth was in a grim line. "I'm not going to touch you again. What happened earlier was nuts. We're both probably stressed after the way the wedding blew up in our faces."

She swallowed. "You sure know how to make a girl feel pretty."

"Your attractiveness has nothing to do with it. But for the record, you could have stepped out of a pigsty and you'd look as hot as ever. You're that kind of woman, Poppy."

Tension thrummed between them, a taut awareness that was becoming as familiar as the scent of the winter-blooming camellias that graced Sonja's porch. Poppy couldn't afford this; her heart was still in shreds from Will. From losing the Attitude by Amber line. From not knowing where her life was headed.

He didn't force her from her silence. "My house sits up and away from the water far enough to not worry about it, not for a good while. It would take a week of rain like this to make the water level near me rise to my house. I did as much to hurricane-proof it as I could when I built it. It's safe and as weather-protected as any place in these parts. And where else are you going to go?"

He had her there. With the airport shutdown and Henry and Sonja's place about to flood, she was screwed. Doubly so. And of course Brandon had a stormproof house. He was a multimillionaire, according to what she'd found on the Internet. Not that she'd spent a lot of time obsessing over him.

"Double dang damn it."

His laughter reached across the cab to her as he pulled back onto the gravel driveway and cut the engine.

# Chapter 10

They worked efficiently together, scarily so. Poppy figured the chemistry that had almost had them fucking like dogs twice so far worked well for other physical tasks like moving furniture and belongings upstairs. Brandon carried the heavier items while she ran up and down the stairs with other items from the floor that weren't too heavy. They got most of the furniture up the stairs together. She let Brandon guide her hand placement on how to edge the large chairs and sofa around the wainscoted stairwell and hallways without crushing her fingers.

"The larger sofa is too big for us to get upstairs." Brandon spoke without a hint of the breathlessness she felt after they set down a big recliner on the stair landing. "I'll prop it on its side and shove it up as many steps as I can, but that's as far as it will go."

Poppy nodded. "Maybe we'll get lucky and the flood won't come this high." As the rain continued to batter the roof and sides of the charming house, she was resigned to the fact that indeed, Henry and Sonja's house was going to flood.

Poppy wondered if the heavens knew about the failed wedding. Did angels throw self-pity parties? She doubted it.

Brandon eyed her luggage, which they'd brought into the house with them. "Take what you absolutely need for the next week or so and put it in this bag. Your suitcases are too heavy and they'll get soaked." Brandon held a white plastic kitchen garbage bag out. "I've got clothes you can borrow, and you can do laundry. Focus on any prescriptions, what you need with you to be able to work. Worst case you can always use one of my computers."

Poppy took the bag, careful to avoid touching his fingers. Their short work of Henry and Sonja's furnishings had forced a sweat from both of them and Brandon's was all tangy male, sexy and dangerously spicy. At least he was warm and not freezing as she'd be if she hadn't showered.

"So you're telling me we're going to paddle to your house in this downpour? The grocery clerk told me to try to find a canoe in case I had to escape." The skies had grown darker and they'd turned the lights on throughout the house. The bulbs flickered on and off as the power ominously fluctuated.

"We're going to take Henry's flat-bottom boat. I made it, so I know how it'll handle the water."

"I didn't know Henry had a boat." She shoved her headache meds and toothbrush into the bag, along with most of the contents of her backpack. "You're sure this will keep my laptop dry?"

"It'll have to, won't it?" He said it like a statement, underscoring the direness of their circumstance.

"Excuse me if I'm not used to swimming my way out of storms." She stood up and blew a stray lock out of her eyes. Brandon didn't miss the gesture from the way his eyes narrowed on her lips. She shrugged. "I'm sorry. I don't mean to sound like such a spoiled little bitch. I'm used to having to stock up for a snowstorm, and when the wind's blowing the snow sideways in Buffalo I know not to go out. We get some major storms in New York City, too. But this, this is unlike anything I've ever experienced. I half expect Noah's Ark to show up on the dock." She looked where she motioned her thumb, out the French doors toward the backyard and deck where only a little more than a week earlier the wedding party had enjoyed pre-festivity cocktails. Shock shook through her at the sight of water covering all but the last few steps up to the main deck that was adjoined to the house. "Holy hell, it *is* the Great Flood."

"And we have the perfect ark for it. Come on, let's go. Wear this." He tossed her a rain slicker and looked at her feet. "Sonja's got to have waders in the garage."

She followed him through the kitchen entry to the garage. Sonja's car sat alone in the double-vehicle room, still dripping.

"When did you pull this in?"

"While you were showering."

She'd never noticed it when they'd driven out in the truck.

"Here, try these." He handed her a pair of flowered rubber boots. She took the waders and stepped into them.

"They're roomy but they'll do. Where's the boat?"

"Around back. We're going to have to work together to get it to the water, but at least that's not going to be very far today." He took a larger, man-sized slicker off a hook and shrugged into it. The drab olive, rubber slicker would look silly if not practical on anyone else. On Brandon, it looked classic.

"Stop staring, Yankee, and get ready to push, pull, and heave this boat into the river." He opened a door to the outside and they faced Henry's boat. Brandon quickly removed the tarp over it before he took the brakes off the hitch and began to roll the boat down a cement ramp.

"I had no idea this boat was here." And she hadn't noticed the boat ramp that was built into the side piece of property, angling down to the river. When she'd arrived last week the ramp didn't catch her eye, as she'd spent her time on the back deck. Goosebumps rose on her forearms and nape as she saw that the water they had to get the boat into was mere feet away, instead of the two hundred yards she estimated it had been before the rain.

"Stay to the side and out of the way of the boat, Poppy. It's heavier than it looks." His instruction was firm, confident, but also empowering. Not one hint of condescension percolated in his tone.

Once the boat was afloat, Brandon pushed it far enough out so that he could pull the trailer back up onto the level ground.

"Won't the water carry that away?"

"It might, but probably not. It's heavy enough to stay put." He waded toward her and took the plastic bag from her hands and tossed it into the cabin, under a protective roof. Thanks to the tarp, the boat looked relatively dry.

Although the deluge didn't let up and she feared the boat would sink. Brandon's arms were at his side and he faced her. "I'm going to have to put you in." He had to shout over the roar of the rainfall.

Poppy's knees were shaking, and she hated not knowing how exactly he thought they were going to survive this. "Are you sure?" She motioned at the water filling the boat.

"Now, Poppy!" His roar shook her and she scrambled toward him, her boots sloshing in the muddy water. A quick flash of a tail slithered across the top of the water near her calves and she screamed.

Strong hands had her waist and she was being lifted up and over the side of the boat, where she landed on the cushioned side benches on her knees with a splash. The deck tilted starboard as Brandon swung himself aboard and landed next to her.

"That was a cottonmouth. Not someone we want to bring back with us." He grabbed her elbow and led her to the overhang that protected the engine controls. Within seconds he had the engines running and was slowly maneuvering them away from the house. They passed the decorative tops of the deck railings and Poppy shuddered. "The water's almost completely over the deck."

Brandon didn't answer but instead was immersed in guiding the boat through and between trees and brush. Poppy knew that water moccasins liked to hang out in trees and decided to not look too closely. The brush of the snake against her rubber boots had been enough reptile contact for her.

She let out a breath of relief when they cleared where she remembered the edge of the tributary was, only to suck it back in as the rain assaulted them from all sides. Combined with the gusts and chaotic current, it made for a ride she'd have associated with white water rafting, not cruising down toward the Mississippi.

"Do we have to get to the main river to get to your place?" Her throat was raw from shouting and they were barely out of the small tributary where Sonja and Henry's neighborhood rested.

"Do you mean the Mississippi? Yes, but it won't be for long. With the current we'll cut the usual time in half." The white flash of his grin under the slicker hood angered and comforted her. She stepped up to him and pulled his hood back as she had hers.

"You need to be able to see better."

His eyes met hers for a brief moment and in their blue depths she saw that he hadn't forgotten her, or what was going on between them. Not at all.

It was probably ridiculous to enjoy the burst of lust he lit low in her center. Downright dangerous, in the midst of a natural disaster, to think about what they could be doing on this boat if the rain weren't coming down in buckets.

"Should I start bailing the water out?" She looked around for a pail. Her plastic bag of all her worldly goods was floating on the few inches of rain that sloshed on the deck. Poppy grabbed it and shoved it up against the windshield in front of her.

"This boat's got a pump. It's doing its job or there'd be a lot more water in here already." He took them around a large semicircle turn and she widened her eyes as she looked through the windshield and saw what lay ahead.

Frothy foam wave caps indicated where the current on the Mississippi raged in all its fury. The same expanse of water that had been as flat as a plate of glass and as calm last week had erupted into a boiling mess of mud, fallen limbs and trees, and water. If she were standing on the riverbank she'd appreciate the sheer raw power of nature. In a flat-bottomed aluminum boat that was being thrown around like it was no more than a toy, she was scared senseless.

Until she looked at Brandon. He was the captain of their adventure, leading them to safety with the confidence only gained from a lifetime of acquaintance with these waters. He whistled and alternatively swore as the boat was jostled and shaken by storm debris and rough currents. If he had any of the same fears as she, he didn't reveal it in his relaxed wide-legged stance at the helm, or in how comfortably he held the wheel. He was a thoroughly modern man driving a boat outfitted with the latest technology, but he might as well be a seventeenth century Caribbean pirate, or one of the French explorers who'd arrived in the river delta three centuries ago. Brandon Boudreaux was as much a part of the bayou as crawdads and the Mississippi, and he had the pedigree to prove it.

"You're staring again, Yankee girl." He shouted over the din of the rain but his eyes never left the water and she wondered how the hell he could see.

"How will you know where to pull over—oh!" The boat pulled into the river and it was like hitting a wall when it hit the current. She flew to the side, against Brandon, who kept his hands on the wheel.

"Hang on to me, damn it! I can't let go of the wheel until we're at my place."

He didn't have to tell her, as she'd already wrapped her arms around his waist and clung like a baby possum to her mama. But Brandon's body was nothing like a soft cuddly animal. All tension and focus, his muscles conveyed the deep concentration his mind enjoyed.

"Sorry!" She gave him a quick, friendly squeeze. This wasn't the time to worry about how he interpreted her gestures. The longer she held on to him, the more the warmth of his body seeped into hers and she allowed herself to relax against him. It was a better way to handle the jolts and jarring slap-downs the bottom of the boat was going through. She'd never complain about having to attend a dinner boat cruise around Manhattan again. As the rain continued she didn't know when or how they'd get to safety.

She trusted Brandon that it'd happen.

* * * *

Brandon had been on the river in all sorts of storms, but the deluge was absolutely crazy—the kind of adventure he'd have loved as a teen or college kid. But with a woman clinging to him for her life, all he wanted was to pull into his dock.

The woman holding on to him continued to intrigue him, at the worst time of his life for any kind of relationship. Sex-only, sex-and-friends, sex-and-romance; no matter what Poppy would be willing to settle for, he didn't have it to give.

And yet, as he faced and fought the roughest ride he'd ever had on the Mississippi, he had a goddamned erection. What the hell kind of rescuer was he?

*A horny one.*

Her hot petite body was all but wrapped around him and a sick, twisted, reptilian throwback part of his brain imagined her going down on him right now. Wrapping first her hands and then her wet, hot mouth around him and sucking until he couldn't take it anymore.

*Thwack.*

A huge tree winged past the boat, and he knew there'd be a dent to pound out later.

Her arms tightened around his waist again and realization struck him as fast as the lightning that had bolted the area earlier. Having Poppy next to him felt real. Comfortable. Expected.

*Natural.*

"Fuck." He had a bad habit of thinking aloud. Her head lifted from its spot on his back, where he felt the heat imprint of her breasts and abdomen through both of their slickers.

"What?"

"Ah, er, I'm thinking about how big of a dent that tree made."

"As long as it doesn't put a hole in the keel."

He wanted to turn his head, turn his body, and take her in his arms. Find out how she knew what a keel was, what it was about her that made him so fucking hard. But if he did that there'd be no figuring anything out because they'd wind up at the bottom of the Mississippi. The realization that he couldn't take his eyes off the current, had to hold on to the wheel to stay on course, sobered him enough to clear away the haze of lust he was thinking through.

"You okay back there?" His voice sounded like a damned adolescent's.

"I'm fine." Her muffled response against his back affirmed what he suspected. Poppy was scared. He might not be able to control how his body reacted to her, but he damned well could make sure she had no reason to fear for her safety.

Except even he was no match for this kind of storm. Time to man up.

\* \* \* \*

By the time Brandon steered them out of the raging Mississippi and through one after another tributary until they were dealing with only the heavy rains, Poppy felt like she'd run a marathon through the Amazon Rainforest. She was soaked inside and out—on the outside from the rain and her body was coated with sweat from the non-breathable material of the slicker. Her teeth had started to clatter as shivers racked her but she didn't care. They'd made it.

"You're awfully quiet, Yankee girl." Brandon spoke loudly but no longer had to shout, as the rain's constant beating was their only companion as they motored up through a marshy area. Even the boat's motor seemed quiet after the roar of the river.

"I'm meditating. This is pure zen compared to what we just went through." She hoped he understood that she meant the river, and not the sexual attraction that had been their constant companion since they'd met on Friday. "That current was insane."

"Are you cold?"

"Naw, I'm fine."

"Liar."

"How far is your place?"

"It's right over there." He pointed past the swamp, past a grove of what might be crepe myrtles, she couldn't tell for sure in the rain and with no blossoms. Her gaze kept going, looking, until it landed on a large but simply lined structure. Its front picture window was the only clue that it wasn't an industrial building.

"Did you design it?" It looked like the two boats of his she'd been on so far—organic to the bayou, practical, functional. "I'll bet you have only the best technology in there."

His laughter was balm to her shivering heart as it wrapped around and through the space between them. "Yeah, you could say I like my toys. Henry likes to tease me that I'd live in a mud house as long as it had Wi-Fi."

"Is he right?" She watched his face closely for any hint of pride or entitlement as he looked out at his property. All she noticed was the soft edge to his eyes, the half grin of his mouth.

"I'm a guy. I get to live my dream every day, building bigger versions of the models I built as a kid. Boats by Gus has allowed me some financial freedom, and I have fun with it, to a point."

He pulled up to a dock that was miraculously above water and killed the engine. As he threw two lines over onto the wooden structure, he jumped out and made quick work of tying them to stanchions painted in the same colors as the Boats by Gus logo she'd seen on his other boat and the T-shirt he'd worn the other night.

Poppy grabbed her bag and made to scramble out of the boat but Brandon beat her, holding his hand out.

Without a word, she held onto him—for balance purposes only. It burned from his heat where he'd touched her because she was freezing.

"Okay, let's get inside and I'll show you around before I have to come out and move the boat."

"Why do you have to move it?"

"The tide. It's going to go a lot higher, maybe by up to four feet, before this lets up." He spoke from under his hood again and was close enough to her that their hoods formed a sense of cocoon around them. Poppy took a step back.

"That makes sense. I've never been a boat person, even though I grew up on the water."

They walked down a long pier to a large stretch of land that formed the bank the house sat on. "Did your family live in New York your entire life?"

"Oh no, I'm not a native Manhattanite. I went there for college, when I met Sonja, and fell in love with the city. I grew up in Western New York, in Buffalo. I don't suppose you've ever been there?"

"Yes, several times. You know there is a huge boating community on Lake Erie, right?" His teasing made the dimples on his cheeks deepen and she felt her cheeks redden in response. What would it be like to really flirt with this man, to be charmed by him? Instead of the tug-and-push of the attraction they kept cha-cha-ing around?

"Yes. I've been to the boat show there. It's amazing to watch the big sailboats out on the lake. I just thought it was for the wealthy, though. Of course, I always thought nothing compared to the force of lake-effect snow storms in Buffalo but after today I've changed my perspective."

They were on his back deck now, but it was concrete instead of wooden and it wrapped around the house. He led them to a side door where he looked into a tiny cup and keyed a PIN into an access pad.

"You do *not* have a retina scanner."

"I do. Backed up with a keypad in case someone pops my eye out to break in." His drawl was emphasized and she could blame it on the exhaustion but she knew him well enough to know he was teasing her.

"Hey, it's the bayou. I'm learning anything can happen here."

So far, all she'd experienced was having her best friend's wedding crash and burn, closely followed by her career. Despair swamped her as she remembered her personal circumstance, which while on a back burner as long as she was stuck in NOLA, was going to come to full spotlight as soon as the storm lifted.

As soon as she could get back to New York.

# Chapter 11

"Make yourself at home. I'm going to check on the generator." Brandon took her slicker and paused as if just noticing how wet she was. "On second thought, go get yourself a hot shower. Guest room is through the kitchen, around back. There are robes and towels in the linen closet. You can wash your clothes later."

"Thanks." She bit her bottom lip to keep her teeth from chattering and made her way through the stainless-steel world that was Brandon's home. At least in the kitchen, where every appliance reflected a fuzzy shape of her drab appearance. A second shower in one day, after being drenched again, didn't exactly appeal to her but the warmth it promised did.

Only after she'd dried her hair did she realize she'd not ever questioned her safety. Brandon's expertise on the water and through the storm was unquestionable. And she'd never felt as though she were going to be at risk here, alone in his house with him. Not that Brandon struck her as any kind of serial killer or perv, but she hardly knew him, truth be told. Big city living had taught her to be cautious when selecting a lover.

"What the hell?" She spoke to herself as she walked barefoot out to the bedroom area and through to the hallway. A. Brandon wasn't a lover, no matter how much her body craved him, and B. She had been in extremis, thanks to the weather. The entire southern part of Louisiana was, judging from the storm.

A long thin faucet indicated filtered water at the sink and her thirst kicked in. She looked around at the understated gray-stained cupboards, trying to guess which one held glasses.

"Last cupboard on the left."

She whirled around, the hardwood floor as smooth as the black granite counters.

"I didn't hear you."

He stood at the other end of the massive kitchen island, in a fresh white T-shirt and faded button-flys. She wondered if he had a weathered pair of jeans for each day of the week.

"How's the water pressure in the guest shower?"

"Uh, fine? Good, actually."

He scrubbed his nape and shoved his other hand in his front pocket. Next to where the button-fly was. *Get your head out of his crotch.* Brandon was obviously taking the high road and making good on his promise that nothing would happen between them. Which was good. Necessary. Maybe a little frustrating. Or a lot.

"I ask because I haven't had many, ah, guests and I wondered if the rain forest shower head really worked."

She looked away and retrieved a glass and filled it. "It works great. You know you just admitted that you only have women who stay with you, and not in the guest room?" Damn it, she couldn't keep her mental filter in place to save her life. "Sorry, none of my business."

He regarded her with a smug expression but not before she caught a flash of surprise. "Correct. None of your business. But if you're wondering, you're right. Except that I usually go to their place if we're going to engage in some fun."

She held up crossed fingers in front of her as if he were a vampire. "TMI. Sorry I said anything. What is your Wi-Fi password, by the way?"

"The network is BBG-5, the only one that will come up. You may not have noticed in this downpour but there aren't any other homes for at least a half-mile radius." He walked over to a built-in desk and wrote the password on a sticky note. "Here. Feel free to use all of your devices at once—you can't slow my system down."

"Thanks." She took the note from him and did not dwell on his hands. He had workingman's hands. Large, muscular, a few calluses. The kind that provided the best kind of friction as he ran his hands over her body.

He caught her glance and held it, too long. Heat pushed up from between her legs to her breasts and she shook uncontrollably. It was all she could do to not untie her belt and drop the robe. She wanted to hide from Brandon as much as she wanted to completely expose herself to him.

"I meant what I said, Poppy. You're safe here. This time together is a matter of circumstance. We're stuck here for as long as the weather pattern holds. Feel free to work wherever it suits you."

"Thanks." A lead weight plumbed her stomach as if he'd said "you're no more than a stranger to me." Poppy looked around at the open, airy kitchen. Anywhere but at Brandon. "I'll talk to you later."

She all but ran to the guest room before she made a complete idiot of herself. Before she blurted out that she didn't have any work to do.

Even more odd was the sense of loss that haunted her as she settled into the guest room. Her living space for the duration. For the first time in her life, Poppy was without a job and with no idea what she was going to do next.

\* \* \* \*

Brandon was relieved that Poppy retreated to the guest room. An hour later he heard the washer and dryer spinning when he walked by the laundry room, so she'd taken him up on his offer and made herself at home.

She'd looked like a lost rabbit in that fluffy white robe. When he'd built the house he'd spared no expense on the decor, and the interior designer had insisted he'd be glad he'd agreed to have the guest room completely outfitted. The only person who regularly used it was Jena, but since she was overseas it'd gone empty. Henry lived close enough to not need it and his parents... They'd visited him here once. That hurt, somewhere deep down, but not as much as he knew Henry was smarting. To have your own wedding blow up in your face because of your parents was unconscionable. He wanted to drive up to his father's offices and punch the old man in the face for how he and his mother had treated Sonja. But that was Henry's circus.

He sat down at his computer and read an email from the investigator he'd hired to find Jeb. No luck on figuring out where the funds were, but a little news on Jeb's location. Apparently, his best friend had disappeared after arriving in Paraguay. What the hell? Who absconded with fifteen million dollars and went to *Paraguay*? Wouldn't Rio or Costa Rica be nicer places to blow Boat by Gus's hard-earned cash?

"Jesus." He ran his hands through his hair, wondering for the thousandth time why he didn't notice Jeb was getting ready to bail in such a spectacular fashion.

"You okay?"

Poppy stood in his office doorway, her eyes wary. Her hair had dried into a riot of waves around her face, the blond emphasizing her caramel eyes.

"Did anyone ever tell you your eyes are the exact color of Southern Comfort?"

"No, but if that's a bourbon then yes." She leaned a hip against the pocket door frame. "Usually they get compared to Jack Daniel's."

"I see you got your clothes washed."

She plucked at her yellow pullover, every ounce of her body filling the delicious jeans that clung to her. "Yeah, I threw in what I'd brought in the bag, too. Everything was damp. At least my computer stayed dry." She ventured into the office. He smelled her—the fancy guest room shower soap, his laundry detergent, and the flowery smell she'd brought in with her from New York. "I thought I'd seen the fanciest laundries onboard the yachts I've been on. But yours is space-age."

"Yeah."

Her eyes sought his; for what, he didn't know. The compassion in them made him want to run, fast. Because Poppy Kaminsky was dangerous.

"Well, I'll go back to work if you're busy." She stood there, obviously not wanting to be alone. Guilt sucker-punched him.

"Have a seat. I'm not getting anything productive done." He nodded at his screen, which thankfully boasted a photo of one of his boats with him, Jeb, and the country's most popular hip-hop artist posing in front.

"Wow, you've sold a boat to Honey Child?" She smiled, her first one since he'd brought her back here.

"He's not as tough as his songs make out. He brought his wife and kids, and the boat has a special infant crib area because his wife was pregnant with twins." He clicked through to photos of the boat. "Do you see what I meant about needing help with the decor? Customers like Honey Child bring their own interior designers with them. But we've, I've, been trying to branch out and come up with a line of sailboats for the average boater. I want to bring quality to everyone."

"That's admirable. You seem to be a real expert at your job." Her voice had grown small again. Probably thinking about her ex on his boat with her former assistant. Married. Brandon wasn't above doing a few Google searches to find out more about a woman who fascinated him, even if the timing stunk.

"I'd like to think I was on the right track with the company, but a few things have happened that are making me question what the hell I'm doing."

"Like what?" She sat down on the easy chair next to his, where he often spent hours with his tablet, sketching out new boat ideas. "You can trust me. There's probably nothing I haven't heard from my clients when it comes to business troubles. Are you experiencing a dwindling demographic, or maybe you need to up your social media presence?"

His laughter erupted and surprised him as much as her. Poppy startled and answered with one of her tiny smiles. God, that bastard must have really taken her through heartbreak city.

"Naw, nothing like that. You know how a guy left you high and dry, Poppy? Well, the same thing happened to me, only I wasn't in love with him. But he was like a brother, my best friend."

Her expression was neutral, her posture open and receptive. "Go on."

And for the first time since it happened, Brandon spilled his guts.

\* \* \* \*

Poppy had lied. Customers didn't regularly share *any* of their private lives with her. Sure, she caught glimpses of their true personalities from how they behaved as she suggested different outfits, styles, or colors. No one told her about their companies going belly up. But Brandon had looked so...lost. As if his dog had died. She'd chalked it up to the wedding and his parents' role in it. No one could blame him or Henry for what had happened, but she understood feeling the weight of shame because of something your family had done. Or in her case, her almost-family with Will. Will, Will and Tori—not two people she wanted to be thinking about right now. Ever, in fact.

"Jeb is solid. He's not a criminal. That's what's making me so crazy."

"He cleaned out your accounts."

"Yes, he did. There's no question it was him."

"Unless he was kidnapped and killed by thugs after he gave them all of his financial and banking information at gunpoint?"

Brandon didn't pick up her attempt at humor. "I know it's crazy but I actually thought about that. That's how out of character this is for him. Jeb is the epitome of a solid guy. He was right next to me, making all the big decisions, from the very first boat we sold."

"Then why is it called Boats by Gus?"

"I founded the company and its basic concepts were all mine. Jeb is my numbers guy, the CPA who also knows the business inside and out." Brandon stroked his chin. "It's the worst kind of feeling, to realize that for at least the last six months, he's been planning this. The private investigator working the case for me showed me how it had to have been at least that much time to figure out how to do it without a hitch."

"What does the FBI say?" At his stunned look she pressed further. "Maybe it's not the FBI, but you did contact at least the local police about this, right?"

He stayed silent for a long while and she waited. Could it be that pulled-together Brandon Boudreaux was as much of a hot mess as she?

"I haven't told anyone besides the private investigator. And you. I keep telling myself to call my lawyer."

She felt the weight of his crisis as if it were her breakup all over again. From the forlorn look on his face, Brandon felt as abandoned as she had.

"You're an adult; by definition you can't be abandoned. This sucks, Brandon, but you have to stand up to it and grab Jeb by the fucking balls!"

His lopsided grin was like a hook, reeling her in. "Did you grow up learning to talk so sweetly, or is it something you picked up in New York?"

"I know Southern women who use 'fuck' way more than I do. And you're avoiding my suggestion." She leaned forward and put her hands on his forearm. His face filled her vision but she didn't allow herself to soak it up as she wanted. Instead she looked him right in the eyes. "I know it hurts, Brandon, but you've got the facts right in front of you. The sooner you accept them and take action to get some of your money back, the better you'll feel."

His eyes were downcast, staring at her hands as she pulled back. Touching him, skin to skin, even something as platonic as his forearms, was a bad idea. Because her skin sent signals to the lust part of her brain and her brain was telling her most intimate parts to get ready and raring to go with Brandon.

"There's no getting it back. If Jeb intended to leave with all that money, he didn't plan to have a way for me to get it back. He's too smart for that."

"Okay, well, you've still got your company. How many people work for you?"

His face pinched up and if he was a decade or two older she'd be worried he'd grab his chest next. "Directly? I have twenty-three managers. I had plans to hire a half dozen more but now that's impossible." He shook his head before looking at her with that intensity that was sexy as hell when he was focused on her but scary when it reflected his despair. "I've got nothing left. I'm going to have to close the company within the month, probably file for bankruptcy."

She stared at him. He didn't know it, but she was in the same exact place. It kept her from asking him about how many employees total, for now.

"Don't you have more orders? For future boats?"

"All the advance deposits are gone, used to order the parts or for overhead. We maintain a large storage facility that's about to lose power, and not from this damn storm." His head was in his hands, his elbows on his thighs as he leaned over in his chair.

To hell with skin on skin and what it did to her sexy parts. They'd have to hush up. She leaned forward and grasped his arms again. "Brandon. I know it feels like it's all over, but trust me, it's not. You're a brilliant boatbuilder. I didn't just read your website, I checked out the media reports. You might have to totally rebuild your financials from the ground up, but you'll survive."

"I'll survive, sure, but what about my team? They're all screwed. They can't wait for me to turn the business back around. The economy's bad enough down here and besides my highly skilled laborers that I've fought to keep, I employ the skilled laborers that can't pick up and get a job anywhere else, not this quickly." He pulled back from her and slammed his hand down on his desk. She winced as if she could feel the pain jolt up his bones. "That's the worst part. Not Jeb's betrayal of me, but my stupidity that led to this. I've put all of these families at risk."

She stood up and walked to the large sliding door on the other side of his office. The rain continued, allowing only glimpses of the water beyond the marsh. It was a metaphor for her life and career but one thing she was good at was motivating others. It was part of being a personal stylist. Yet her skills that she'd prided herself on were incapable of bringing Brandon out of his pit. And he was in a deep one, all right.

"There is one job that might make a difference."

She spun to face him at his quiet declaration. "What?"

He sighed. "It's such a long shot. I wasn't going to even consider it when the offer came in last month. But now it might be all I have left." He stood up and joined her at the window, his hands in his pockets. His handsome features reflected the shadows of rivulets from the window and he looked like the saddest clown she'd ever seen. She didn't like clowns, but if Brandon were a clown she thought she might.

"Have you ever heard of San Sofia?"

"The island in the Bahamas?" He nodded. "Yes, I actually helped a Broadway actress get ready for a gig down there, for a corporation's annual conference. She wanted to be professional, but comfortable she wasn't performing for the crowd."

"Well, San Sofia is an island nation. It's independent and has its own president and everything. My lawyers checked it out, and I had a few conversations with the State Department. They're having a huge opioid problem, just like ours in the U.S. They want to contract for a dozen of my boats to help them monitor and protect their coastline."

"Do you mean you're going to build military boats? Like, navy gunships?"

"No, no. They want the more modest line of yawls—sailboats with engines—fully equipped with all the gizmos and gadgets we're known for. They have their own coast guard that works with ours, and that's where the enforcement part will come in. Our Department of Defense will work with them on fitting out weapons as needed. I just have to produce the boats they want in the amount of time they want them."

"How much is the contract worth?"

The figure he named made her reach to the windowpane to steady herself, to feel the hard surface of the glass to make sure this wasn't a dream. "Brandon, Boats by Gus is going to be just fine. Say yes and tell your employees that it might get tight for a month or two but that you'll make it up to them. Give them bonuses at Christmas. It's win-win."

"I'd have to win the contract first, Yankee girl. An island nation doesn't put all its money in one boatbuilding outfit."

"So win it."

He shook his head and looked at her. They stood only inches apart but the gauntlet he threw down, while invisible, was palpable. "It's not my gig. I don't know the first thing about protocol, and I'd have to ensure our own government that I'm doing this on the up and up. There are huge corporations, shipbuilders that regularly produce platforms for the global economy, vying for this. I'm literally a guppy in this ocean."

"You don't strike me as a coward, Brandon. You're a self-made man who built this business from the ground up. You're going to quit now, just because your best friend broke all your trust and took all your money?" She couldn't help the grin that spread across her face.

He looked at her for several moments, unflinching. She'd pushed too far, encroached on his private life where she had no business. The guy had been nice enough to give her shelter during a hurricane and she'd done nothing but antagonize him since she'd arrived here. And the attraction she had for him, it was insane, out of her control.

As was the warmth of an emotion she dared not identify when his face slowly broke into an answering grin. "You've got me there, Yankee girl. You got me. But if I do this I have to have the right demeanor for the government meetings. Hell, I don't even have a conservative suit to my name."

"You have suits though, right? You said you did."

"Of course. But they're not the trim, white-shirt red-tie type. What I have are more suited for cocktails with my more financially sound clients. Linen. I've never seen a G-man in a linen suit." His self-deprecation was a huge turn-on. Brandon exuded confidence but not the narcissistic kind she'd discovered Will was full of. Brandon was financially sound, or had been, and yet he never lumped himself in with his super-rich clientele. She liked that about him. It was a big part of her motivation to help him out of his rut.

"Well, Gus, it just so happens that you're looking at one of the finest stylists this side of the Mississippi. I can turn a toad into a slick CEO in no time."

"Only if you'll let me pay you."

"Consider it rent for the emergency lodging."

# Chapter 12

"You don't have to do this, Poppy. It sounds all fine and good when there's nothing else to do in the middle of a storm, when you're stranded here. But I'm not one of your celebrity clients, Yankee girl." Brandon stood in all his sexy glory in front of her, his back to one of many of the door-sized mirrors in his closet. He wore a suit as finely cut as any Poppy had purchased for her customers. It was day three of being stormbound, day three of advising Brandon on how to carry himself.

It was day three of pure torture for her sorely neglected lust.

"Quiet. I can't hear myself think." Which was true. Her thoughts were drowned out by her incessant desire for him. She held up several different ties, settling on a silk cranberry. "Change your shirt. White's too stark. Try the pale blue." She turned toward the racks of clothes, mostly very bayou, very casual, to avoid looking at his naked chest. The stillness behind her told her he wasn't moving.

"You don't have to get all shy now, Brandon. I'm the one you were trying to hump next to Sonja's car, remember?"

"I'm trying to keep from getting ill is more like it." It'd been like this since they'd agreed she'd coach him through his fashion and protocol choices. Banter but never the all-out flirting that would get them into hot water higher than the bayou's flood.

"Okay, you can turn around."

She turned and looked him over. "That looks good. You have one 'conservative' suit, after all." She made air quotes in the small space.

"It feels so damn stiff." He tugged at the tie but she looked south when he said 'stiff.' "Stop staring at my crotch, Poppy."

Heat singed her cheeks and she deliberately shifted her attention back to his jacket. The navy suit, pale blue shirt, and contrasting tie were perfect. Except. "Maybe we should try the lemon tie."

"No. Red is the most conservative I've ever worn, and it's better to err on the serious side, right?"

"Hmm." She tugged on his shoulders as he finished tucking his tie in and buttoned his suit coat. "This fits you perfectly."

"It wasn't off the rack. I had it made in Hong Kong on a whim."

"Obviously." She walked back around to face him. "Now let's go over your pitch. First for the State Department, then for the ship buyers from San Sofia."

He tugged at the tie he'd just knotted. "I've got it, Poppy. I'm tired of going through it. You must have a ton of work to do for your nationwide brand launch."

"No, not really." It wasn't a lie. She'd neglected to mention that she didn't have the job anymore. If she said it aloud, it'd be game over for her denial, which was keeping her pretty steady at the moment. "Any idea when the Wi-Fi will be back?"

He slipped off the tie. "No. It's one thing to have the generator, as it ensures power. But I can't control access to the satellites. When the weather is this heavy, no one is getting a signal."

Thank God. If he had a signal he might be able to catch the news that her huge home decor deal was kaput.

"No problem." She wandered around his huge master bedroom, somehow grateful for the cocoon of the pounding rain. It'd been relentless, like nothing she'd experienced before. "Do you think the French Quarter is under water?"

"No telling, but there's a good chance it's not. The rainfall can be isolated in local areas, completely flooding neighborhoods out, while the next down gets no more than a few showers."

"Like snow bands in the Northeast."

"I suppose so." He moved around in the closet, his voice muffled. She used the chance to slip out.

"I'm going to get lunch going."

In the kitchen she surveyed the dwindling fresh veggies and fruits in the spotless refrigerator. There was enough to whip up a spinach omelet so she set to work. So far Brandon had either set out the supplies for sandwiches or heated up one of the frozen meals he said his housekeeper made on a weekly basis for him. The least she could do was cook for the man who'd given her shelter in a storm.

More than he knew. Being in the spacious home, so far from the tiny cramped studio she lived in, allowed her to almost believe there was hope for her life beyond New York. Almost.

"That smells fantastic."

She felt his body heat behind her and peeked sideways at him from her place at the stove. His legs were too bare under the long shorts, his chest too big in one of his T-shirts. The hair on his chest peeked over the collar and her fingers tingled.

"Sit over there and I'll bring it."

"Uh, aye aye, Captain?" He backed away as if she were a rabid dog. She felt like a crazy person, tiptoeing around this sex god without allowing herself to give in to her baser instincts. His once-over felt like a blow torch held only inches away.

"Sorry. Maybe it's cabin fever." She hoped he'd believe her and not see that besides giving her shelter, he'd given her time to heal enough to allow her to believe that she'd make love again, feel the raw, unadulterated waves of passion with someone. Not just someone. Brandon.

His heat was behind her again, and his breath hit her nape in the exact spot needed to make her wet. The delicious shivers she'd been ignoring started in her lower back, radiating up around her breasts and back down to her center. "Who's looking at who now, Gus?"

"We have an agreement. I meant that you can feel safe here. And frankly, I'm not in a place to make this any more than what it could be. I don't have anything to offer you."

She clicked off the flame, slid the omelet to a gray hand-thrown ceramic plate. They both knew what he meant by 'this.' "Like I'm in a place to forge more than a make-out scene up against my best friend's car." Another quick glance out of the corner of her eye revealed that Brandon wasn't latching on to her attempt at humor. She set the spatula down and turned to face him.

Her hips brushed his abdomen and she took the half-inch step she had left, her ass hitting the stove knobs.

"Careful." His hands were at her waist, pulling her away from the knobs. Away from danger.

But he was the most dangerous item in his slick contemporary kitchen.

The expanse of granite that topped the island counter behind him reflected the overhead recessed lights and she saw herself splayed out on the surface, eager and ready for him. Her hands shook and she clutched them, digging her fingers into her palms. She couldn't touch him or her willpower would snap. "I can't. We shouldn't." Who was she trying to convince? He had to see her desire.

"No, we shouldn't. Not at all." His mouth moved excruciatingly slow, each enunciation its own come-on. She reflexively licked her lips and was rewarded by the tiniest flare of his nostrils. She got to him, too.

"Although, we've managed to keep up a business relationship for the past few days. You've been true to your word." And he had; he hadn't as much as squeezed her hand or arm, or brushed against her. As if maybe, just maybe, he was fighting it too.

"We have. I have." He placed his hands on the counter behind him and the skin at her waist tightened at the sudden break from his touch. Brandon's eyes watched her, soaked in her expression. He cocked his head. "I'm having a hard time not giving in to what we've got, Yankee girl." He breathed in deeply, his nostrils flaring. "We do this, we agree it's with no expectations."

She nodded. "A buddy fuck."

His cheeks had a faint tinge of pink and she couldn't identify the feeling that twirled in her core at his obvious reaction. Delight?

"What about after, when I take you to the airport?" The muscles on his jawbone twitched.

"What about when I call an Uber and get myself to the airport?"

"You're my kind of woman, Yankee girl." His gaze felt like he had X-ray vision, the way he took her in, from her face to her toes. She wished she'd worn her best lingerie, the hundred-dollar bra and matching thong that she'd left in her drawer in Manhattan. When she'd given up on love.

Scratch that. Love had nothing to do with this.

"Meet you halfway." He let go of the counter, putting his body mere inches from hers. Brandon held out his hands, palms up.

"Deal." She slid her hands over his, taking her time, allowing their palms to meet. The friction of skin on skin had her clenching her thighs. They stood and stared at each other, their hands engaged in an erotic touchfest, and she was gratified to see that his chest was moving up and down quickly. As if he might be panting, too.

"No regrets?" As turned on as he obviously was—she couldn't miss the ginormous erection straining his board shorts—he was still leaving her an out. And she knew that he'd let her turn around and walk back to the guest room without a word. And they'd go on working together to help him land the only contract that had the ability to save his shattered business.

"None."

His hands stilled and he maneuvered to hold one, tugging her to follow him. "Come with me." Not to his boat, or as a rescue from rising waters.

She relished the intimate grip of their hands as she followed him down the hall to his master suite.

\* \* \* \*

He'd made his king-sized bed with clean sheets that morning, thank God. And he'd not even tried to fool himself that he'd changed the bed on his own, without waiting for his housekeeper's weekly visit, for anything other than hope. Hope that somehow he and Poppy would get to this point, no matter how illogical and disastrous his brain told him it was. Brandon was tired of logic. It was what had changed his mind about not diving into a physical relationship with her. Poppy made him feel things in the last days he'd thought long buried, and some emotions were even new, though unnamed.

"I like that you made your bed."

"How do you know that I made it?"

"I don't mean that you washed your sheets—I saw you doing that yesterday, by the way. I mean that you take the time in the morning to make sure it's neat. Shipshape."

"I figure I have so much other shit all over the house that I need one organized thing to my name."

"Gadgets and nautical history books aren't 'shit.'"

\* \* \* \*

He cupped her face with his hands, the softness of her cheeks smooth under his calloused fingers. "You ready for this, Poppy?" His erection strained against his shorts and he fought the urge to turn her around and take her bent over his bed, right now. The waiting had been too tortuous to waste the attraction between them on a quick fuck, though.

"Positive." She turned her head and grabbed his finger between her teeth. Holding it captive while staring at him with her drowsy brown eyes, she licked and sucked on it.

The mood of slow anticipation shattered. Brandon buried his fingers into her hair, holding the back of her head as he pulled her mouth to his. Poppy's fingers ran along his shoulders, his neck, before she grabbed his nape and dug her fingers into his skin. She was drowning in their chemistry, too. The kiss in the rain had been revelatory but this was sex at its sinful best. It was so bad it was sacred, the way her skin flamed wherever he touched it. As if they shared an invisible connection and the heat of his fingers reached her before his hands settled on her. On her lower back, her front, her breasts. When he held her breast and squeezed, his thumb running over her peaked nipple, Poppy pushed her pelvis against his middle and wrapped her leg around his.

"Oh. My. God." She leaned her head back, exposing her throat to him. His tongue traced up its length and he savored the salty sweet taste of her. Not spun of sugar, his Poppy, but made of something stronger. Deeper. He couldn't wait to lick her everywhere.

"My turn." Her fingers made short work of the tie at his waist and he helped her shove the shorts off, over his erection. When she grasped the hot length of him his scalp tingled.

"Poppy, you'll be the death of me."

"You feel very much alive." Sinking to her knees, she took him in her mouth and with what remaining sanity he had left he looked down to watch her. She smiled against him and he groaned, his fingers running through her hair.

Brandon pulled away and pulled her up against him by grasping her upper arms. "Not so fast, Yankee girl." He spoke low and rough against her ear, needing to be inside her. She moaned and ground against him. Another few seconds of her hot mouth on him and the party would have ended way too soon.

Brandon craved her.

"You're way overdressed for this meeting."

"I am." She lifted her arms over her head. Her breathless reply was the supreme turn-on. He instinctively knew that Poppy was totally in the moment, totally with him.

He'd already undone her bra clasp and it lifted away with her tank top. He moved his hand over her soft, feminine belly, his fingers making a slow, deliberate trek toward her wet heat. He tugged at the waistband of her panties but instead of helping her out of them he went for broke and stuck one, two fingers between her swollen lips and into her hot center, just as he'd done on the gazebo.

"What, you have a signature move?" Her last word came out on a moan. His cock strained, needing release. Not until he was sure Poppy had hers. Because when he got her on the bed, rational thought would be an imaginary concept.

"No. It's my Poppy move. I can't resist your hot, wet pussy." His voice rasped against her throat as she undulated on his hand, riding it with abandon. He loved her total lack of self-consciousness.

"Brandon!" At once a scream and a moan as mini-spasms clutched at his fingers. She grabbed his shoulders to keep her balance as he moved his fingers rhythmically. He brushed her clit with his thumb and Poppy exploded. He held her as she rode the waves of bliss, his arm wrapped firmly around her waist. As her climax ebbed, she opened her eyes.

"Oh my." She slowly shook her head. "That was—"

"Just the start, Yankee girl." He moved both hands up and down her back, his teeth nipping at the skin on her shoulders, her throat.

"Brandon?" Her hands started to move, spending time on his pecs, his abs, and making a quick trip to his erection. God, he wasn't going to last long enough for her.

"Yeah?"

"We're still standing."

"Not for long."

He'd replayed the mental tape of her in the French Quarter garden over and over. Now he had a new memory. He could drown in her whiskey eyes, eyes that were glazed from her orgasm, her lips parted as she panted. He fought with his control as he lowered her to the bed and followed her, lying on top of her.

"God, you're so hot, so tight." He kissed her long and deep and just about came out of his skin when her hot hand clasped around his cock started stroking. He wanted to lie on his back and just let her do it, take him to where she'd been. It'd be just as quick.

"Not yet, sweetheart." He lifted up and moved down, licking her from her throat to her sternum to each breast, taking extra time with her nipples. "You are so damned sexy, Poppy." She arched her back, giving him full access to her breasts, and her stomach as he continued his journey. Her body tensed as he approached her sweet spot and he chuckled.

"Get ready to fly, Yankee girl." He had no more patience and he shaped his mouth around her, licking her clit and soaking up the wetness that was pure Poppy. She was beauty and sex and sin in one package and he'd thought of nothing but this since he'd seen her standing on Henry's deck.

He wanted to savor her all night, but it wasn't going to be this time around. They were both too worked up, had waited too long. When her insides started clenching and her fingers dug into his scalp as she yelled out, he smiled against her. He lifted his head and watched her float back to earth, the flush over her breasts and neck, her cheeks red. "That feel good?" He got on his knees and reached into the nightstand for a condom.

"Just wait."

"Fuck me, Brandon."

Without hesitation he complied, thrusting into her in one deep shove, their simultaneous groans echoing around the room. He waited a few seconds to allow her to get used to him. "You okay?" Forehead to forehead, bodies locked together.

"Mmm. Please, Brandon." She bucked her hips and he didn't need any further urging. He thrust, pounded, rolled his hips against hers, sinking into her hot center as if he'd die if he couldn't be there. Poppy met him push for push, gyrating at the perfect instants to drive him wild.

He hung on until she tightened around his cock and when he let go her gasps followed him into a stratosphere of sexual sensation he'd never experienced before.

After several minutes and dozens of shared gasps for air, he rolled to the side and held her. They came down from the sexual high together, arm in arm. It was quiet in his bedroom, the afternoon light casting a kind of yellow glow he hadn't noticed before. Shit, he'd never noticed a lot of anything before Poppy.

Had he ever lost it like this with another woman? No. And he'd only known her for mere days.

He was so screwed.

* * * *

As the storm passed, two more days did. He and Poppy worked well together and he enjoyed her company.

"I think that if I'm going to help you win a contract to save your business I should at least have an idea of what you do on a daily basis. What do you have to offer your client that no one else can?" Poppy sat cross-legged on the rug in his bedroom—he noted that she never, ever sat on his king-sized bed. As if by avoiding that she was handling the sexual tension between them all neat and tidy. He loved how her legs were long enough to cross like that, showing her sensual thighs off along with what he thought might be the result of hours of fancy yoga classes in New York.

"Brandon? Did you hear me?"

"Yes, sorry. You want to see the shop? It's nothing to write home about." Secretly he puffed with pride at the idea of taking her there, as he did whenever he gave a tour of Boats by Gus.

"Spare the modesty. You're a salesman, remember?"

"Jeb always handled this part of the business."

"It seems odd to me that an accountant was also your sales rep. I mean, aren't numbers people usually introverts?"

He grunted. "Not Jeb. He's the smartest person I've ever known, but he's a people person, too. How else would a kid orphaned at age nine, from the wrong side of New Orleans, weasel himself into my family?"

"Explain."

He blew out a breath, wanting to sit next to her, hell, lie next to her, no, put his head on her lap and tell his story. Ridiculous.

"Jeb's been my brother since we were nine. He and I, and Henry, hung out and played after school regularly. He had a scholarship to the private Catholic school we went to—his mom was a single mom and he never knew his father. When his mother was murdered, he didn't come to school for weeks, kind of disappeared. Except to come talk to me. Eventually I went to my parents and asked them to let Jeb stay with us." He shook his head. "The one thing they did right in their lives was let Jeb stay with us as much as he wanted. An aunt raised him, and he lived with her, but he spent a lot of time at our place. I want to be able to say it was to look good in front of the Parish Council, or shine up my father's political résumé, but it was none of that. It was solely to help a poor kid out." He paused. "Come to think of it, having Jeb around kept me out of their hair, too."

"So you really feel you've lost a brother, because Jeb is your friend. That explains why Henry didn't seem so affected by it." Her astute observation threw him. Was there anything she didn't miss?

"Henry and Jeb weren't as close—you're right, he was my friend. When we went to college together it cemented our relationship. Then Katrina hit, and my folks made the move north. Dad kept the office down here, where Henry and Sonja work, but the firm headquarters is in Baton Rouge."

"When did you and Jeb start thinking you'd go into business together?"

"It was a natural fit, and while I hate to sound all New York and hipster, it happened organically. Jeb always had his eyes set on law school, but then realized he loved numbers more and went for his CPA. He's the one who I have to thank for pushing me to start my own business. I'd planned to work at one of the local shipbuilders for a while, learning my craft and the business end of it."

"What changed?"

"I interned at three different shipbuilders through college. Katrina wiped out so much. With all the incentives offered by the federal, state, and local governments, it was the best time to start a new business." He laughed. "I was scared shitless."

Poppy didn't laugh with him, but her smile and the understanding gleam in her eyes let him know she got it. She got *him*.

* * * *

Poppy watched Brandon open up and spill his guts to her. She reveled in how invested he was in his business. As much as she'd thought she loved styling clients, had she ever felt so connected to it? Shame washed over her at the realization that she'd done it more for fame and fortune. She'd have to look at it later, more closely.

"What about the other shipbuilders in the area? The ones you interned for—didn't they want you to work for them after you graduated?"

"I didn't have to. It wasn't a commitment, as I didn't take any scholarship monies from them. And I didn't have any interest in the hardcore commercial shipbuilding industry. I wanted to be more local, more custom." He looked away, out through the huge wall windows and at the expanse of water that stretched as far as she could see. "I never thought I'd be trying to win a commercial contract like this."

"We have to be straight on one thing, Brandon."

His eyes, back on her, were shadowed. Guarded. "Yeah?"

"Are you only doing this for the money? Because that's a good enough reason, don't get me wrong. But if your heart isn't in this project, it's going to show when you go up in front of the San Sofia reps."

He didn't move save for the tiny blood vessel near his left eye. It clearly pulsed in time to his rumination.

"If you asked me this a month ago, I'd have said that of course I was only doing it for the money. But two of my employees have lost their kids to heroin overdoses. I'd say it's become a little more personal for us."

"How many employees do you have, total?"

"Just under a thousand."

"Hell, Brandon, you made it sound like—"

"Like it was just me and Jeb?" He rubbed the back of his neck. "Yeah, that's because that's how it's been, in terms of the decisions we've made. We started with five other employees, but as we've grown, the production output has increased, obviously. And I've got pressure from my employees to do bigger projects, like the other shipbuilders in the area. They see a government contract as insurance that they'll have a job, even in a bad economy. Being at the behest of the mega-rich for sailboats isn't enough to keep the company afloat through the rough times. And when the economy goes south, our flat-bottom boat sales fall off."

She stood up, needing space from the intensity of his energy. Pure angst poured off him. No wonder he'd been so crazed, so grumpy. He was supporting one thousand people, that many families. "Take me to the boatyard, Gus."

He stood up and stretched. "Aye aye, ma'am."

She turned back when at the door. "Can we get there or is the flooding still an issue?"

He laughed. "Yankee girl, this is boat country and boats are my life. We can always get wherever we need to." He looked out at the water again. "I think we'll be able to drive no problem, but the water's the best way to see Boats by Gus for the first time. We'll take my flat-bottom."

"I'll get my boots." Or rather, Sonja's waders. Unlike the first few times she'd boarded Brandon's boat, she couldn't ignore the burst of long lost emotion in her center. Joy.

# Chapter 13

Brandon maneuvered the boat up to a huge pier that was covered with cranes, lifts, and Poppy thought she identified cradles for the untested boats. Where she'd pictured a quaint aluminum Quonset hut type of office, with maybe a huge factory-ish facility behind it, Boats by Gus encompassed a vast amount of concrete next to the river. Three buildings that looked like airplane hangars lined up in a row, with a multitude of smaller buildings sprinkled in.

"Here." He held out his hand and, in a motion that was becoming far too familiar and practiced, she accepted his boost up onto the pier.

"Thanks." She made a point of looking all around. "Is all of this yours? I mean, Boats by Gus?"

"Yup. The small flat-bottoms are manufactured here, in the closest warehouse. The next one is where the custom sailboats happen, and the furthest is for custom commercial vessels."

"So that's where the San Sofia ships will be built." She tugged on his arm, unable to conceal her interest. "Come on, let's start there."

Brandon didn't move. When she looked up at him his face was in that "the shit's about to hit the fan" expression.

"What is it?" God, had she said something stupid already? She had to help him land this contract because she needed the cold hard cash to save her own business. But now there was something more going on, something deeper that she didn't want to identify was motivating her. "Are you thinking it was a mistake to bring me here?"

He blinked. "No, not at all. In fact, you need to see this, you're right. I don't want to lead you on, though, Poppy. You realize that the odds of me winning the San Sofia contract are the same as having a year without rain in the bayou, right?"

Poppy didn't respond. She couldn't. Brandon had to be able to dig deep and muster his own motivation. All she could do was coach him.

Brandon let out an exasperated breath and grasped her elbow in a brief squeeze. "Come on."

\* \* \* \*

He thought he'd appreciated Poppy's bourbon eyes in all settings—outside on the water, inside while it was storming, under the bright lights of his kitchen. Seeing her eyes widen in reaction to the vastness of his third boathouse facility took the cake.

"You've got plenty of room here to build the types of boats you were showing me." She craned her neck to view the top of the rounded roof. Their voices were tiny in the huge space, making their tour intimate, somehow. That and it was Sunday, so no one was about except for his security staff, who only came through here on their regular rounds.

"Yes. We could easily make six of the requested twelve in the first year of the contract."

"Wait, the first year?" Poppy bit her lower lip. "Is that customary? Forgive me for being obtuse but I'm used to working in an industry where I can have just about whatever I want when I want it. I've never had to wait a year for anything."

Brandon's brow arched. "Boats take a long while, and a little longer at Boats by Gus because we're known for attention to detail and custom work."

"But you're competing against builders that have some of this automated, right?"

"Yes. And that's the bitch right there. We've known for a while that we'd have to accept some automation in order to compete with the mainline builders. I wanted to do it on my time."

"It strikes me that this is your time." Amber eyes on his, brooking no argument. She shrugged. "Shit happens, Brandon. And the worst stuff is never on our timetable. What you still have control over is how to approach it. You refuse to report Jeb's theft yet, and even if you did, like you said, the money's gone. As I see it you don't have a choice. You have to win the San Sofia contract."

All the accusations he'd had against her helping him were blown out of his consciousness with the single purpose of saving his company. With Poppy's unabashed observation.

"I do."

"How long would it keep your company running?"

"The contract will take two years, start to finish, to deliver all dozen vessels. I'd have to hire on twenty-five percent more workforce."

"And keep everyone else's pay the same?"

"That includes a ten percent bonus for each employee, new and established, for each year of the contract."

She whistled. "That's incredible."

"There will always be the next contract to get after this, though." He never wanted to be in the business of fighting for contracts, depending upon governmental budgets. It smacked too closely to the political work his father had done.

"Brandon, that's called 'life.' There's always the 'next' whatever. That's not what matters." She put her hands on her hips and he thought she was going to stamp her foot in those ridiculously large rubber waders. "What matters is that you've already got the San Sofia orders. Once you start thinking like this, you'll have it."

He stared at the woman in front of him, wondering where the hell she'd come from, and how on earth she'd landed in his bayou.

"What?" Tilted head, highlighting the sunbeam streaks in her wavy hair.

His arm lifted as if an unseen being did it for him and he stroked a lock of her hair behind her ear. Her ears did have a little point to them, maybe this was some kind of a dream.

"I thought Louisianans had the market on woo-woo stuff. I never expected affirmation coaching from a Yankee."

Crawdad-red streaks appeared on her cheekbones and he dropped his hand. His fingertips tingled from the contact with her smooth skin.

"But you may have a point." He spoke quickly as she remained silent. Had he pushed a boundary by touching her? He'd promised to not touch her and yet his hands, his body, craved her. "Let's get on with the rest of the look-about."

\* \* \* \*

Poppy wanted to shout to the rafters in each of the boathouses Brandon walked her through. It didn't surprise her that she was excited for the prospects of Boats by Gus, by its ability to land an international contract. Her job for the past eight years had been to encourage and motivate her clients to discover their own style and express it without apology. So it made sense that she'd be able to transfer this skill to coaching Brandon through a critical career turning point. Well, more than that. It truly was make-or-break for him. Like she'd thought her Attitude by Amber contract was.

What startled her, snuck up on her like a cottonmouth in the muddy tributary bayou waters, was the way she felt she shared Brandon's pride and sense of accomplishment for his entire company. He'd created this from the waterline up, providing a singularly exceptional product both to high-end and average working buyers. And employed a significant number of New Orleans natives.

"You spend most of your time here, you said." They stood on a platform next to a sailboat that looked completely finished to her untrained eyes. Brandon's hands kept running over the wooden part of the hull as if it were a purring cat. Being a boat seemed like the best idea right now.

"Yes." He pointed to the bottom of the keel. "That's all fiberglass, custom molded in the building we just walked through. This part is always custom, something unique to our sailboats."

She couldn't help it, she laughed. "When I think of sailboats I see smaller boats with a single sail, a family with a dog on it. These, these are works of art."

"Thanks." He must have received thousands of compliments from boat-smart people and yet a humble expression of gratitude for her appreciation.

"You've really created something special here."

"I didn't do it alone."

"You're not alone now, either."

He turned his face from the smooth wood to her, and the speculation in his eyes sparked with amusement. "But you are. You're alone in this big empty warehouse with a rabble-rouser."

"Is that a warning?" Her voice fell to a whisper on "warning." Bam! There went her insides, all squirrelly, and instigating the pulse between her legs again. Not that she needed anything to kick-start her sexual awareness toward Brandon.

"May I?" He leaned in infinitesimally, his meaning as clear as his Louisiana sky–blue eyes. Which were half closed, anticipating her acquiescence. Smart man.

She closed the distance between them, all of six inches, and pressed her lips to his. When his eyes closed she did the same.

Brandon grasped the back of her head and wrapped his arm around her waist, pulling her in tight. Unlike the other times they'd locked lips, he didn't haul her up against him. He left it all to the touch of tongue on tongue, his every stroke heating her center to a scorching need she didn't think was possible to quench.

Poppy strained to press against him, needing to press her breasts against his chest, to feel his erection against her liquid center.

"Not so fast." He chuckled as he nipped her lower lip and left firm, hard kisses along her jaw, his tongue flicking in and out. The combination of pressure and heat from his tongue made her knees turn to molasses. "I've got you, Poppy. Trust me."

It was her turn to laugh. "On a wooden platform twelve feet up from a concrete floor?"

He lifted his head from kissing her throat and regarded her. His gaze revealed nothing except the heat they shared. "You're the first woman I've ever kissed here."

As if a bucket of ice water had poured over her heart, Poppy flinched and stepped backward, out of Brandon's reach. She had to put space between them. Between her and the crazy, sexy way he drove her to the edge of her control. And he'd only kissed her.

"Careful." He let her go but kept his hands on her upper arms. "Are you okay?"

She shrugged out of his grasp. "Sure. But I think it'd be a good idea to get off this platform."

"I can do us one better." The devil-may-care spark in his eyes undid her. She raised her eyebrow at him and he grinned. Poppy caught a flash of heat that sparked off Brandon's eyes as he turned to face her on the platform that surrounded the yacht.

"Do you know, Poppy, that this boat already has its cabin fitted, right down to the furnishings?"

She licked her bottom lip. "It seems as though it's balancing only on the edge of the keel."

"No. If that were true we wouldn't be able to stand so close and still be safe." He took a step toward her, shrinking the space between them to mere inches.

She grasped the railing, unable to move anywhere. Unable to look anywhere but up at Brandon. His face, chiseled like stone in the shadows thrown off by the large structures in the even larger shipbuilding.

"Aren't you concerned one of your employees will see us?"

He shook his head. "Climb up the ladder, Poppy."

She looked up at the sturdy but temporary ladder that led up to the deck of the yacht. Her insides were vibrating with her need for him. Somewhere inside her, in that little chamber of her heart she walled off from everyone, even herself, she had a sense of importance. Destiny. As though going

with Brandon up into the boat meant more than flirting and a possible
sexcapade to break up the long weekend after a major storm.

Poppy shot Brandon a grin and went up the wooden rungs, more like
steps, conscious of him watching her, watching her ass as she climbed
aboard. The thought of him observing her made her legs feel as though
she'd just completed a rough spin class at her city gym, and her breath
hitched with the familiar tempo she was coming to recognize as how
Brandon made her feel.

She stepped onto the oak deck and moved aside to make room for
Brandon. It was easy to distract herself from her pure want by looking at
the beautiful simplicity of the vessel.

"This deck is marvelous." She crouched down to run her hand along the
smooth finish. Poppy had been on her share of upscale boats and ships but
this was different. It was smaller than most sailing yawls, yet the obvious
attention to detail and custom finishing made it appear far richer, far more
precious than a big oil baron's yacht.

"I help lay the wood lengths myself." He was next to her, their knees
touching. "Not all of it, but enough to know it'll all fit together properly. I
also have the finest ship builders in the country." He said it with obvious
pride but not with arrogance. Brandon's pride was in his workers and their
product, not his own talents.

"You're happier here than in the other plant."

"Not happier. It's more a matter of being where I know I fit in. I can
work at any shipbuilder, designing vessels and helping get them produced.
But this"—he stood up and took her hand to help haul her up—"this is
my passion. No question."

Did he see the way her cheeks heated when he said "passion"? Poppy
didn't know but she knew that she wanted this man. She wanted his
passion to be focused on her. It wasn't just his unshaven stubble that
seemed incongruous with the sharp hue of his eyes, or the way he was
able to reduce her to a puddle of need with one sultry appraisal. Brandon
knew her, got her, with little or no effort. They were tuned in to the same
fateful frequency.

Poppy felt like she knew Brandon, too—maybe better than anyone.
Which was silly, as he'd dated women longer than she'd known him,
hadn't he? Certainly she'd had a couple of longer relationships. And she'd
been engaged.

Yet her week with Brandon had forged bonds deeper than any she'd
ever known possible when she was with her ex. And she knew Brandon

hadn't revealed the disastrous state of his business to anyone else he was close to. Instead of going to anyone he already knew, he'd relied on her.

"What?" He stood close but not touching.

"You relied on me this week."

He slowly nodded. "Yes."

"And I've trusted you enough to stay with you." It wasn't just the storm. She knew that now.

"Come here." He enveloped her in a warm hug and she willingly went, savoring his scent as it underscored how safe she felt with him. She heard his heartbeat under his pullover and T-shirt and her fingers tugged on the material.

"Poppy." His sharp intake of breath on her name sent a shock of awareness through her and she lifted her face to him, her lips to his.

"Not right here." He looked around the warehouse from where they stood atop the sailboat and nodded at the entrance to the cabin. "Want a personal tour of the living quarters?"

"I think it's mandatory, right? Since you wanted me to think about doing some interior design work for you?" She would have been embarrassed by how throaty her voice was, how obviously turned on he had her. Except he groaned at her query and pushed on her lower back.

"Quick, Poppy. Before I throw you down on this deck."

She climbed down the half dozen polished wooden stairs and found herself in another world. But Brandon's patience was as thin as hers. His hands were on her shoulders, turning her around, and when those same hands trailed down to her ass and pulled her up against his erection, Poppy didn't care if they were in a custom-built sailboat or dugout canoe.

* * * *

Brandon's control snapped and he covered Poppy's sweet mouth with his, eager to show her how hot she made him, how hot he found her. Her tongue circled around his with matching abandon and he couldn't stop the low growls that percolated in his throat. He tore his mouth from hers and trailed down her throat, shoving up her top and freeing her from it when she lifted her arms overhead.

His top came off next, with the work of her agile fingers and when the same fingers undid his jeans and reached into his boxers to grasp his hard cock he couldn't wait.

"Poppy, I'm sorry, but I have to have you now."

"How do you want it, Brandon?" Her eyes glowed with sexy want and something strummed deep in his chest. This woman understood him.

"Right here."

Her answering smile was all he needed. He turned her around, helping her shove out of her pants, catching the most beautiful look at her perfectly formed ass. She arched her back and showed him what he wanted. What he needed.

"Give it to me, Brandon." Her voice caught and the feminine sound had a direct line to his dick. It was all he could do to focus long enough to roll on a condom.

"Let me put protection on."

"Hurry."

He reached between her legs and was stoked to find her wet and ready. Without hesitation he entered her in one thrust, loving how she took him without anything but a moan of pleasure, bracing herself against the galley counter. Poppy knew his need before he did and she met his thrusts with total freedom.

"So. Fucking. Wet." He moved again and again, wanting this to last forever but needing the intensity of release he'd only ever felt with her.

"For you." Her words puffed out as breathless as a cloud and it only excited him more.

"Are you close, babe?" He reached around her waist and circled her clit with his fingers, needing her release as much as his own.

"Brandon!" Her scream of pleasure was his only warning before his world exploded into pure pleasure. He allowed the wave of sexual release to wash over him and become more.

As his breathing slowed he leaned over her, still inside her, not wanting to break their connection.

"Poppy." He whispered her name to her spine, kissed the bumps of her vertebrae.

"Mmm."

"I think we just christened this boat."

Her laughter rolled over him, the pleasure not unlike what their joining had just unleashed. Brandon stilled. Poppy's warm body was under his as she remained bent over the counter, resting her head on her arms. Their legs touched at every point possible, and he couldn't get enough of the silky smoothness of her skin next to his.

It hit him clear as a Louisiana autumn sky. Poppy was more than a friend to him. More than a girlfriend, or fuck buddy. But what, he didn't know. Which was kind of a relief, because he didn't think his heart could handle the answer.

\* \* \* \*

Poppy felt Brandon stiffen, and not the kind of stiff that had just given her the most intense orgasm ever. She swore she heard his heart's windows and doors systematically shut closed as they pulled apart and dressed. Unlike when they'd torn each other's clothing off, now they dressed themselves.

"The bathroom's not functioning yet, but there's one off my office."

"Thanks. I'll make it until then." Damn, even she sounded brisk and businesslike. She snuck a glance at him but his expression revealed nothing as he shrugged into his pullover, closing off the view of his chiseled chest.

"Let me show you the rest of the cabin." He took her through to the four-bunk bed area the client was going to use for his children, a guest bedroom, and the master suite that included a shower as big as hers in New York. The attention to space utilization intrigued her, as did the comparatively bland cabinetry and furniture.

"Are all of your boats designed the same, inside?"

"Pretty much, yeah. Unless the buyer has a definite idea for what they want, in terms of colors and styles. Now you know why I want to hire you to help me with this part."

"It's very impressive." And it was. The only things she'd add to the living quarters would border on whimsy—fabrics for the bedding and key eye-candy items like a vase or wall hanging. "And I'd have to adapt my ideas to be able to be nailed down and secured in the event of rough seas, correct?"

"In the event of any seas. It doesn't take a whole lot to get things tossed around down here." Brandon didn't do any of his usual flirty moves in the sleeping area, and she bit back a laugh. They hadn't even made it to the bedrooms before they'd had to be together. Again.

"Let's go down to my office."

She followed him through the narrow passageway back to the galley kitchen where they'd made ingenious use of the smooth counter, and back up onto the deck.

As when they'd come up onto the scaffolding, Brandon went down the outside ladder first and motioned for her to follow. His chivalry was something she wanted to poke fun at, but knew it was futile. He'd charmed her out of her panties with his good manners.

Once on the warehouse floor, she waited for him to lead the way. He stood next to the boat, looking up at the keel from the bottom.

"Where to next?"

"We've got the main office to go through, which is nothing to get too excited about." He turned and looked at her. "I didn't mean to send you running scared up there, Poppy. When we're together I seem to lose any ability to be reasonable."

She gulped. "You didn't scare me. I wanted it as much as you. It was spectacular. I'm coming off a bad breakup, and I've never been so comfortable with another man, so it's weird for me."

"Me, too. About the comfortable part." He motioned for her to walk with him as he led them to the exit. "Do you have any questions about the company now that you've seen it up close?"

He changed the subject and she went with it. Examining the fact that she felt safer with Brandon than she had in a long, long while—and so soon after a major breakup—was akin to wrestling an alligator. She didn't have the expertise or inclination to explore either option. Sometimes it was easier to let her heart catch a break.

# Chapter 14

"Where are you?" Poppy spoke to Sonja, whose incoming call alerted her that her phone was working again. Since she and Brandon had, um, broken in his newest ship's kitchen counter, she hadn't even checked it.

"I'm safe and with a friend." Sonja's voice was flatter than normal but not as scary as Poppy had anticipated.

"I thought Henry was with you?"

"He's not there?" Oh shit. She heard the concern, the worry, and maybe a little bit of anger in Sonja's voice.

"No. I thought he was going to find you. But it's been crazy weather here. This is the first phone call I've been able to take in almost five days."

"Yes, I saw the reports. You still have power at the house?"

"I, ah, I'm not at your house." She quickly filled Sonja in on how she'd ended up at Brandon's. "But it's all worked out. He needed help preparing for a big meeting and I've been able to help him with his prep."

"Well, that's a turnaround from how you two were sniping at each other when you met."

"How are you feeling? Morning sickness? Have you told Henry?" Poppy wanted to know the answers to these questions as much as she was unwilling to share what had happened between her and Brandon. How could she share what she didn't understand?

"I'm doing well. And I can't tell Henry about the baby if I haven't seen him, can I?"

"So you haven't even talked to him?"

Silence, then a shuddering sigh. "I can't face him right now. I've been such a coward."

"You're not a coward, Sonja. What's the real reason you ran away?"

"I read about you in the news, Poppy." Sonja had her own way of avoiding the hard questions. The hairs on Poppy's nape stood up.

"What's in the news?"

"That the biggest retail deal for a fashion and home decor line in a decade has been canceled. That Attitude by Amber has been tanked. Oh boo, what are you going to do?"

Poppy fought the tears that burned to fall. Then sat straight up as a bolt of realization jerked her out of her self-pity. "I've got to go. Glad you're okay." She threw her phone down and raced from the guest room, needing to find Brandon.

He was at the kitchen counter, sipping a cappuccino while he thumbed through his iPad.

"Hey." A quick glimpse of blue eyes as he gave her an even quicker once-over. Did he already know?

"Good morning, Poppy. You've figured out the cell coverage has resumed. I heard you talking to someone."

"Yes. It was Sonja. She's fine, but hasn't spoken to Henry yet." She fidgeted. "I need to tell you something."

"Let me guess." His eyes were on her again but the heat wasn't sexual. He was *pissed.* "Are you going to admit you've lost your entire career? Your New York City business was one thing, but now you've torpedoed your Attitude by Amber line. How long have you known about this? Were you hoping to endear me to you with your styling ways so that I'd hire you on permanently?"

"No, no. And the work we did together is gratis. I won't take a penny from you."

"Bullshit, Poppy. You expect me to believe that a woman of the world like you didn't deliberately deceive me about your work situation? Do you even have money to fly back to New York?"

She swallowed. "Yes. It was a round-trip ticket, I can change the return anytime." Not that she was going to. She'd figured out what she wanted to do with her business, and New Orleans was where she wanted to start a pilot project of sorts. Nothing she was going to share with him. Not now.

He didn't say anything, just sipped his coffee with his eyes boring a hole through her. And made her realize that she actually cared about his opinion of her. They'd all but agreed to keep their connection sex-only, with a dose of her helping him out for the San Sofia contract bid. Neither of them wanted more. She certainly didn't.

So why did her heart feel like an invisible hand was working it like Play-Doh?

He got up from the stool and walked to the deep stainless sink, rinsed his cup out. "The airport's open as of noon tomorrow. Let me know when you need a ride."

"But what about your meeting for the anti-drug boats?"

"It's been postponed until next week. You'll be gone by then."

"Wait a minute, Brandon. I'm sorry I didn't tell you about Attitude by Amber being tanked. It's not been my best time, these past couple of months. There's no way I'm leaving NOLA before you're done with the meeting and land the account. Because I know you will."

His eyes reflected scorn, disappointment and maybe a glimmer of need. As in he needed someone to believe in his ability to get back on his feet. She knew what that was, how low you had to be to be willing to give something your all, to trust someone else so completely.

"Take me back to Sonja and Henry's—the power's got to be back on there, right? I'll drive back here as needed to help you prep. We can go over the presentation at least one more time. I'm guessing you'll be interviewed more than once if you get in the running for the contract." He didn't get to shut her out like this. Her helping him had been more than a nice gesture. It was what had saved her in her darkest moment.

He regarded her with what might be doubt but she hoped it was more like disgusted disappointment. Because what they'd shared last night, all night, had been more than scratching each other's itch and she couldn't bear it if he hated her. Like Sonja not wanting to acknowledge her doubts about fleeing the wedding, her need of his acceptance was nothing she wanted to acknowledge.

"Let's not make this more than it is. Was." He spoke slowly, his face guarded, the scars of Jeb's betrayal smoothed over by his detached stance. She saw underneath it, though. "You're still on my payroll, until I land the San Sofia contract. I'm not going to take rent from you, Poppy."

It made sense to accept something for her work, even though it had been fun to style Brandon. And she wanted to appear as professional as he when it came to a firm boundary between work and play. "I won't take a penny unless you do get it. I meant it when I said to consider it my rent, but I'm okay with you paying me, after you get the contract. You can pay me like an agent. We can agree to a flat fee or a percentage." She meant it. She'd have to come up with another way to fund her initial legal bills if San Sofia walked, but she'd worry about it then. Maybe her lawyer would consider giving her an advance on the expectation she'd get to unfreeze her assets soon.

"I thought we at least had the start of a friendship." She placed her hand on the counter, hesitating. No one had made her feel at once full of esteem and afraid of her next move. "You can play 'Gus' all you need to, but I've seen Brandon. That's who I'm here for. Not the sex, although that was intense, not your stormproof house, but for you."

He picked up his iPad and held it to his chest as if it were a shield. "I accept your continued professional support. We'll go back to Henry's to get Sonja's car, if it survived the flood, so that you can come and go as you need to. If it's in need of a dry-out then you can continue to use one of my vehicles. If the 300 series isn't working out, I have others. You'll probably want to stay here, though. And you're welcome to. It'll take a couple of weeks to get all the utilities back on in Henry's neighborhood, not to mention to get the river stench out of the downstairs."

He seemed to overlook that he was incredibly fortunate to be mostly independent of the grid that drove the average Louisianan's life, but she didn't call him on it. And to throw out that he had a BMW that he'd lend to her so casually was another sign that they were from different worlds. Any extra money she made she sent to her mother and sister. She'd paid for Ginger's college singlehandedly, and had purchased a small-town home for her family in one of the nicer suburbs of Buffalo. None of her family lived like they had when she was young, at the hands of brutality. Abuse from the one man they should have all been able to trust, her father and her mother's husband.

He looked up at her. "You're being awfully quiet. Am I pushing you into staying here?"

Could she handle staying in this house, in close quarters with Brandon, for another week? She definitely needed Internet and electrical power because not only was she supporting Brandon as a client, she had her own work to do. The idea had sprouted in the midst of her pity party and blossomed as she'd helped Brandon lay out suits and set up his PowerPoint presentation.

"No, not at all. I'm used to being more independent, living in hotel rooms as needed." But she didn't have the funds for that, and she needed more time to set up her next career move, and Brandon's house worked for her. She was comfortable here, if she ignored the almost constant sexual tension. And that wasn't uncomfortable, exactly.

"I promise I'll give you all the space you need, Poppy."

"I know you will. I'll stay here but you won't know I'm around. Unless you have a question about your prep for your meeting for the San Sofia contract."

He set down his iPad and stalked around the counter toward her. She held her ground and lifted her chin. If she could hold his gaze maybe he wouldn't see the quakes that started the minute he moved closer. He stopped a foot from her, reached out and tugged on one of her locks.

"Thank you, Poppy." His fingers ran along her neck, his thumb brushed over her bottom lip.

"For what?" Geez, did her breath have to get behind her voice like that? She sounded like one of the women in the bars who'd all made it clear that they were available to Brandon. And yet he'd taken *her* to bed. She could blame it on the storm, they both could, but neither of them was that shallow or immature. They'd done what they'd wanted to. What did this man see in her?

He leaned in and kissed her, as if it were their first. His lips were firm, his tongue warm and reassuring as his mouth moved over hers. She leaned in, her hands on his chest, and kissed him back. When he lifted his head he pressed his forehead to hers. "Thank you for being here."

"I could say the same." Who'd rescued whom?

He straightened and the take-no-prisoners business expression was back in place.

"That's how you need to look."

"What?" His head tilted, his total focus on her. She loved it.

"When you have your meetings for the San Sofia contract. You look confident, intelligent, and like anyone who'd turn Boats by Gus down is a loser."

He blinked. "I'll keep that in mind. Let's go get your wheels." He walked out of the room and she waited for the relief to hit her. Relief that she had a respite, time to regroup. It wasn't going to be easy, staying here, trying to remain detached from an emotional entanglement. Not with Brandon's masculine stamp in each room. Since her business assets were frozen and she was down to nil in her bank account, a free bed and all the technology she needed was heaven sent. Instead of relief, she felt a fluttering in her belly that had nothing to do with the new career path that had started to form in her mind. Nothing to do with having a dry place to lay her head at night. Nothing to do with being able to stay in New Orleans and avoid the harsh critical spotlight of her New York City colleagues and clients.

The fluttering was the unfurling of an emotional landscape she had yet to traverse. Attraction, desire, chemistry, instant-crush; she was an expert at these. This sense of belonging was something else altogether, and it scared the grits right out of her.

She grabbed her purse and ran after Brandon, who'd disappeared into the hallway where the garage was connected.

"Coming!"

\* \* \* \*

The next couple of weeks flew as Poppy began to put her new career into motion. After canvassing all of NOLA for the perfect storefront, she decided to give herself a break and a treat at Café Du Monde. She bit into a hot beignet and savored the instant rush of pure white flour and sugar to her brain. It was the perfect formula for her kind of crack. New Orleans–style donuts, consumed at this tiny table in a corner at New Orleans' most famous café, were a sensory treat for her. No one recognized her, or if they did, couldn't care less. The lack of celebrity attention was a new freedom she was afraid to count on.

"What are you doing here?"

She jolted at the sinfully sexy voice. A voice that had whispered the dirtiest words in her ear while he'd made love to her. Had broadened her concept of hot sex more than once.

"Playing tourist, obviously." She looked up at him and consciously wiped the sugar from her lips with her napkin, lest he think she was ogling him. In one of the impeccable suits they'd agreed upon for his meetings he towered above her and everyone else in the chilly morning air. Several heads turned to take him in and she realized that in this city, Brandon, or rather *Gus*, was a celebrity.

"May I?" Only then did she notice the white paper bag in his hand, the grease spots spreading. He held a cup of chicory coffee in his other hand—she could smell the warm aroma.

"Have a seat." She shoved out the wrought iron chair across from her and he sat, immediately eliminating her sense of privacy in a crowd. But not her safety. Brandon did a lot of things to her insides but she always felt safe around him. Protected.

"You're up and out early today." He bit into his beignet, watching her over the sugared fried dough.

So he'd been paying attention to her schedule? Even when she'd gone to sleep in the guest room? That remained her firm boundary. Record-setting multiple orgasms and all, she couldn't risk falling asleep with Brandon.

"I had some things I wanted to do."

"Seems you didn't need to get this dressed up to walk around the French Quarter."

"What are you doing here?" She didn't have to respond to the interrogating. He licked his fingers before taking a long sip of his hot drink. "I had an early appointment."

"With the Department of State?"

"No, that was yesterday. I met with my private investigator and lawyers." She focused on her second beignet, marveling at how quickly the little donuts disappeared from her bag. Brandon needed to talk and she owed it to him to listen. Wanted to listen.

"I'm at an impasse. Without reporting it to the authorities, I'm never going to stand a chance of getting one dime back from Jeb."

"Maybe it's time to rip the bandage off." She wasn't going to repeat herself. He already knew her opinion. Friends didn't steal your entire net worth and disappear with it.

"I can't, Poppy. If anyone gets wind of this, especially our government or San Sofia, the deal will be dead in the water. They need to have total confidence in Boats by Gus." He crumpled his empty bag and pushed it to the side.

"Then plan to file a report as soon as you land the contract. You will get it, Brandon." She believed it, she wasn't paying lip service to him as she might have other clients. Other clients were concerned about how they looked to the outside world. Brandon was, too, but she saw the sincerity in his desire to work with the tiny island nation. He wanted to help stop the drug runners, to be on the right side of life.

"Have you ever had a lifelong friendship go south on you, Poppy?"

"Lifelong, no. Sonja and I have been solid since college, and I still have grade school friends back in Western New York. But I know what betrayal is." Like him, she'd lost everything in terms of her career. Unlike him, she wasn't one deal away from restituting her business. That was going to take a complete do-over on her part. And years.

"What are you thinking about?" The warmth had edged back into his tone. It made her heart sing and she didn't want her heart or any other part of her singing for Brandon Boudreaux. It was easier when he iced her out, as he had after finding out her brand line deal was sunk. Or when they were having mind-blowing sex, preventing her from thinking about what she was risking by getting so close to him.

Too close.

"I'm thinking that you have a chance to get your company back on track. That's one more than most folks get when they lose a job. Most have to start over."

"I am starting over, Poppy. Maybe not with the kind of work I do, or even how I do it. But for the first time in my life, I'm on my own."

* * * *

He watched her amber eyes widen as she took in his words, her mouth working as though she were going to challenge him.

"If anyone can do something on his own, it's you!" Her smile was forced along with her Positive Poppy banter. He let it go.

Since the storm had lifted Brandon was rarely in the house. He couldn't be near her, not without wanting to be *with* her, and he was no good for her. He'd overreacted to the news about her brand line, too, which really pissed him off. If their relationship was laid-back, if he was the man he knew she needed right now, the last thing he could expect from her was all the intimate details of her failed business. Poppy needed a rebound relationship, which he was willing to be. Anything more would spell disaster for both of them. He had to focus on saving his livelihood and she had to get back on her feet, too.

He'd given Poppy a key fob, hoping he'd be able to allow her to simply be a roommate with benefits. But it was impossible. He wanted her and she allowed him to have her every chance they got. Even better, she wanted him and wasn't shy about it. And while he expected she'd be in and out he didn't know what she did all day while he was gone. Seeing her sitting here in the Café Du Monde, dressed to kill, had shaken him. He'd been immediately drawn to her, immediately recognized her.

Brandon's meetings with the government officials had gone well and tomorrow he met with the actual representatives of San Sofia who would decide whether or not he'd get the contract.

While he'd been busy building boats and going to the preliminary meetings, Poppy had apparently been doing some business of her own.

"I appreciate the sentiment, Yankee girl, but there's nothing I do alone in my industry. From my team to all the contractors and agencies we work with, it's a team effort."

"Do you mean to sound condescending toward my job, or is that just an extra talent of yours? I know that you think fashion and celebrity stylists are frivolous, but I do happen to make a difference in the world, too. It might not be helping in the war on drugs but I help people to feel better about themselves each day."

"What kind of people are you talking about, Poppy? You mean you make rich, privileged people feel better about being so selfish with their financial blessings?"

"That's not fair. Your clients are ten times as well-off as mine. They have to be, to be able to afford one of your sailboats. If you want to throw down on demographics, bring it." Her chin jutted, actually jutted, over the table and the gleam in her eye was one of hostile intent.

"Do you want to punch me, Poppy?"

"No—well, maybe just a bit. Yes. Yes, I want to punch you right in your nose. You know nothing about what I do."

"I know that you've helped me prepare for my toughest contract interview yet. And since it's going to be my last negotiation unless I win it, there's extra pressure. Your styling and coaching has got me this far. I'm grateful."

"Then why all the commotion about what I do, if it's relevant or not?"

"Because I like the way your eyes sparkle when you're mad." Christ, had those words just come out of his mouth? So much for keeping it above board around Poppy.

"I'm not mad. I'm annoyed that I have to continue this conversation with you and the millions of men like you who don't get what I do for a living."

"Do you get what you do, Poppy?" The rug had been pulled out from under her, and in the ugliest of ways because it had been very public, very in-your-face.

"I know that I provide services tailored to each individual client, not the same for all. Clients seek me out because they see the newfound confidence in their friends and colleagues who've used my services."

Her bottom lip trembled and he wanted to crush it under his mouth. To lick away her doubts. "I'm sure they do. And…I shouldn't have said what I did. I promise I'll find something else to get your blood boiling. Not your career."

She didn't reply but the grim line of her mouth softened. He let the silence stand as he puzzled over the bubbling feeling in his chest. As if his heart was letting a little more light in.

\* \* \* \*

Poppy couldn't escape the unexpected rendezvous with Brandon at Café Du Monde fast enough. He had rattled her cage as usual but this time he'd not stopped at the bars. He was inside with her, egging her on with the harsh whips of her own recriminations. She had lost sight of why she'd taken up being a personal stylist in the first place. The event in her life that had inspired her to pursue making people feel their best no matter what. She shook away the awful memory, reminding herself that she was safe, her mother was safe. No one would hurt them again.

She leaned her head back on the driver's seat as the AC powered up. The BMW was the epitome of luxury and she loved every minute of driving it. Brandon knew she would, because she'd liked driving Sonja's Beemer. When she'd retrieved it from his garage she saw several other vehicles including a no-nonsense Ford Fiesta she'd have been happy to use and told him so. He'd dismissed her offer and said that she was doing him a favor by giving the high-end car a workout. Her phone rang and she lifted her head, looking at the dashboard's hands-free display. A thrill ran through her when she saw it was one of the boutiques she'd left her card at this morning. She pressed the accept button.

"Poppy's Do-Overs." It felt so good to have her own sense of a job again, to have a new business.

"Poppy, it's Bianca from Fresh Lines. You were in our boutique earlier?"

"Yes. It's nice to hear from you again." She tried to stay calm and not sound too eager. Professionalism over despair.

"I've taken a look at your brochure, and your business is just what I need right now."

"Wonderful." She fought against screaming her gratitude. After months of spiraling into the crater the breakup from Will had blasted in her heart, jubilation was a stranger. But a welcome one.

To her delight, the boutique owner wanted to hire her to conduct monthly presentations about how to be your own fashion stylist.

"I can start this week if you'd like."

"That's great. I'll put you on the schedule for Saturday morning. It's the perfect time when the new moms want out of the house to shop."

"You think my audience will be mostly young mothers?"

"Oh no. There will also be a couple of empty nester women who are regular shoppers, and the news anchor saw my post about your services on Facebook and wants to hire you for a private session!"

"This is fantastic. As promised, you'll get ten percent of my commission. I can bring a contract by tomorrow."

"Actually, I have a different idea for that. I have an entire room in the back that I use for storage, but I have plenty of space on the third floor to move my extra inventory. What would you say to using the main-floor storage room for your office? If you expand as you'd mentioned, I'd love for my shop to be your headquarters here in New Orleans. Until your income is steady, I'll charge you rent based on the customers you bring. Totally on commission."

It seemed too easy. Too quick. "Answer me this, Bianca. Did you do a background check on me?"

Bianca's warm laughter conceded guilt. "Not per se but I did Google you. I thought you looked familiar! And for the record, your ex is a douche."

"Ah, thank you?" Poppy trusted her gut and no alarm bells had gone off with Bianca.

"We'll finesse the details tomorrow, but until then may I suggest that you join the NOLA Chamber of Commerce? The next meeting is this week and it'd be the perfect networking opportunity for you."

"I'll do that. Thanks again, Bianca. I really mean it."

"My pleasure."

Poppy smiled as she disconnected the call. Driving Brandon's car was a treat but she'd have to find her own car soon. She didn't own a car because it wasn't needed in New York. If she found a place to live anywhere outside of downtown NOLA she'd need a vehicle. Plus Louisiana was better seen by car.

Or boat.

New Orleans was giving her a chance to circle back and reinvent Designs by Amber. For starters, she'd changed the name to Poppy's Do-Overs. Instead of attracting high-end clients, she hoped to encourage established women in established careers to take a professional inventory and see if they were living their dreams. Part of her business model was to donate a set percentage to battered women's shelters, and she hoped to offer her services at the actual shelters. She'd done work with social workers in New York City when she'd first started in personal styling but her charity work had fallen to the side as her time constraints grew.

That had been a big mistake.

She needed hard cash to put down on a new place to live in New York and a new shop. Brandon's work would be the bulk of what she needed to get going, but it wasn't going to help her immediate needs. And she had to face facts. Returning to live in New York full time was not an affordable option. Not yet, and maybe not for quite a while.

Hence her setting up a new website and having business cards and brochures printed on the cheap in a local office supply store. She'd spent the past two weeks since the storm handing out her card to every boutique owner within the city limits. It was humbling work after what she'd accomplished in New York, but she was starting over. With negative-nothing, because her reputation had been so damaged.

It wasn't going to be easy, or quick. But it might be lasting. A new life and career in New Orleans. As long as she promised herself that she wasn't doing it for anyone but herself. Allowing the tiniest speckle of hope for a more lasting relationship with Brandon would turn NOLA into New York all over again. Up until Will she'd never relied on a man, never considered a lasting relationship. She'd never make that mistake again.

# Chapter 15

Poppy leaned over to the slick contemporary nightstand and shut off her phone's alarm, ruing the early hour. Until she looked to her left and saw the sunrise spill over the water. She'd figured out that the guest room overlooked Lake Pontchartrain, while the living area of Brandon's house had a spectacular view of the Mississippi. The house's unique position had kept it from flooding during the storm.

Sonja and Henry's place hadn't been as fortunate. The bottom floor had seepage damage that didn't look that bad to Poppy but Brandon assured her it would necessitate the entire hardwood floor being ripped up and replaced. He'd already hired a mitigation contractor for Henry, but with the high numbers of damaged homes it might be weeks before the house was repaired.

Poppy ran a hot shower and laid out her outfit. She'd picked up some pieces with Southern flair, such as a blouse or skirt, while keeping her signature sleek lines intact. Turned out that if people shopping in the boutique recognized her, they were happy to have a "famous stylist" help them with their wardrobe choices. They didn't care about the rumors of her mental illness or lack thereof.

She walked into Brandon's kitchen and found a bright yellow note next to the espresso machine.

*Left early for meeting. Meet me for brunch at 10:30?*

Brandon had scribbled the address of the restaurant at the bottom of the slip of paper. His strong scrawl reminded her of his lovemaking-deft, polished, but with enough wild to keep her on edge, wondering what he'd do next to bring her to another delta-shaking orgasm. The man knew his way around her body, that was a given. And she was trying to keep her heart out of this by always insisting on going to sleep in her separate room, apart from him. As if she could pretend it really was sex-only.

Getting involved with anyone after all she'd gone through with Will had to be a rebound. That was the only logical conclusion. She had no other way to explain the constant craving she had for Brandon. His body, for sure, but his humor, the sense that he completely understood her.

She took the note and neatly folded it. Nothing wrong with a little rebound action.

\* \* \* \*

Brandon sat in a comfortable chair in a minimally appointed waiting area of one of New Orleans' top law firms. He knew it was one of the best because his father owned the top firm in the area. It was a mystery to him why Henry hadn't landed this account. If the San Sofia procurement team had been handled by the Boudreaux firm, Brandon might have groveled enough to ask Henry for a leg-up on the competition.

Of course, that would be illegal and Henry didn't do anything outside of the lines. Brandon didn't either, in fact. And he wouldn't want to put Henry at risk, ever, but he wished like hell he could confide in his brother about Jeb disappearing with the company funds. Henry would have succinct legal advice for him, as he always did. But he'd forevermore judge Jeb, and Brandon wasn't an idiot. He knew that Jeb and he's business partnership stuck in Henry's craw. Henry never said as much, but it was there in the way they didn't talk about anything but the most shallow aspects of Boats by Gus. Which was fine with Brandon because he had no desire to hear about how the old man was treating Henry to bonus upon bonus, how losing one son made him pour his focus on his remaining two children.

"Mr. Boudreaux?" A woman in a suit that fit her body like an alligator's skin stood at the front of the waiting area. Brandon stood and walked past the half a dozen or so other contenders for the San Sofia contract and gave the executive assistant his killer smile.

"Thanks, Mary Beth." He motioned for her to go first through the door and into the carpeted passageway. "How's it going so far today?"

He didn't miss her checking him out. Was certain she wanted him to notice, in fact. Her cat green eyes were offset by a smooth olive-toned complexion, made all the more enticing by her long, straight brunette locks.

"It's been the usual, but I think it's about to get more interesting." Her perfect brow arched over her eye and he caught her message. He waited for the usual thrill of a flirt to swirl in his chest but…nothing. Mary Beth was his perfect type—brunette, tall, confident.

She absolutely wasn't a bleached-blond petite woman with the sharpest tongue this side of the Mississippi.

"Gus? What do you think?" She knew from his file that he was the company's namesake.

"I think the competition is fierce. No one wants to stand out and risk losing a multimillion-dollar contract."

Disappointment warred with annoyance in her eyes and he offered her a bland smile this time.

"You're probably right."

"Any tips for me before I go up to bat?"

She laughed. Low and throaty, and he suspected she caught a lot of big fish with it. Two weeks ago he'd have been one of them.

Now all he could see in his mind was how Poppy looked in her yoga pants and sloppy T-shirt, sipping chamomile tea as she looked at her phone. It was only because they'd been spending so much time together, both needing human touch.

"They're not an easy crowd. Limited funds, for the type of boats they want."

"How many of these kinds of contracts do you work each year?" If this didn't work out, maybe he'd have another chance before he had to shut down Boats by Gus.

Mary Beth shook her head. "Hard to say. We don't get a lot of foreign nations in here. But I've only been with the firm for five months. As soon as I pass the bar I'll either be offered a position or I'll find another place to work."

"Well, thanks." They'd reached the door to the conference room.

"Anytime, Gus. But you know that already, don't you? Good luck and I hope you have something to celebrate after this." Somehow, she knew he had another woman on the line. He'd been definite in his boundaries with her. This was new territory for Brandon. He'd cared for more than one woman in his life, but none that left some kind of invisible stamp on him. Discounting it to nerves, he nodded.

"Thanks, Mary Beth."

*Showtime.*

* * * *

"Hello?" Poppy had wanted to let the call from her lawyer in New York go to voicemail but she'd never been a chicken.

"Poppy, good to hear your voice. How are you doing?" Louise's tone revealed a rare glimpse of compassion. Usually the Manhattan attorney was strictly business, no-nonsense.

Poppy looked around at her new office in the back room of Bianca's boutique. "I'm doing very well, thank you. What's up?"

"The initial suit from your former assistant is weak, as you already figured out. She doesn't have anything going for her, honestly. I expect the judge will throw it out."

"But she doesn't have any assets, either." Except Will. "How will she make reparations for the damage to my reputation and business?" Anger pushed heat into her face and she stood up, needing to pace. "I lost the deal for Attitude by Amber."

Silence. Even her loquacious attorney whom she'd known for five years was lost for words.

"I'd hoped the reports I read were incorrect."

"Nope. Absolutely accurate. Done, gone. No payment rendered."

"I'm sorry, Poppy. I do wish you'd called me with this as soon as you were informed. You need to countersue."

"There was nothing you could have done. They were adamant. Frankly I'm surprised they waited this long to put out a press release. As for countersuing, I want to be divested of any ties to those two idiots as soon as I can."

Louise's sigh sounded hurried. "Listen, it's imperative that you countersue. I've known you for too long, Poppy. You're too giving and while I admire your spiritual intention, because that's what it is, legally I cannot advise you to let anything go."

"This is why you're my lawyer, Louise." She thought about it but didn't need to. "Yes, let's go for it. What do you need me to do?"

"Nothing right this minute. I'll file the petition against Will and Tori, since they're married. There might be a way to free up enough of your funds to at least pay for your legal fees and help you get started again."

Poppy toyed with shiny plastic Mardi Gras beads that spilled from a clear plastic container on her desk. She wanted to create an entire palette from the bright purples, greens, and golds. "I've come up with a new business plan but I can't go full speed ahead until I have what's left of my funds. I still have a few loyal clients in New York, I'm exploring some other options for a new career." It would be much, much slower than her Attitude by Amber deal. Regional to NOLA, and only if she was very,

very lucky. And it would never be as lucrative as her stylist business. But it might be the most satisfying thing she'd done to date. Since that time right after Hurricane Katrina, when she'd volunteered alongside Sonja.

"It may take months to get to your corporate accounts again. You had something put away in your personal funds, right?"

She managed a shaky laugh. "No. I'm flat broke because, like the overconfident stylist I was, I put just about all of my own money into my business." She told Louise to call her as soon as she had word on the judge's decision, and disconnected the call.

"Hey." Bianca stood at the door, a large empty basket on her hip. "I didn't want to interrupt your call but I'm going to move the rest of this stuff out of here." She placed the basket on a shelf and Poppy helped her fill it with assorted scarves, wallets, and belts. "Were those new clients?"

"No, unfortunately, not yet. You didn't interrupt anything, trust me." She paused, then decided to jump in with both feet. "I know we haven't known each other long, and you've already given me an office, but since you've read up on me, you know my former executive assistant is suing me for copyright? She claims that my sunflower design was her idea."

"Was it?"

Poppy laughed. "That woman couldn't draw a stick figure, much less use the graphics program I did to come up with that logo. And I had it copyrighted before she started getting a paycheck from me. She's messed with the wrong person."

"But she got your fiancé." Bianca's expression was open and sympathetic. "You wouldn't be human if you didn't want retribution."

"A few weeks ago, yes, I wanted to claw her eyes out and kick Will's balls up to his nose. Now? I'm looking for other ways to enact revenge. Isn't living well the best revenge and all that? I want to grow a new business, the one I've started here with you."

"I couldn't help overhear that you lost your deal for your own brand line?"

"Yes. My one big regret. The buzz over the breakup and my erratic behavior was too risky for the retailers." She shrugged. "It still stings, I can't lie. But if it had gone through, I wouldn't be standing here and dreaming up ways to empower women with fashion in New Orleans, would I?"

Bianca smiled. "No, you wouldn't."

"So you're in? My plan is to establish a solid base here in downtown NOLA before trying to expand. Frankly, I don't see it going out of the local area."

Bianca's wide grin flashed her affirmation. "Bring a pen when you bring me the contract." The bells over the boutique entrance chimed and Bianca left to greet the customer.

Poppy couldn't help it. She did a crazed happy dance on the spot.

* * * *

Poppy peered up at the sign "Flapjack Heaven" and compared the address to Brandon's note. Yup, she was in the right place. "Dive" didn't describe the dirty-windowed café, and she was using "café" in the loosest sense of the word. She was ten minutes early and she looked up and down the street for a nicer coffee shop to wait, but she stood far off the French Quarter, on a side street that more closely resembled an alley. It was an odd place to show up to wearing her sexiest thong set under her outfit.

She pushed open the front door and an ancient brass bell clanged overhead. The greasy-aproned man at the cash register didn't look up, merely continued to scroll through whatever on his phone screen. In the middle of the wall, a rectangular opening to the kitchen revealed several cooks, all industriously whisking, flipping, and ringing the bell on the counter across said window. From a back door two servers rushed in, each grabbing armloads of plates laden with pancakes, French toast, and grits before they disappeared through the same swinging door.

"I'm meeting someone for brunch." She stood in front of the cashier. He looked up as if she'd caused him an extreme inconvenience.

"Go pick out a table." He motioned over his left shoulder with his head and went back to his phone.

Poppy looked around the tiny front of the building, where there were no chairs, no benches. She walked back toward the only other door, wondering why the hell, with all the incredible places in New Orleans to eat, Brandon had picked this dump.

She shoved open the swinging door, bracing in case one of the servers came crashing through at the same time. A few short steps across an Art Deco–era tiled corridor, with *his* and *hers* restrooms on either side, and she opened a second, screen door onto a courtyard garden. She was embraced by an enormous lush tropical escape from the hot, humid street with nothing remotely urban in sight. Red- and violet-hued macaws hung out in giant cages, tearing with relish into mango slices. The sweet chirp of songbirds flitted down from the high tree boughs that covered the space, allowing shafts of sunlight to float down when it wasn't obscured by clouds.

Only after she inhaled the sweet jasmine, touched the leaves on a low-hanging magnolia branch, did she notice the patrons. And what looked like dozens of servers, not just the pair she'd seen earlier. Tables were scattered all through the parklike setting, most in their own alcove to offer privacy to the diners. The place was packed and she had to walk deeper into the garden before she spied an empty table partially obscured by a hanging palm tree branch.

"Coffee?" Her bottom had barely hit the cushioned chair before a waiter in a crisply pressed white shirt, rolled sleeves, and with a linen towel over his forearm smiled at her, his shiny silver coffee pot reflecting her stunned expression.

"Yes. Please." She noted the tiny silver pitcher of cream in the center of the table. "I'm meeting a friend—I'm not sure he'll find me in here."

"No problem, we'll send anyone who describes you back here." The waiter spun and walked off before she had a chance to laugh at his response. The inescapable New Orleans charm reached into her chest and hugged her heart. It wasn't the first time since she'd landed at the airport almost three weeks ago that she'd felt it. Only now, it wasn't the simple thrill of being in a new part of the world. It was more definite, as if the city were wooing her.

She poured a dollop of the rich cream into her cup and stirred with the exquisite silver filigree coffee spoon. The first sip was pure pleasure on her tongue. She closed her eyes and soaked up the scent of the fresh brew, the surrounding vegetation, and the flowers. Allowing a sigh to escape her lips, she existed in this moment as if none of her Manhattan transgressions ever happened. If it were only this simple. *Maybe it is.*

Solid footsteps on the crushed-seashell path forced her eyes open and she gazed up into the brilliant blue of Brandon's contemplation. He took in her hair, her eyes, lingered at her lips before going down along her throat to the cleavage she'd left professional but still obvious, telling herself she hadn't left the extra blouse buttons undone for him. She hadn't been anticipating their brunch like it was a date or anything. *Liar.* His gaze continued its downward sweep, and the way he looked at her bare toes in her gladiator sandals made her press her thighs together. A movement her short skirt couldn't hide, and one that Brandon didn't miss. He slid into the seat across from her and nodded at the server's offer of coffee, all the while keeping his eyes on her. A seductive smile lifted his mouth as he noted the heat in her cheeks.

"Good morning, Yankee girl. You look incredibly sexy, as always."

"Hey." He had her breathless and wet and he hadn't touched her yet. 'Hey?' As if they were more than friends or associates meeting to discuss his meeting. His meeting. "How did it go?"

"In a minute." He reached over the table and kissed her, full on the lips with a tantalizing quick lick of tongue. Poppy breathed in the scent of Brandon as much as she savored his taste. He drew back and his eyes sparkled, his skin crinkling. "Isn't this a nicer way to start the meal?"

"Um, if you're into putting on a show." She couldn't stop the blush if she wanted to, and knew her face had to be the color of the crepe myrtle behind her.

He opened the menu and after staring at the barrier between them, Poppy did the same. Good Lord, there had to be no less than three dozen versions of flapjacks to include gooseberry and gumbo.

"Is there any kind of flapjack they don't have?"

"No."

"What are your favorites?"

"Strawberry. Sometimes peach." The way he said the fruits made it clear that he was thinking about something other than brunch. She jumped back as he snapped the menu down and leaned toward her.

"Peach like your skin and strawberry like your nipples after they've been in my mouth." His smile was the devil incarnate challenged only by the way his eyes glittered.

She leaned in, because in the short time she'd known Brandon, she'd learned that any sign of weakness only encouraged him to keep teasing her.

It wasn't always teasing. A vision of him taking her from behind as she bent over his massive kitchen island set her center into the low, steady throb that demanded relief. She crossed her ankles and kept her knees straight ahead, avoiding his feet.

"I liked it when we did that, too."

She laughed. "Give me a break. You're a mind reader?"

"Close enough, from the way you're trying to catch your breath." His gaze lowered again to her cleavage. "I don't think I've ever seen you in a regular business suit."

"That makes sense since when I'm home I like to be in workout clothes." The server appeared and kept her from obsessing over how she'd said "home" as if she lived here. As if she'd let it slip to Brandon that she was hoping to make New Orleans her home. It was too soon to tell him. She was doing this for her, not a man, not a relationship.

She clenched her eyes shut for a minute, shaking her head. Brandon ordered peach pancakes and she picked banana nut. The server warmed up their coffees and left. The wall of green next to and above them leant an air of romantic intimacy to their table, and Poppy leaned back. She could enjoy a unique dining experience without worrying about whether Brandon figured out the track of her thoughts. It wasn't as if they were like the other couples here, the ones who were completely into one another.

"You okay?" The dainty white porcelain coffee cup was tiny in his hand, but he wasn't awkward handling it. Everything seemed to come naturally to Brandon.

"I'm great. Just clearing my head of silly thoughts."

"Care to share them?"

She sipped her coffee. "No thank you."

He laughed. "Poppy, when are you going to learn that you can trust me?"

"I do trust you. I trust you to be who you are." Guilt nudged her. She didn't trust him enough to let him know she might stay here. She put her cup down on its saucer. No more seductive lines. "So tell me. What happened with the contract?"

Brandon's pleasure pushed a smile across his features and she knew in that moment that he was a modest man. Humble, even. Not like in bed when he loved proving his vast skill.

"It went well. As well as it could. There were several other boat builders there. I recognized a few of the company names and spoke with them in the waiting area. There were some reps from companies that I'd never heard of, too." He rapped his knuckles on the linen tablecloth. She noted how a sprinkling of yellow-orange pollen across the table from the single hibiscus bloom in the vase contrasted with the dark hair on his forearm. "This is a big deal, bigger than I'd imagined. The good news is that I don't need to deal with all of the intricacies of the U.S. Government—that's what the law firm representing the San Sofia government is going to take care of. They'll make sure whoever gets the contract has all their ducks in order, which is a huge relief."

"Does the firm represent you or the San Sofia military?"

"Both. The San Sofia team has their own set of attorneys, of course, looking out for their best interests. The law firm here keeps the rest of it running smoothly."

"Could Henry help you with this?"

His hand stilled and he moved his head to crack his neck. "Right now I'm not in need of any legal help. That will come in to play after I get the contract."

"So you didn't get the offer yet?" She wanted him to succeed, to have the lift out of his rock bottom that he'd given her when he'd asked for her help.

"Hang on. I did okay in the presentation, and I feel I answered all of their questions and concerns to the best of my ability. According to Mary Beth, the firm's intern in charge of the administrative process, I was the only one they showed that much interest in. On the way over here she texted me that I'm one of three callbacks for next week."

"Why do you have to wait a week? I'd have thought San Sofia would want to go to contract as soon as possible. You said the boats are needed to fight their opioid epidemic, right?"

He nodded. "Yes. They've got help from the U.S. Coast Guard for now, but it's never enough. And there has to be a week between the interviews to allow for recording the process with our governments; federal, state, and local."

"It's the same in New York City. Everyone gets their piece of the pie." What she'd accomplished in a month in New Orleans would take several months, even a year or two, in New York. She'd lucked out when she walked into Bianca's shop.

His eyes darkened when she said "pie" and she silently cursed him. Would they ever have a conversation that wasn't laden with sexual innuendo?

"A piece of—yes, death, taxes and all that." He reached across the table and grasped her hand as it lay on the table, surprising her with the sudden intimate gesture. "I wouldn't be this far without you, Poppy. You asked the exact questions I needed to be prepared. I don't think there was one you hadn't thought of in advance."

She ignored her pulse as it jammed in tune to her attraction to him, somewhere alongside her throat. She swallowed. "I was using your notes. Anyone could have helped."

He shook his head. "Kill the modesty, Poppy. You got me all pretty on the outside"—he motioned with his chin to his suit—"but more important, you played the role of inquisitor to a T. You were correct—the folks they sent were mostly civilian politicians. Only one had worked with the military when they served in the U.S. Navy years ago. No question was too simple or too complicated. And I was prepared." He lifted her hand to his lips and kissed her knuckles, the warmth of his mouth too brief before he let go and leaned on his forearms. "I've got a good chance of landing this account, and you're a big reason why."

"I'm glad I could help." It was on the tip of her tongue to tell him she'd decided to set up shop in NOLA. But she couldn't. It'd only place unreasonable expectations on what they shared.

Brandon detailed the interview and she replayed all the work they'd done together the last two weeks. It took effort to shove aside the visions of the incredible sex, something she'd have to address later, on her own, when Brandon wasn't around to see her unguarded expressions. They had worked well together in and out of bed, and she had to admit the satisfaction that thrummed through her was the result of both of their recent successes. The same sense of purpose she'd had when she worked with Sonja down here in the bayou all those years ago, after Katrina had decimated the area.

"Here you go." Their server placed large white china plates heaping with pancakes on the small table. "Will you be needing anything else?"

Brandon looked at the syrup on the table and shook his head. "Nope, I'm good. Poppy?"

"I'm good, too."

\* \* \* \*

Brandon liked how Poppy dug into her flapjacks the same way she'd jumped into helping him prepare for the San Sofia negotiations. Her manners were impeccable, no doubt the result of her many social obligations in New York. But polite protocol couldn't hide the way she devoured her brunch as if she never had to watch her calories. It reminded him of how she gave herself completely to sex, savoring each touch, each sensation. He adjusted his seat.

"Glad to see you're enjoying your meal."

She grinned through a mouthful of banana nut flapjacks, a drop of maple syrup on her chin. "Delicious."

He leaned forward and swiped the syrup away with his forefinger, then licked it off. Poppy's eyes grew wide and he laughed.

"You're too easy a flirt, Poppy."

She swallowed and took a long drink of her water.

"You're relentless."

He laughed. "What made you get into fashion?"

She studied him for a moment before sliding her gaze to the bright pink flower in the table's vase.

"I never picked fashion as a career. I studied psychology in undergrad and expected to go into social work."

"Social work. That's a vocation, not a career."

"Yeah, well, I wanted to give back to the world for being able to get out of—I mean, go to college in the city and start a new life."

He leaned back, taking a break from his stack of flour and sugar. "You know about my family—all you need to know happened the wedding weekend. What about yours?" He watched her closely. She never brought her family up to him. He heard her talking on the phone and assumed it was to family but didn't want to pry. And if she was speaking to a love interest, he didn't want to know. Although Poppy didn't strike him as the type to keep two or more guys on the line, not right after such a major breakup. And if he had his druthers he'd keep her occupied for the foreseeable future. As long as he got the ship contract. Without it he had nothing to offer her.

"Brandon, did you hear what I just said?"

"Sorry, I drifted."

"I asked if you're really certain you want to hear all of this. It's pretty standard, actually."

"Try me."

She blew the curled lock of hair off her forehead and he watched her lower lip puff out. "My mother raised my younger sister and I. Our biological father was out of the picture by the time we were walking—my sister's eighteen months younger than me. Mom, well, she has the worst taste in men."

"In what way?"

"In the stay out of their way or they'd kick the shit out of you way." She grimaced. "I know it sounds awful to someone from a normal home, but getting knocked around was part of our lives for so long, through three different boyfriends, the last one a stepfather, that we didn't know how bad it was."

"I don't believe that. We always know when it's bad like that."

Her eyes flashed on his. "You've been in an abusive family?"

"Not physically. Emotionally and mentally? You saw my parents at the restaurant. Do they look like the epitome of warm and caring to you?"

"No. It's sad that with two sons like you and Henry, and I'm sure your sister, too, that your folks never opened their minds."

Her observation drove a wooden stake through the part of his heart that was off-limits to all. He'd shut if off from his parents after Hurricane Katrina. He'd opted to never discuss it with his siblings; it wasn't their fault that their parents had made such a mess of things. And he didn't blame Henry or his sister for still engaging with Hudson and Gloria. It was their choice, their conscience.

"Brandon, are you okay? You look like you've seen a ghost."

He took in the concern in her eyes, the uncanny way she could tell whether he was daydreaming or thinking about something deep like his lack of relationship with his family. How had this happened, in only four weeks?

"I'm fine." He shifted in his seat and pushed away his plate. His appetite had disappeared with the cold reality of his life. "Keep talking."

"So, my mother's last husband had a violent temper. Nothing new to us, we knew as kids to clear out of the house if one of her husbands or boyfriends came in drunk and pissed off. But by the time I was thirteen and Ginger was eleven, we knew too much. And we'd become the parents to our mom." She fiddled with the tiny silver sugar spoon that stuck out of the covered dispenser. She wouldn't meet his eyes.

"Ginger woke me up one night when the fighting was getting particularly intense between Mom and our stepdad. It wasn't loud and that was the problem. I knew that when it got quiet whatever was happening was probably really bad. As in deadly. I made Ginger lock herself in our bedroom, and told her to call the police on my cell phone. She didn't have one yet. We had to wait until we were teens, Mom's rule." She reached for a vining flower and caressed the soft white petals.

"I crept downstairs and found the bastard straddling my mother, his hands around her throat. She was pushing at him, still breathing, but I knew he had her right at the point of her letting go. I still don't know how I did it. I grabbed this old milk-glass lamp with a frilly shade—do you know the kind I'm talking about, the white glass that looks fragile but it's really heavy?"

"My grandmother had some." He and Henry had knocked one over with an indoor plastic golf set, much to his mother's horror. Their grandmother had laughed and swept up the shards as if it were a dime-store purchase.

"Yes, this lamp, it was from my mother's mother. I took it and started hitting him over the back and head. It surprised him enough to let go of Mom, and she was able to crawl away once she caught her breath." Her shoulders shuddered and her eyes had a distant focus. His arms trembled from the want to hold her, comfort her. Instinctively he knew that if he touched her, did anything to shake her out of the nightmare of a memory, she'd shut down. So he waited.

"He was so angry. I could tell he didn't see me, that he wanted to get rid of whatever, *whoever* had stopped him from hurting my mother. I'm damned lucky he was drunk and tripped over the leg of our end table. He was chasing me into the kitchen—I was trying to get out of the house. We only had a front door, which we kept closed most of the time, and the side door off of the kitchen. I knew that if I got out of the house he'd come after me and then Mom and Ginger would be safe."

She grew silent and his compassion for her ordeal internally wrestled with uninhibited abject rage at her stepfather.

"Did you make it out? Before he could hurt you?"

She shook her head. "Only to the kitchen door. He had me cornered, but then the police showed up and it eventually worked out."

Brandon suspected there was a lot more to the story in the "eventually worked out" part, but didn't press. Poppy looked as agitated as she had when he'd gone to get her from Henry and Sonja's during the storm. And he didn't want to ever see her plummet back into the panic attack she'd had that first night.

He should have realized then that this woman wasn't a passing distraction for him. She wasn't a fuck buddy or business colleague, either. She was… Poppy.

She ran her slim fingers over the white tablecloth. "It sounds pretty awful compared to your upbringing, I'm sure."

"It was awful and I'm so sorry you went through that, Poppy."

Slowly she lifted her gaze from the flower, to the plants surrounding the table, and finally, rested it on him. "Thank you."

Damned if he didn't feel an invisible line between them, as strong as any ship's line, wrapping around his heart.

* * * *

Poppy considered herself an expert at judging people, at least from an energy perspective. She could always tell if someone had anger issues, or was putting on a show to the world while suffering on the inside. Brandon wasn't so easy to read, and she knew that was part of what made him so damned hot to her. The challenge of figuring him out.

Right now she really wished he was more transparent. She'd never felt more exposed, not even when he'd taken her clothes off the first time and laid her out on his bed, his eyes devouring every nook and cranny of her body.

He leaned back and the movement pulled his dress shirt taut across his chest. His tie had an aqua-blue diamond pattern and the color brought out the turquoise flecks in his eyes.

"Nothing to thank me for, Yankee girl. It's my privilege to hear your story."

"More like my history." She was not defined by that time in her life. She couldn't be.

"History has a way of hanging around. If we're lucky it's the best threads that weave into our mainsail."

"Say what?" She knew he was talking about sailing but boating wasn't her bailiwick.

"The mainsail, the largest sail on a boat. I'm using it as a metaphor for life."

"I didn't know 'poet' was on your résumé alongside 'naval architect.'"

That blinding flash of his teeth accompanied by his deep dimples brought out the masculine cleft in his chin. "I minored in English Lit, focus on early American poetry."

"That sounds...intriguing." From Brandon, it did.

"It was a good counterpoint to the engineering classes I needed for the naval architecture certification, that's for sure."

"You don't have to act like it's all okay, that you don't think less of me because of how I grew up." She remembered Will's incredulous expression, followed by flat-out denial when she'd mentioned her childhood. Will hadn't even wanted to make the trip to Western New York with her to meet her mother and sister. He'd finally relented and they'd stayed in Niagara Falls for a single night before he declared they should go to Toronto. Will found Buffalo boring.

"Your background only makes me admire you more, Poppy. You've accomplished in less than three decades what many never do in a lifetime."

"You should know. You've done the same in many ways."

"Yeah, we're a couple of overachievers. Each for different reasons, though. So you were saying you originally wanted to be a social worker?"

"Yes." She fiddled with her utensils. "But then in college I got a summer internship in the Personal Stylist department of a major department store. I was hooked. Being able to pick out clothes I'd never afford for others to wear, and to help them feel better about themselves was pure fun. I used those skills that one summer here, when I came home with Sonja for spring break. It was right after Katrina. There was so much homelessness, so much devastation."

"The people who could afford a stylist weren't suffering." Brandon's face was still, as if he had his own flashbacks to deal with.

"I know. I didn't work as a stylist in the traditional sense. I volunteered at a church with Sonja. We handed out clothing to families who'd lost it all. They came in to get whatever their gift certificates and prepaid store credit cards couldn't cover."

"I remember the gift certificates. So many businesses donated them for years after the storm."

"Right. But you can't get back everything, not without an income. So many were out of work for months, or had to move. The women and their kids would come in, looking for something fun in the piles of donated clothes that poured in from all over the country, the world. I'd help them piece together outfits. They could use their gift certificates to affordable department stores to get basics like tank tops and T-shirts, and then find a donated designer scarf or bag to accessorize."

"I'm impressed."

She shrugged, but her cheeks warmed from his praise. "It was so easy for me. It was then that I decided to look into becoming a personal stylist more seriously." And now she wanted to do more by doing what looked like less. Support women through disastrous circumstances into the change they needed. Her New York career seemed like a previous life, a faded memory.

Realization jerked through her. What was going on here? In New Orleans, in Brandon's home, in her heart?

Was she learning to let go of when she'd been wronged and move ahead?

"Is it because you've been working on something different in the shop you told me about?"

Now would be the perfect time to tell Brandon that she was making her work here permanent. That she was staying.

"A new project always helps with attitude, doesn't it?"

* * * *

Brandon picked out a bunch of daisies for the kitchen island. Only because he wanted to make a nice dinner for both himself and Poppy tonight, not because the flowers reminded him of the daisies painted on Poppy's toes the evening he'd met her.

He wound his cart through the aisles, taking extra time on the cuts of steak, wondering if Poppy even ate meat. He hadn't paid that much attention, thank God. Relief granted him a brief respite from his concern that he was becoming too invested in what Yankee girl thought of him. What he thought of her. He was thinking of her too often, too much. He had a business to save, after all. But just when he thought he had her figured out, she brought up something that totally sideswiped him. And not because she knew she was knocking him to his knees, stirring up shit he'd thought he'd forgotten. Like when she'd been talking about working here after Katrina hit, and mentioned the gift certificates. That was a tough time for his city. Brandon had wanted to cry when he saw other New Orleanians still struggling to find a job or pay for groceries for their kids. And his parents had packed up and left, started over far away. To him, they'd ignored what had happened.

"Hey, Gus. How you doin', sugar?" He was caught in the ice cream aisle, looking for the flavor he'd stepped on during the start of the storm. When he'd had Poppy up against the car.

*Fuck.*

"Hi, Brandy." He greeted the cashier whose presence was a legacy at this Piggly Wiggly. Brandy LaCroix's family had known the Boudreauxs ever since they'd all gone to the same parish church. "Just getting some things for dinner."

"Looks like you're having a date."

A date.

"No, nothing like that at all. You know me, Brandy. If I wanted to impress a girl I'd take her out, not burn steaks on my grill."

"Save the self-deprecation for someone who believes your bullshit, Gus Boudreaux. I still remember the time your mama brought you and your brother in here, trying to get groceries while she was sick as a dog, pregnant with your sister, Jena. You were raising hell in the carriage, throwing out everything she put in it."

Brandon shifted from foot to foot, looking around to see if he was blocking anyone who needed to get around them.

Brandy put her hand on his forearm. "How are your mama and daddy? I haven't seen them in years. As you damned well know."

"They're well." He didn't mention he'd last seen them at Henry's failed wedding rehearsal dinner, and that was the first time in a year that he'd laid eyes on them.

"Please tell them I said hello. I'll let you get back to it—come see me when you check out if you please." Brandy sashayed down the aisle toward the back where he dimly remembered there was an employee break room. He'd dated a girl in college who'd worked here part time.

Brandon looked at the ice cream selection again. He'd made meals for girlfriends before, this was nothing new.

But Poppy wasn't his girlfriend. God, she'd cringe if she ever heard herself referred to as that, especially after her spectacular betrayal by her loser ex. He recoiled again from the term fuck buddies, as they weren't buddies and…

Jesus. Joseph. And Mary. They weren't fucking. He'd made love to Poppy Kaminsky. They were lovers.

He was in love with the Yankee girl.

# Chapter 16

Poppy left the boutique by six, when Bianca closed on Tuesday nights. Bianca said they stayed open until eight on Thursdays and Fridays when more women were apt to want to shop, with the weekend in front of them. As she drove home to Brandon's she reflected on how she wasn't even choosing her work hours any longer. And it was okay.

The front door of the house smelled like polished wood from the Southern sun hitting it all afternoon. She placed her palm on the smooth oak, impressed by the heat that wafted off. When she entered the foyer the woodsy scent was immediately replaced by a delicious aroma from the kitchen.

"I hope you like steak." Brandon stood at the island stovetop, whisking something in a salad bowl while two steaks sizzled on the stove's grill plate.

"I do, but I don't expect you to cook for me." She placed her bag and laptop carrier on a stool and stood across the island from him. They'd made do with convenience food and if anyone did cook for both of them, it was her. She felt it was a good way to pay him back for occupying his guest room.

"My pleasure. I forgot how much I enjoy doing this." His eyes remained downcast, focused on the sauce or dressing he was making. He dipped a finger into the bowl and lifted it up, licking it. "Needs more mustard."

He reached over to a jar of European-style mustard and scooped out a teaspoonful. Only then did his gaze meet hers, and she jumped at the crackle of sexual tension.

"I, um, never made homemade dressing." He'd caught her ogling him. Again.

"Everything's better homemade, Poppy." He grinned and she picked up a potholder that was near her and threw it at him. Par for her lack of athletic prowess, the padded square landed in the salad bowl. Brandon was splattered with yellow drops.

"Oh, I'm so sorry." Fruitless words as laughter bubbled along her chest cavity, up her throat, and she burst out in a fit of giggles.

Brandon said nothing as he calmly dabbed at his white T-shirt, his forearms, and dropped the dishcloth into the sink. When he turned back toward her, she watched his face, which at first glance was a work of ambivalent detachment.

Too late she recognized the sparks of heat in his eyes, the same warning she had whenever he was about to get sexy with her. He was around the island in one fluid motion and she turned, poised to flee.

From what? *What are you running from?*

Familiar arms wrapped around her waist and pulled her back up against his front, her ass shaping around his erection. Brandon's breath was hot on her throat as he kissed the side of it, chuckling like a tiger holding a rabbit. She was that easy, that ready, that fucking hot for him.

"I've wanted this all day." His hand pushing her skirt up from behind, his fingers grasping her ass. She wriggled to give him better access, reached for her waistband and shoved her skirt down, revealing her lacy black thong.

"Jesus, Poppy. You're beautiful." His tone lost its teasing and flirty tone, the raspy staccatos matching the tremors running over the skin of her belly and thighs.

His touch was her hot beignet with sprinkled sugar. She'd never get enough. Before her heart rate was out of control, her resistance melted by his touch, she pushed his hands and arms off her waist and turned to face him. Lagoon-blue eyes half-lidded with his need gave away how turned on he was. As did the rock-hard erection she unbuttoned his jeans to get to.

"Poppy." He put his forehead on hers, his plea clear. He needed the relief he'd so willingly given her, so many times. Her fingertips traced along his lower abs to the hair that grew in a perfect line to his groin, where she let her fingers enjoy playing in the springy, coarse curls. With a last shove downward, his jeans and boxers fell to his ankles and his cock burst free from its enclosure.

His groans were music and the only affirmations she needed as she lowered to her knees, the cold kitchen floor hard and certain against her skin. Poppy was full of need but instead of needing Brandon inside her—she trusted this would come later—she was compelled to please him, to send him where he'd flung her. To the place where daily worries and once-in-a-lifetime catastrophes melted away and all that mattered was touch and feel.

Poppy breathed in his purely Brandon scent, musky with a twinge of salt, as if he'd been born of the bayou and had always been here, waiting for her. When she took him in her mouth his legs tensed and his hands went to her head where he ran his fingers through her orgasm-tousled locks. She sucked and licked, using her tongue to convey her own need for his release, while her hands cupped him and pressed him in the most intimate places. His climax hit him as hard as hers had, judging from the animalistic cry he let out as his cock stiffened for the last time before release. She caressed and cared for him with her mouth as his spasms continued, until his breathing let go of the frantic hitches and his cock reflected complete satisfaction.

"Poppy." He hauled her against him by her upper arms and buried his head in the crook of her neck, his arms loosely around her waist. "You're killing me."

"What? Wasn't that what you wanted?" She bit back a laugh and waited for him to acknowledge her teasing. Instead he cupped her jaw with his hand and lifted her face to his, seeking something in her gaze she wasn't sure she had to give him. Wanted to give him. Could afford to share.

Had she ever felt this organically connected to another man? This had never been the feeling around Will. Sexy, pleasurable, sure. But knowing it would never be as good as this ever again with anyone else? No. Brandon was her first.

The thought jolted through her as she stood in his arms. Brandon wasn't a random rebound hookup.

Holy hell.

* * * *

"You're an amazing woman, Poppy Kaminsky. Where did you come from?" Brandon whispered to her, not wanting to let go of her waist. This was a first for him. He'd just had the blowjob of his life and his dick was already indicating it wasn't enough. He wanted Poppy in bed, all night long.

He felt her stiffen, and braced himself for her recriminations. Poppy had made it clear she was on a man hiatus and that their shared chemistry was part of her post-breakup rehab. She didn't want commitment and he was sounding like a whimpering, needy toddler.

*Son of a bitch.*

"Hey, relax. I'm not getting too serious here, don't worry."

Her eyes came back to his and where he expected relief he saw another emotion, a reaction that he wasn't seeking but inspired elation deep inside his chest.

Disappointment.

Could it be possible that Poppy had changed her mind, that she wanted more out of this? He mentally shook his head. Neither of them wanted a serious relationship, they'd said as much more than once. And they were each entrenched in their geographical areas. He didn't see either of them moving. Although New York City held a different connotation for him when he pictured being with Poppy on the streets, in a café, in a fancy restaurant. On a bed in her loft apartment.

"I know you're not serious." She pushed on his chest and he let his arms drop. "I'm just getting a lot of things in order with work right now. I'm distracted."

"You're telling me that you were making lists in your head while blowing me?"

She smiled. "I am multitalented but no, I wasn't thinking about anything but you."

He hated himself for being so selfish but he knew he had to move now, before Poppy started thinking about anything else too deeply. He leaned in and kissed her full on the lips. With any other woman it would be a sensual way of saying thanks for such a hot sex session. With Poppy it quickly turned into a prelude for more when she opened her mouth fully to him, seeking out his tongue as he licked along her lower lip.

"Keep it that way. No thinking until we're done." He lifted her into his arms and wanted to pummel his chest like a freaking moron, he felt so much more alive, so capable around her.

"Um, Brandon?"

"Yeah?" He had them around the island, headed for his bedroom.

"You might want to take the steaks off the grill and turn the stove off. Unless you think we'll only be a minute?"

\* \* \* \*

Five minutes later, he settled her on the clean sheets he'd put on this morning, two days before his housekeeper was scheduled to do it as part of her regular routine. He hadn't been thinking he and Poppy would end up here again for sure, but just in case.

"Your sheets smell like lavender." She stretched out on the mattress, her livid blond hair reflecting golden streaks in the fading daylight. "We need to close the blinds."

"No one can see us but the alligators, honey." He quickly got rid of his shirt and took his time peeling her black thong off. "Jesus, do you own any plain underwear?"

She didn't answer but instead got her top off, her breasts spilling over the demitasse cups of a pink-on-black bra. Brandon's cock forgot about the epic orgasm Poppy had just wrought from him and was ready to go, aching for the release only Poppy's pussy gave him.

"You're beautiful." He licked her breasts along the edges of her bra, keeping his weight on his forearms and knees. God, he could be inside her in one slick thrust. It would be so slippery, Poppy's arousal evident in the way her walls clenched around him.

Not yet.

"Brandon, please. Don't wait." She writhed and bucked her hips in small, deep circles. "I need you."

"How?"

"Inside. Now. Do you want me to beg?"

*Yes.*

"Hang on. What's the hurry? The house isn't going to burn down."

He licked his way down her abdomen, loving the dips and curves into her belly button and alongside her silky hips. His teeth couldn't help but nip at her hip bones, protruding above her adorably slightly rounded tummy. "I love that you're a real woman, Poppy. So sexy. So voluptuous. Open up for me, babe." His hands reached up for her breasts as he settled between her legs, where he deeply inhaled her intense arousal before he teased her with his tongue. Her wet folds were lusciously swollen and she tasted of sex, yes, but more, woman.

His woman.

"Brandon." His name was never spoken like this before. As if her entire survival depended on him.

"Enjoy it, Poppy." He delighted in her gasps, the way she grew incredibly still, how her pussy started throwing off spasms before the orgasm fully hit her, when she cried out loud enough to wake the baby egrets incubating in eggs out in the bayou. How she sat up halfway and gave him a bemused look.

"I have no idea how you do that, but oh my God, Brandon." She flopped back down and he licked her again, until she was on the edge, ready to come in the way only Poppy could. Fully and with no distractions. He quickly raised to his knees and donned a condom.

Only when Poppy met his gaze with her flaming whiskey eyes did he thrust into her. He'd planned to go slow, to cycle his pumping with his pelvic circles, just like so many women he'd been with enjoyed. But planning wasn't something that worked with Poppy in his life. He became a man, an animal he didn't recognize or maybe knew too well. The primal beast that he and his guy friends joked about but he never let loose, always kept a tight leash on.

There was nothing but freedom with Poppy as he thrust again and again, harder, faster. Her words and gasps encouraged him and with one final shove he jumped off the edge of his control into complete release.

\* \* \* \*

"This tastes pretty good for cold steak." Poppy was ravenous after their bedroom gymnastics. She reminded herself that she had to think of what they were doing as nothing more. Why torture herself?

"I know something that tastes a lot better." Brandon's voice echoed in the large kitchen as they sat on barstools at the granite counter. His smug smirk would be an affront from any other man.

She waved her fork at him. "You don't have to say that. We're buddies, remember?"

He grunted and chewed on a huge chunk of rib eye, lazily holding his glass of red wine as he studied her. "One thing you must have figured out about me already is that I don't say anything just for the hell of it. You're a beautiful woman, Poppy."

"Thank you." She took a small sip of her wine. "I'm not used to talking afterwards."

"About sex? I think this is the second-most fun thing about having great sex."

"Kind of like a debrief?" She snorted. "So that I'll do better next time?"

"So that I'll know what you enjoyed most and I can make next time the stuff of your dreams."

She steeled herself to meet his eyes but he'd already moved on, cutting off another piece of steak with casual ease.

"I'm hoping tomorrow will be the last interview or presentation I have to do for this contract. Are you up for a practice session after we're done eating?"

"Absolutely." Supporting Brandon as he prepped for the San Sofia contract was comfortable, familiar ground.

Unlike the tangible connection between them. Poppy couldn't ignore it any longer. To a Yankee with a heart that had been shattered like hers, however, her relationship with Brandon was the equivalent of wading barefoot into the muddy, snake- and alligator-infested bayou waters.

# Chapter 17

"Here's a perfect color for your skin tone." Poppy pulled a frothy lemon-yellow scarf off the boutique shelf. "You can wear this with the blouse you have on, as well as with a knit T-shirt or even a dress. Scarves are the quickest and often the least expensive way to update your wardrobe."

The customer who'd wandered into the shop tilted her head. "So I don't have to buy an entirely new wardrobe?"

"Absolutely not."

"Good, because I can't afford it right now! My boys are teenagers and all of my extra money goes to groceries. But I need some updating. I just got a new position." Evident relief added a glow to her smile. She looked over the accessory area again, her gaze landing on a pale blue wrap. "What about this?"

"Perfect." Poppy continued to work with the woman until it was certain the customer was happy with her purchases. The bell on the front door rang out as she left and Poppy heard hand clapping behind her. She turned to see Bianca with a grin that split her face in two.

"Well done, Poppy. You've got the touch! Exactly what this shop needed. Where were you last year?"

Poppy shook her head. "I wouldn't have been able to sell anything that wasn't already in stock. Your eye for color and texture is incredible." She fingered a pink scarf she'd coveted since she started working with Bianca. "Look at this design—I can find peach and blush and fuchsia in any department store. But you've found the perfect shade of pink, a peony pink, if you will, that coordinates with both cool and warm color palettes. And it's in a lighter cotton blend. That's a talent."

"Stop being coy, Poppy. You're the best at what you do or you wouldn't have such a huge business in New York."

"Had."

Bianca's face dropped into compassion. "I'm sorry. No news on the lawsuit being dropped?"

"Not yet. My lawyer is certain it will be."

"I want the best for you but I have to say that selfishly I'd love to keep you all to myself!"

"I'm serious about starting an office here, Bianca. If you'll have me, I'd like to make this my permanent location in NOLA."

Bianca squealed. "Are you serious? That's amazing! Yes, yes, yes!" She clicked toward Poppy on her stiletto sandals, her full tulle skirt bobbing as if in agreement, too. "Thank you so much, Poppy. I won't let you down." She whispered fiercely into Poppy's ear.

Poppy hugged Bianca back. "Let you down? You're the one who gave me a break. I could have been anyone and you trusted me enough to give me part-time work." Poppy had been spending almost forty hours per week here while Brandon worked on the San Sofia presentation. She'd come in early today and was staying longer, waiting to hear if he'd received an offer. It was too anxiety-provoking to be at the house with him, not that he'd be there.

And each time she went back to his house, she was reminded that she needed to go back to her own home. New York. Her time in New Orleans was never supposed to be more than two weeks, and she'd doubled that and then some.

"I'm going to get some of your new order organized." Poppy walked into her office not a moment too soon. Fat tears started to roll down her cheeks, tears that had nothing to do with gratitude toward Bianca or relief that it looked like her new business idea was a viable one.

Her sorrow was closer to her heart, the heart that had found healing in NOLA with a certain sexy bayou bachelor.

\* \* \* \*

"Poppy?" The soft feminine voice reached her through her intense scrutiny of a wardrobe selection for a new client—the fifth in as many days. Poppy looked up and her mouth popped open as she saw Sonja, standing awkwardly inside her studio office.

"Sonja!" She stood up so fast that papers and scraps of fabric fluttered to the floor, some of them scrunched under her mules. Poppy didn't care as she embraced her best friend. "Oh. My. God. When you go big, you go big! How are you feeling?"

Sonja shrugged and gave a wan shadow of her usual smile. "Par for the course. I throw up until noon, then crave salty crackers until dinner, when I wolf down as much as I can without getting nauseous again."

"Here, have a seat." She gave Sonja her desk chair and sat on a stool. "Tell me what's going on. When did you get back?"

Sonja looked around the studio, turning a full three hundred and sixty degrees before sitting in the offered place. "I think you have more to tell me. You've done all of this in less than a month?"

"Yeah. But I had help. Bianca is a dear and I'm so lucky it worked out. Without her, I might still be pounding the pavement for a job."

Sonja's knowing gaze offered no sign of compromise. "You still underestimate yourself. You'd be working wherever you want to. You just needed time to regroup. And about that, how's Brandon?"

Poppy shook her head. "No way. You first. A runaway pregnant bride trumps anything going on in my life."

Two worry lines appeared between Sonja's brows. "About that, Poppy... you're still the only one who knows."

"What?" She couldn't believe Sonja had kept her pregnancy from Henry all this time.

"I haven't seen Henry in person yet. I took an extra week of vacation, and I've decided to go back to work at the Boudreaux firm as before, here in New Orleans. I don't have to deal with his father except once or twice a month, and it pays the bills. Plus Hudson begged me not to quit."

"You're kidding. That bigot doesn't want a lawsuit, me thinks."

"I thought that at first, too, but he sounded sincere and believe me, I see it all in the courtroom. I think the wedding fail was a huge wake-up call for the family, especially Hudson and Gloria. It's one thing when the son who's always been the independent one breaks ties, but when the conformist—Henry—threatens to never speak to them again, that's reason to reevaluate your motives. Plus with their sister out of the country, it hit them hard that all of their children were gone."

"Did Henry tell you this?"

"No. His father did, and then his mother called me. Of course with her, it's hard to tell. She's probably secretly thrilled that the wedding is off, for now. I think she'll always be the kind of mother who doesn't accept whomever her children decide to be with. She's been calling the shots for so long in that family." Sonja's narrative trailed off as she fingered a length of pale cream ribbon. "They'll feel differently when they know they're going to be grandparents."

"When are you going to tell Henry?" Poppy had hoped they'd been together all this time, working it out.

"I'm not sure. I've got a little while longer to get away with looser clothing. But I will tell him. I don't want it to be any kind of bargaining chip in our relationship moving forward, though."

"Phew! So you agree you belong with him?"

Sonja's smile grew sad. "I believe he's the love of my life. But that's not enough for a lasting relationship. The fact that we even allowed his parents to come between us at all is a deal breaker. We're through. It's over."

"What exactly did they say to you, Sonja?"

Sonja shook her head decisively. "No. This is a conversation for me and Henry. When the time's right."

There was more Sonja wasn't telling her, Poppy was certain. She understood keeping some things close to the heart. "I understand, of course. But know that I'm here when you want to talk, okay?"

"Deal. Now, what about you?"

"Do you remember how I loved working with you when we came here for spring break in college? Handing out the clothes after Katrina with your church?"

"How could I forget? Do you know, I still have some of my church members asking about you. You were such a big help and you know you have a natural knack for boosting people's spirits. They never forgot all you did."

"Actually, I think it's the other way around. I find nothing more exciting than the look on someone's face after I've helped them narrow down their style and figure out a way to live comfortably in it." Now she'd add affordably to that list. Why hadn't she realized sooner that she wanted to make more of a difference in people's day-to-day lives?

"And you're going to do this here, with Bianca? Until you go back to New York?" Sonja acted casual but Poppy knew her best friend well enough to see the catlike observation going on.

Poppy smiled. "You're sitting in the office for Poppy's Do-Overs. And not only will I have this business, working with Bianca, I've committed to putting ten percent back into the community. Not only in dollars but in time. I'll set up shop at the local battered women's shelter, or have them come here, whichever they find safest and most comfortable. Yesterday I met with a single mom and her teenaged daughter. I got to help both of them pick out clothes and put outfits together. The mother is going interviewing for jobs, and the daughter is prepping to apply to college."

"Girl, I'm so proud of you. Will you take it national as soon as you can?"

Poppy's stomach dropped at the thought of expanding "No. An office here, *only* here. I don't want any hint of a franchise business model and I want the local community to be able to trust me."

"That's fantastic!" Sonja gave her a quick hug. "I'm so glad. I often thought you'd be happier doing something a little more grounded."

"I don't know about 'grounded.' At least in terms of a job. I was the one who wasn't living in reality, back at my old job. This, this feels right. As if I've returned to myself. That sounds stupid, doesn't it?"

"Not at all. So tell me, where does Brandon fit in all of this?"

Sonja's question was clear. "I'm not doing this for a man, if that's what you're really asking. Brandon and I are friends. I helped him get ready for some business opportunities, and he gave me a place to stay during the flooding. Speaking of which, how's your house?"

Sonja gave her a measured look but didn't push her, for which Poppy was grateful. It was hard enough starting all over again with her vocation, her livelihood. Losing the man she never really had, the man who'd healed her through the worst time in her life, that was something entirely worse. And nothing she was going to discuss with anybody, even her best friend.

"It's a mess." Sonja's assessment said volumes, and not just about her home.

"I wanted to go back after the storm and stay there, but the damage mitigation team still had all the fans and plastic covers up. Said the mold threat was too great for me to stay."

"I was able to get my things. I've moved out, ahead of Henry returning, and rented my own place. It's not far from here, actually. I'll be able to walk to the firm office if I want to."

"Sonja, I'm so sorry."

Sonja shook her head. "Don't be. This is all for the best."

Poppy wasn't so sure.

* * * *

Brandon walked with purpose to Poppy's boutique. He knew it was called something else but to him, it would always be hers. Anything she touched was hers. Including him.

The thought should scare him, make him want to shake her off. Instead, he wanted more of Poppy with each passing day. And it wasn't because she'd helped him prepare to win the San Sofia contract. He knew that now because, in fact, he hadn't gotten the contract. He'd lost the big government deal.

Yet he felt like a winner, and he still wanted her. He needed Poppy in his life. But how he was going to convince her of this eluded him. He knew he had to try, though, because he'd learned enough over the past month to grasp that sometimes life didn't give you second chances. He might have one with his family, a way to find common ground, to see if he'd misread some of what he thought had been his parents' blatant racism. Poppy, however, was once in a lifetime. There'd be no second chances with other women.

His heart pounded as he neared the boutique. Trying to explain to Poppy why she should stay in New Orleans with him scared him more than any of the negotiations he'd been through for the contract that in the end hadn't happened.

His cell rang and he wanted to ignore it but it was his private investigator, Stanley.

"Tell me you found Jeb."

"I have. He's in Asuncion, Paraguay.

"That makes no sense." Brandon thought for a moment. "When is he coming back here? With the money?"

"He's not, and he doesn't have the money any longer, not in any of the accounts I could access. None of it."

Disappointment flared into anger. He completely trusted Stanley and believed him. The retired FBI agent ran a part-time PI firm and had come highly recommended. He'd used Stanley's services before, for background checks on clients who had shady reputations. Boats by Gus didn't do business with crooks or drug dealers.

"Jesus. He blew through fifteen million dollars in a month?" So he'd lost it all, thanks to Jeb. And his own personal blind spot. "How did you find him? And how do you know the money's gone?"

"I called in a few favors from former colleagues. I have contacts in Paraguay but no one seems to know why he's there. Or if they did they can't tell me."

"So it could still be something legit." He could give Jeb one last chance.

"You're being naive, Brandon. I'm not your attorney but I suggest you talk to him. Better yet, report this. A man who stole from your company is not your friend, no matter what your history. Do you want to be implicated in whatever business he had in South America? We're talking some life-altering circumstances, Brandon. Drug running at best, weapons smuggling at worst."

"No, wait on it for now. Let me talk to my lawyer. Thanks, Stanley. I'll get back to you." He quickly connected to his lawyer who picked up immediately.

"Brandon."

"I need help." Brandon filled him in, his decision solidifying as he did.

"You're going to report this, right?"

"That's why I called you. Yes. And I'm going to need you with me when I file my report, to make sure Boats by Gus isn't implicated in whatever Jeb was involved in."

"This isn't going to be a slam dunk. There could be charges pressed against you for being complicit to Jeb's actions if they were illegal. You're going to have to explain why you waited so long to report Jeb's theft, Brandon. If he was involved in drugs or munitions you could be on the hook for funding it."

"But you're my witness, as is Stanley."

"Meet me at the police station in fifteen minutes. We'll file your report. Have your PI call it in to the FBI."

Brandon stared at his phone after he disconnected, waiting for the shock to hit him. He was about to report Jeb, his brother in all else but blood, to the authorities. Instead of regret, determination formed into a single solid ball of steel in his gut. He'd be damned if anyone would take Boats by Gus from him or his ability to pay Poppy for her part in getting him this far.

Poppy. She deserved a man who stood up for what was his, not someone holding out hope when it was clear he'd been robbed. Poppy was right.

He stood in front of the boutique, watching Poppy's profile as she talked with a customer. It wasn't time yet. Giving the boutique a cursory glance, he turned away. As he walked back to his car he threw the flowers into a trashcan. He'd get her new ones later, when they had something to celebrate.

* * * *

Poppy took the call from her lawyer with trepidation. "Tell me something good, Louise."

"The good news is that we have a court appearance in seventy-two hours."

"That's quick! How did you do that?"

"Well, that's the not-so-good news. I promised you'd be here to testify."

Poppy groaned. "I thought you said it would take months."

"Getting your funds, yes. But scoring a slot with the judge this quickly is too much of a boon to try to move it. The judge wants both you, Will, and Tori in front of a mediator appointed by her on Friday morning, eight o'clock." Louise's no-nonsense tone crashed through the protective cocoon Poppy had allowed New Orleans to weave around her.

Brandon was the safest part of the cocoon and yet the most dangerous to her sanity. No, that wasn't true. Her feelings for Brandon were what were making her crazy.

Poppy stared out the office window. It'd been a long day with no word from Brandon on how the contract bid went. A text would have been nice.

"Poppy, you still there?"

"Yes. Friday fits my schedule perfectly. It's time for me to come home and get my affairs in order so that I can get on with my life." She wanted to file for her new business LLC, and she needed the money that had been frozen with her former EA's lawsuit to do so.

"So I'll see you Friday?"

"Yes. See you Friday, Louise."

Her phone buzzed almost immediately after she ended the call with Louise. Brandon. She inhaled deeply, hoping to keep the disappointment out of her tone. And realized with a shock that she was incredibly let down that she'd have to leave New Orleans, leave Brandon, for any length of time.

Holy fried okra.

"Hey."

"Hey yourself. I was wondering if you'll be home for dinner tonight?" His voice was the balm she needed.

"I was going to stay late but I don't have the energy right now."

"You okay?"

"No. Yes. No—it's been a long day and I haven't had the success I'd hoped for. I knew this was going to be a long haul, the new job, but..."

"Come home now, Yankee girl."

She ignored the many layers to the word "home" and complied. As always, Brandon got her. He knew she needed to lick her wounds. And she hadn't even shared her legal news with him. For the first time, she keenly wished she'd met him at a different time in both their lives. A time when she had nothing to worry about but how good they were together.

At least they'd still have tonight.

* * * *

He wasn't sure what made him do it. He stood surveying his domain, the result of most of a day's work.

The sun was starting to set and it threw the screened-in porch into a rosy gold light, something he'd appreciated from the dock more than this room. It was chilly out here as the day's warmth dissipated, but anticipation revved his motor and made him feel the room might be too hot for what he'd planned.

He'd made sure the space heater was good to go, and the several dozen candles he'd lit flickered in the quiet space. He'd pulled the futon he usually napped on out into a full-size bed and fitted it with satin sheets. Brandon was particularly proud of the satin sheet bit, as he'd picked them up while out and about earlier, gathering supplies for tonight's main event.

He was going to make sure Poppy knew she could trust him. That he was her friend and confidante first, lover second.

His dick hardened at the thought of how they'd make love tonight and he had to admit, in the few minutes before she'd be home, that it was difficult to remind himself at times that he wanted to be more than her sex buddy. It wasn't as if he was promising her anything more. But lately her expression had grown grim, less playful than when they'd first agreed she'd stay with him at his house. She said she was excited about her new job in town but her enthusiasm took a hit each time she tried to act as if she were still the big stylist she'd been in New York.

He knew that rough spot. He'd been fighting to keep the shipyard running as if fifteen million hadn't up and disappeared in one moment, one flight to South America.

And he still hadn't found Jeb or the money. There was nothing past his verified arrival to Paraguay, and Brandon no longer had the means to launch a private search in a foreign country.

All Brandon had left was the hope of a future job. The possibility of it. And Poppy.

The familiar tap of her leather-soled sandals on the hardwood floor echoed deep in the house behind him. Poppy was home.

\* \* \* \*

Poppy dropped her bag on the granite counter and scanned the great room for Brandon. Only when her gaze landed on the open double French doors did she realize he was on the porch. She smiled, grateful for the excuse to sit down and look at the water for the last remaining minutes of daylight. She'd change into more comfortable clothes in a bit.

As she walked through the doors she saw his silhouette against the edge of the room, his back to her.

"It's beautiful tonight, isn't—" Her words jammed in her throat which had tightened measurably as she took in the scene. Candles, dozens of vanilla white candles, were scattered about the room. On the window ledges, the small table tops, the wet bar that also served as a hot beverage station. The futon where she and Brandon had enjoyed many a morning coffee or afternoon cocktail was unfolded and flat, covered in shimmering linens. Linens with—wait, were those rose petals strewn across them? Brandon's body turned as if in slow motion and when his eyes met hers they were glistening, his smile sure and bright. "Yes, you are beautiful tonight, Poppy."

She clutched at her throat, her chest with her hand as she motioned with the other. "What, what is all this?"

"It's a toast to you. To the fact that we've successfully cohabitated for the better part of a month without either one of us losing our shit."

"Oh." His expectant expression collapsed and she closed the gap with three steps, grabbed his face on either side and kissed him soundly on his lips. "Thank you. You are a wonderful man, Brandon Boudreaux." She let her hands rest on his shoulders and noticed the crisp linen under her palms, her cheek as she rested her face against his chest. He'd dressed up for her.

But why?

"It's a little over-the-top, isn't it?" Hesitation and embarrassment crept into his voice.

Unwilling to lift her head from the comfort of being able to hear the vibration of his voice, she blindly reached up and placed a finger on his mouth. "No. It's perfect."

Normally he'd already have her finger in his mouth, sucking, making her wild with her need for him. For this she pulled back and looked at him. "What's wrong?"

"Nothing's wrong. I wanted to surprise you. I thought you could use it."

More than he'd ever know. "I can. I do." She stepped back and looked at the sunset, close to its climactic finale. The candlelight grew more vibrant as the dusk wove into twilight. As her gaze skimmed the room she noted a new piece of furniture.

"You have a telescope?" She'd never noticed it.

"It's the first clear night since the storm went through. Do you realize we've had rain showers every day since, on and off?"

She laughed. "Yes, I do. Have you seen my hair?"

His eyes glowed with desire. His hands reached out and he combed her curls with his fingers. "I've seen every inch of you, Poppy."

Awash in the familiar heat of her reaction to him, she felt a tug she hadn't with him. Maybe not with any man. "Brandon, I..." She didn't know what he wanted. What she was willing to give. And she still hadn't told him she was staying in NOLA, but alone.

He dropped his arms. "Come here." He pulled her to him, her back nestled against his front, and they stood for the several long minutes it took the sun to drop beneath the horizon. It was primal, two human beings watching their world go from day to night. It was *Architectural Digest* perfect, with the expert layout of the screened porch that was larger than any patio she'd been on. It was textbook sexy, with the candlelight, the bottle of champagne on ice that she'd just noticed, and the bed that looked like a seduction scene from her favorite romance movie.

"Are you hungry?" His breath moved the hair atop her head, warming her scalp and making her turn around. She wanted to face Brandon.

"Very." She sniffed. "What's that?"

"The marinade. It's warming up on the grill." He stepped away and walked to the wet bar. "Can I make you a cocktail? The usual?"

"Sure." She watched him as he measured the liquor, poured it over the ice cubes in the old-fashioned glass, added simple syrup and soda water. He stirred it and threw in a slice of orange. "Here you go."

"Thank you. Cheers." She held up her glass and he clinked his, half-empty, against hers.

"You can stay here or come out with me to the grill. The mosquitoes shouldn't be too bad."

"With all those citronella plants I can't imagine one bug would dare to fly near here."

He laughed and it warmed her belly to know she'd put that smile on his face. She wondered if she had some kind of sociopathic tendency because for the life of her she couldn't remember ever deriving so much pleasure from knowing she'd made a man smile like that.

Of course, no man smiled like Brandon.

Brandon lifted the cover off a sauce pot on one of the gargantuan grill's side burners and the delicious aroma of fresh celery, garlic, and parsley hit her. "That's amazing. What are you making?"

"Crawdads." He took plastic wrap off a stainless-steel bowl he'd retrieved from the porch refrigerator and tossed its contents into a steel mesh basket. "I marinated them in my secret recipe, and the marinade is reducing down by half. Once these babies are done we'll throw them on top of the rice."

"Where's the rice?"

"In the rice cooker on the kitchen counter." He grinned. "I couldn't finagle to fix everything out here, as much as I wanted to."

"I can go get the rice."

"No, you're going to relax and enjoy the entire night. I mean it, Poppy. You've done so much for me these past few weeks. Let me do something nice for you."

She squirmed, wiggling her toes in her sandals. "You gave me a roof over my head, Brandon."

"A roof you could have had at a hotel during the flood. You agreed to stay here, with me, and you've seen me through my darkest time."

Hope flared in at least two of her heart's chambers when he said "through."

"Brandon, does this mean that you got the deal?"

"What? Oh, no." He sighed and flipped the crawdads over and over, each turn unlocking more of the heavenly scent. "I didn't get the big deal. There's still a chance for smaller jobs materializing as offshoots of the main contract, but I'm not counting on it. I've heard nothing." He looked like he had more to say but stopped himself. As if he was protecting her from what he thought was inevitable. He was going to lose Boats by Gus.

She placed her hand in the middle of his back and rubbed in circular motions, trying to give him the comfort he unwittingly gave her each time he told her he thought she was the most creative person he knew, or when he listened to her suggestions for how to dress and carry himself during those grueling interviews with the San Sofia government officials.

"No news is good news, in this case." Unlike her case, where the news is what had decimated not only her styling business but Attitude by Amber, too. She let her arm drop and let out a long breath before she took a decent sip of her drink.

"None of that, Poppy. Not tonight." Brandon closed the grill lid and placed the basket of perfectly cooked crawdads on the stone ledge that surrounded it. "This is about you enjoying a perfect Louisiana evening."

"With the perfect Southern gentleman?"

"What I'm planning to do to you, Poppy, is not the work of a gentleman." He pulled her to him and gave her the softest, sexiest kiss. His tongue merely skimmed her lips, where their only body contact occurred. She had her drink in one hand and could have circled his neck with the other but let Brandon work his magic and lead the way for what her center told her was going to be a Cajun-hot night.

* * * *

Brandon poured them each a glass of the crisp Sauvignon blanc he knew was her favorite. The extra effort to get it today was worth seeing her shy smile.

"You remembered?" She looked from the bottle's label to him, her gaze soft and open. Completely different from the hard, injured woman he'd first spotted on Henry's dock.

"There's little about you that I could ever forget."

Her smile vanished and she blinked. Damn it he didn't mean to scare her off.

"That's…that's the most ro—, I mean, nicest thing anyone's ever said to me." Poppy's blinks yielded a large solitary tear then dropped down onto her soft cheek. He reached over and wiped it away, taking the opportunity to caress her.

"I never want to be the reason you cry, Yankee girl."

She shot him a wobbly grin. "These are the good kind of tears."

"To good friends who also happen to be great in bed?" He held up his glass and was relieved when his attempt to make her laugh paid off.

"You've been true to your word, Brandon, I'll give you that." She clinked his glass. "To friends."

Did that mean she still only considered them friends? He didn't think they were more, but then again, he didn't think about his friends all day long. Save for Jeb, and even then he was thinking more about all the money Jeb had disappeared with.

"What's wrong? You look like someone stole your favorite Pokémon card."

Irritation niggled in his belly. "Nothing's wrong. It couldn't be better, sitting here with you."

She stared at him, the kind of look that always preceded a deep dive into his psyche. "This is so kind of you. You're a kind man."

"Ah, that's not a word I've ever been accused of before."

"Then you don't hang around people long enough for them to see this side of you." She popped a shelled crawdad into her mouth and chewed. "Mmmm. This is heaven."

"Thanks." Actually, the way her full lips formed around her food was heaven—more like paradise. He stifled a groan and remained quiet. He was determined as hell to make this night special for her. She deserved it.

"Spill it, Brandon."

He didn't pretend to not know what she meant. She knew him well enough. Too well, hell yeah, but they were past the point of him playing cool and detached, save for in bed. "I did this because you were so upset on the phone, yes, but also because I meant it when I said I owe you everything for helping me through the past few weeks."

"But you haven't got the San Sofia contract. Don't you want to wait until then?"

He shook his head. "I told you, it's unlikely I'll get it. And it's not as important to me right now." He reached over and grasped her hands, which she'd placed on the table when he started to speak. "You gave me back a belief in myself that I thought was gone for good. I know that the chances of Boats by Gus surviving are nil, but I know I can start over. I can land a job with a local shipbuilder, or even relocate if I have to. My life isn't the sorry mess I thought it was a month ago."

"Same."

Disappointment rose in his chest when she tugged her hands free, but then washed away in the roar of awareness that hit him as she stood and walked around the small table to where he sat.

"You've saved me too, Brandon." She tugged on his arms until he sat parallel to the table, and he watched in fascination as Poppy lowered herself to her knees in front of him.

"Poppy, as much as this is an incredible idea, tonight is about you."

"And so it is. Let me do what I want, Brandon." Her hands and fingers moved with lightning speed and his shorts were unbuttoned, the zipper down, her hand around his hard cock before he could utter another word.

"Do you like that?" She tightened her hand around his length, her other hand cupping his testicles. Brandon hissed and she smiled. The woman was pure pleasure and agony wrapped in the most beautiful package.

"I love it."

\* \* \* \*

She'd slept with Brandon. All night.

The morning after Louise's call and Brandon's tender lovemaking, she'd fallen asleep in his arms on the futon. When she awoke there was a steaming mug of coffee on the end table and no sign of Brandon. She'd crept by the closed door to his office and heard the earnest, low pitch of his voice. He was working already.

There was nothing left for her to do but leave.

Poppy packed a few remaining items into her suitcase. The same one she'd arrived with just over a month ago. It felt more like lifetimes ago. She wasn't the same woman.

It was easier this way, with no time or chance for a farewell round of sex. It wasn't just sex anymore. Not with Brandon.

She had to get out of Brandon's house, while she still could. Unlike the relief leaving New York had given her, flying out of the bayou filled her with dread. It reminded her of being a kid in Buffalo and knowing that she had to make that 9-1-1 call for her battered mother, for their safety. Because it meant something else had to end. Another one of Mom's lovers had to go, another hope that maybe this time would be different crushed.

The flashback evaporated at the echo of Brandon's footfalls in the hallway. The same thrill she always felt when he appeared shot through her, followed by an ugly sense of betrayal. *Her* betrayal. But how could leaving Brandon be a betrayal—they had no commitment, no agreement except that she'd get a commission for styling him, which she'd refused. He stopped outside her open door and the sight of his tall, familiar frame made the ache in her heart turn into a full-fledged bleeding stab wound.

"Hey, Poppy." He leaned into her room. "Wait—what are you doing?"

"Packing. I have to go back to New York."

"Since when?"

She looked at him, his expression a combination of wariness and something else that eluded her. Anger?

"Since I've decided to redo my business model." She didn't want him to see her face, not too closely. Her careful composure would never hold up under his intense scrutiny and she had to stay strong.

"Poppy, I'm sorry that I haven't been able to pay you yet."

"I've already told you it's on me. And this isn't about money." Not really. Yes, she needed money, but the court hearing would help, she prayed.

He entered the room and stood next to her in front of her luggage, too close for comfort. "Then what is it about?"

"I need to go, Brandon. I shouldn't have stayed here for so long. My home base is New York and I'm in the middle of changing my entire corporate structure." More like launching a new career.

"You couldn't predict the storm, the flooding." He spoke of the weather but his eyes were on her, pleading for—what?

"No, but I could have gotten an apartment or an efficiency. Or…" She didn't want to say it.

"Gone back to New York sooner." He lifted his arms to her, but as she kept folding clothing and placing it neatly in her luggage he let them drop. "You regret staying here."

Arrow right to the heart, that one. Maybe her aorta, even. "I don't regret the fun we've had, Brandon. But we agreed, we're buddies, right? And I owe you so much—you helped me have a project to focus on when my life was falling apart." At the wounded shock in his eyes she shook her head. "No, no, not that." She motioned at the bed. "Our sex wasn't the project—I mean coaching and styling you for the San Sofia contract."

"I was a goddamned *project*?" His voice was low but the ferocity of his anger vibrated with each syllable. "Tell me, Poppy, how many of your previous clients did you fuck with such abandon? Is that part of the styling package, the one where you take a sorry son of a bitch at his rock bottom and bring him back to life?"

"Stop. You know it's not about that." She wasn't going to talk about their physical relationship. She couldn't, not without caving and throwing her arms around him and sobbing. Because it wasn't about anything physical. Not totally. This was a matter of the heart, the soul. Had she felt this way about Will, or any other man?

"You were so busy in your office, I didn't want to interrupt. I'm taking it you got the contract?" She kept her hands moving, needing to at least look like she wasn't hanging on his response. She wanted Brandon to succeed so badly—he deserved it, had earned it.

He stood there, and if it were yesterday or a week ago she'd know for certain that he was fighting his exasperation with her, overriding it with his need to physically have her, the way she needed him inside her. Except in the quiet dark morning he looked angry, and his anger was yielding to an emotion she never expected to receive from him.

Disappointment.

"No, I didn't get the contract. Once the officials involved discovered that one of my trusted employees was in a highly suspect foreign country most likely participating in illegal trade of either weapons or drugs or both, Boats by Gus lost all credibility."

Her fumbling hands froze midair. "I'm so sorry."

He shrugged. "Shit happens."

"You'll find your way." She forced a smile, hoping it hid the sickening swell of nausea she fought. Her help hadn't contributed to a win, after all.

"I'm still going to pay you for your time, Poppy. I'll need to file bankruptcy, liquidate assets. Depending on where I land I'll reimburse you in installments if I have to, but you'll be reimbursed. I'm sorry about this."

She waved her hand at him. "No, no. It was gratis, believe me. And you didn't get the contract, so who can say what I contributed? I have a little nest egg put away. I'm fine." She lied and knew that he knew she was lying. Zipping the case shut, she looked at him.

"Thanks for the place to crash, and the meals, and the—"

He took two long strides and wrapped his arms around her, pulling her to him. Poppy didn't fight him, couldn't resist his mouth as it closed on hers, marking her with a trademark Brandon kiss. Sexy, sensuous, but this time tinged with a new taste. Sadness. Regret, maybe. "It's been real, Yankee girl." He stepped back. "How are you getting to the airport?"

"My ride will be here in five minutes."

He nodded. "Travel safe."

"I will." Awkward didn't begin to describe how she felt wheeling her suitcase through the large house, her insides hollow, empty of any emotion. Until she was safely belted in the back of the Uber lift, her bag in the trunk, and looked at Brandon's house for the last time. As the bayou wind blew through the lowered windows, she let the anguish hit her. How had she been so stupid to think Brandon was only a rebound lover?

* * * *

Brandon stood on his back deck staring at the water after Poppy drove off. He felt like his skin had been rubbed bare, as if Poppy was a bandage ripped off an oozing scab. Except Poppy had healed him in places he hadn't known had been hurting. And given him a vision of what an intimate relationship could be.

He thought of himself as a deliberate man. He knew his persona as Gus in Boats by Gus was a free-living, down-in-the-bayou dude, but he never made a business decision without forethought. Turning Jeb in to the authorities had been deliberate, as regretful as he'd felt for his once best friend.

Going after the San Sofia contract had been deliberate, a way to expand his business, give back to the world in general, and to save his company.

Letting Poppy go as easily as she'd zydecoed into his life, that had been deliberate, too. But at what cost?

The cost to him was irrelevant.

The fact was, no matter how much it tore up his insides, he couldn't hang on to her. He had nothing to pay her, nothing to show how he'd support her. And how could he even consider asking her to stay when he stood to lose his house?

He reached into a potted plant and grabbed a handful of river rocks. One by one he tossed them into the river, waiting for whatever was inside him, building steam, to pop. He'd done the right thing, letting her go. That was the mark of a mature man, right?

Then why was he so fucking miserable?

# Chapter 18

Poppy sat next to Louise, across from Will and Tori, in the mediator's office space on the thirty-seventh floor of a skyscraper.

The attorney mediating the case sat at the head of the conference table, his gray hair in sharp contrast with his horn-rimmed glasses that Poppy suspected were holdovers from the mid-twentieth century and not a recent hipster purchase.

"The State of New York impresses that to solve this conflict amicably and without the time and attention of the Supreme Civil Court is preferable to all parties." He put down the paper he'd been reading from. "Look, folks, let's get this straight. I don't want any bickering, no emotional ringers"—he looked pointedly at Tori, or rather, Tori's growing belly—"and no histrionics." He looked pointedly at Poppy.

She wished she could speak up and tell him what a misogynistic term that was, but in fact, she had been over-the-top hysterical during Will's parents' anniversary party. Was she the same woman who'd thrown that punch bowl across the parquet floor?

"Are we in agreement?"

"Yes, sir." Poppy spoke up as Tori looked to Will for confirmation. An unexpected burst of compassion for her former assistant washed over her. The young woman really did appear to be besotted with Will. Will, for his part, appeared cool and together, but she saw the fear in his eyes. The same look he'd had when he'd originally come to her, needing to feel confident in his suits as he went up against his Russian business counterparts.

What a fucking wimp he was. How had she not seen this before?

As the mediation wore on, Poppy deferred most of her statements to Louise. Louise knew her position on everything and more importantly, how to express it without giving away anything vital to the case. Poppy's main goal was to get out of this room with her business back in hand, and her operating funds back in her control.

"Ms. Kaminsky, please explain when you first realized Ms. Callis was attempting to gain control of your business."

"Do you mean when she started screwing my then-fiancé?"

"Ms. Kaminsky." The mediator's tone was her first warning, as Louise's quick squeeze of her thigh told her.

"Um, sorry. When she launched her own website with my logo, approximately one week before her nuptials to Wi—Mr. Callis."

There. That had to be a more appropriate statement.

"Ms. Callis?" He looked at Tori, who shifted in her seat, her hand firmly grasped by Will's atop the smooth polished table.

"Yes, well, I did use her logo but it was because I had helped her come up with three of her latest home and fashion coordinating concepts. The ideas that sold Attitude by Amber."

"Which your rabid lawsuit put an end to, fuck you very much." The words escaped Poppy's mouth effortlessly, and she felt about a hundred pounds lighter.

"Ms. Kaminsky!" If the mediator had a gavel she imagined he'd knock her upside her head with it.

"Sorry."

Louise didn't even issue her own echo of the warning this time. She'd known Poppy too long. If Poppy was going to be outspoken, there was nothing Louise or anyone else would do to stop her tirade.

The mediator went on for another five minutes, during which Poppy found her mind going back to the boutique in New Orleans. Her new office there. Will. Will kissing her, licking her…

"Ms. Kaminsky?" This time the lawyer sounded genuinely concerned.

Poppy blinked. "I'm sorry." Tori and Will stared at her, their hands in a death lock together atop the conference table. Why she had ever thought that was what she wanted, she'd never know. But she knew that she'd figured out what she wanted. And it wasn't here in a stuffy office building with the likes of Will and Tori around. Poppy wanted the scent of gardenias and the white magnolia petals beckoning her to stay a while. She wanted the scent of brackish water and the feel of the blanket of humidity that made her hair frizz. She wanted New Orleans.

*Brandon.*

She took in a deep breath, exhaled, and placed her hand on Louise's forearm. "Forgive me, Louise." She looked at the mediator and gave him a quick smile. "Allow me this, please."

She faced Will and Tori, meeting each of their gazes before focusing entirely on Tori.

"Tori, you know that you were my intern, then my assistant, and I promoted you to executive assistant only because you're damned good with a schedule and you never missed my coffee times." Indeed, Tori had always ensured a double-mocha-triple-whip latte was on Poppy's desk midmorning and midafternoon. "You know nothing, however, about graphic design or design of any nature. You certainly had nothing to do with any of *my* designs. The documentation shows that. You've got what you wanted—your husband—and you have a child on the way. I'm willing to give you my local, New York City client list"—she ignored Louise's gasp—"if you'll agree to take down my logo from your website and divest yourself and your business of anything related to Designs by Amber." Poppy saw no reason to bring up her new business name, or to mention that she'd already undertaken the steps necessary to obtain a new logo. "Also, you must drop all claims against me."

Now Poppy faced Will. "Or I'll take you both to court for defamation of character and sue you for what I stood to earn from Attitude by Amber in the first two years." Will's eyes widened and she knew she had him. Money was how to talk to Will.

"That doesn't sound very fair." Tori's voice was high and whiny, another trait Poppy wondered how she'd put up with for as long as she had.

"You're being too quick here, Poppy." Louise whispered harshly in her ear. "Let's call a recess."

"No. I'm sorry. You can do your job now." She remained quiet but allowed herself to glare at Will and Tori in alternating rounds of if-you-could-read-my-mind as Louise knocked out an agreement with them and the mediator.

"I just don't understand how you can agree to this so quickly, Will." Tori's face was contorted in a most unbeautiful manner. Instead of the supreme satisfaction that would have coated her shattered heart a month ago, Poppy saw the reality of the couple that sat in front of her.

"We're starting a new life together. We don't need this. You and the baby don't need the stress." Will's ministrations to his bride should have been enough to make Poppy to dive over the table and scratch both their eyes out. She looked at her watch. The sooner this was over the sooner she could get back to her new job, her real life. The reminder of NOLA and

Brandon stilled her impatience. As much as getting back to working with Bianca and living near Sonja was going to be wonderful, the thought of a life without Brandon seemed grayer than a New York fog.

Poppy walked out of the mediation with her head high and her shoulders back. When she knew she was safely out of sight of the participants, she did a quick soul-pumping jig in celebration. She'd finally done it. She'd figured out who she was and what she wanted to do with her life. Where she wanted to *live* her life.

The *who* she wanted to share her life with would have to wait, for now.

She looked at her watch and picked up her pace toward the elevators. If she worked quickly, she'd be able to leave New York by early next week.

* * * *

Brandon hated being alone in his house. Strike that, he hated being in the house without Poppy. He finished up the scrambled eggs in the fry pan and doused them with a hefty shake of his home state's best hot sauce. Food and searching for a new way to reboot his business were the only sure things these past weeks.

And how much he missed Poppy.

His doorbell rang and he looked at the pop-up window on his phone, which he pressed to open the mic. "Come on in, bro."

Henry appeared in the kitchen a few minutes later. "Hey, Brandon."

"Want some eggs?"

"Naw, but I'll take some of that coffee."

"Help yourself." Brandon stayed in his seat at the counter, shoveling eggs into his mouth.

"What do you hear about Jeb?" Henry put the carafe back in place and slid onto a stool next to Brandon.

"He's back—it was all a misunderstanding." Brandon mentally went over the story he, Jeb, and the FBI had agreed upon.

"Taking fifteen million dollars was a mistake?" Henry's incredulity made Brandon laugh.

"Yeah, well, no. It wasn't Jeb who took it—it was some foreign hacker. So Jeb thought he'd cut them off at the knees, you know how crazy-smart he is with computers. Problem is the hackers out-witted him and cleared his bank account, too."

"Man, that sucks. What are you going to do about Boats by Gus?"

"That's the negative-fifteen-million-dollar question." He stood up and got himself more coffee. Since Poppy left he had a hard time shaking the foggy wisps of melancholy from his thoughts. Caffeine staved off total despair.

"You're telling me the U.S. Government won't help you in this circumstance? You've been robbed by a foreign entity. I know you have recourse." Lawyer Henry came out in full force.

"You know, this is the most animated you've been since you got back." As in back from taking off for weeks after the wedding-that-wasn't. "Any contact with Sonja?"

"No. She'll be coming back to the firm, though."

"It's just you two in the city office, right?"

"Yes." Henry looked out the window, making it clear he didn't want to talk about it. "I spoke with Mom and Dad. They feel like shit."

"Sure they do."

"No, really. I think they've finally realized their overreach in their kids' lives." Henry looked at him with the same blue eyes he had. "They said they were reminded how much they missed when they saw you at the rehearsal dinner, and when Jena didn't come back for the wedding."

"Jena can't come back, not while she's been called to active duty."

"They seem to think she could have delayed reporting for this stretch of service. Taken leave or something." Henry looked at him. "Brandon, what's wrong? You look like hell, man."

"Nothing. Everything."

"Anything besides the business stuff going on?" At least Henry had dropped the Jeb discussion. But his brother had his knowing smirk firmly in place. "Woman trouble, maybe?"

"I don't have any problems, per se. I also don't have any woman, in case you haven't noticed." He waved his hand around the room.

"Something happened between you and Poppy." Henry said it as fact.

"Why do you say that?"

"Come off it, Brandon. You couldn't take your eyes off her from the moment you met her."

"Nothing happened before the storm, at least…" He stopped, remembering the gazebo after the wedding fiasco. "After I got her out of your house we worked together to prepare me to put a bid on a government shipbuilding contract."

"And?"

"And, and I don't know. We connected." He wasn't going to spill it all to Henry. His memories with Poppy were precious gems that he wanted to keep safe in a drawstring bag in his heart's deepest chamber. "I've never felt so at ease with a woman before. But I have nothing to offer her, not with the business up in the air. And now, my business is getting back on track but what am I supposed to do? She left. She belongs in New York anyway. Her whole life is there."

"What do you mean you don't have anything to offer her?"

Brandon stared at his brother with complete disbelief. He loved his brother, respected Henry as the brains of the family, but sometimes his brother was obtuse. As though no one had problems if he didn't. "Henry, I have no income, my business is in shambles. It's not the time to ask a woman to share her life with mine."

"It's the best time to ask, bro." Henry rinsed out his mug and put it in the dishwasher. Sonja must have trained him because Brandon couldn't recall a time when Henry had ever done any kind of household chore whatsoever when they were kids.

"How did that work for you and Sonja?" As soon as the words were out his stomach clenched in regret. He slammed his hand on the counter. "I'm sorry, Henry. That was a dick move."

"It was, but I'm not taking it personally. When your heart's hurting it's amazing what shit can spew out of your mouth. Believe me, I know."

"Tell me what you meant."

"You're at your lowest. You don't want a woman who only wants you when you're flying high, do you? You want the girl who'll stay in it through the rough patches, and whomever you chose will have to understand the rough patches can get painfully tough. You're always at the mercy of the next contract, right?"

"Yes, but no differently than you relying on new clients walking in off the street."

"I disagree. People will always need legal help. Boats aren't a necessity—unless you start building boats that are needed by higher profile customers like governments. Like the San Sofia contract you told me about."

Henry walked around the huge island and gripped Brandon on the shoulder. "You've got to swallow the Boudreaux pride and go after her. Or regret it the rest of your life."

"Are you telling me you went after Sonja after she left the church?"

Complete dejection coated Henry's expression. "No. I'm telling you don't be like me. Don't be the one who has lifelong regrets."

# Chapter 19

"When are you going to tell Brandon you're back?" Sonja sat across from Poppy in the tiny coffee shop two buildings over from the boutique.

"When are you going to tell Henry he's your baby daddy?"

"Touché." Sonja tapped Poppy's coffee cup with her wooden stirrer.

"I don't know, Sonja. I keep thinking I'm letting my pride get in the way by not letting him know I'm back. But if he wanted me, he would have come after me. He hasn't even texted once!"

Sonja reached for her second small scone and Poppy grinned. Sonja caught the smile and narrowed her eyes. "What?"

"It's so fun to see you give in to your hunger in a normal way." Sonja had always been nutritionally conscious, scolding Poppy's penchant for street hot dogs and pretzels.

Sonja rolled her eyes. "Trust me, I'm lucky I have an appetite this morning. Most days my head's in the toilet."

"I'm sorry. That has to be hard. How far are you?"

"Seven weeks. I only knew as early as I did because I'm like a clock, and I immediately felt different. Deep down, I knew."

"You've got to tell Henry."

"I know. I also know he'll figure it out in the next month or two anyway, as we work together."

"How did it go today?"

Sonja shook her head. "I don't want to talk about Henry. This is about you and how you're going to get the guts to go after your happily ever after."

"Whoa—I don't do 'ever after.' Not after Will." Even she didn't believe her words. And Will seemed like a distant memory from a past life.

"Waving the bullshit flag here, girl. Will isn't worth our breath. Now Brandon, the way he looked at you when you met—I saw something there, Poppy, even in the midst of my anxiety. That's saying something."

"He talked me down from a full-out panic attack in that bar, the first night." She sipped her cappuccino.

"I wondered where you'd gone. Was it instant chemistry?"

"Downright combustible. But we didn't act on it as soon as you'd think." Visions of them lovemaking in Brandon's bedroom, as lightning flashed about the room, sprung tears. "Oh. My. God. This is so inappropriate." She bunched up her napkin and dabbed at her cheeks, her eyes. Dark mascara and eyeliner streaked the white paper. "Let me guess, I look like a raccoon."

Sonja was laughing too hard to reply. Poppy waited for her friend to calm down and wondered if pregnancy made every emotion heightened. She couldn't imagine feeling more vulnerable than she had these past weeks. Because the highs and lows of her emotions since she'd met Brandon were more than she thought she could handle. And she missed the rollercoaster ride.

"Oh, Poppy, you are so in love with this dude."

"We've only known one another for what, a month, barely?"

"Come off it. You know the time doesn't matter. How did you feel with him, from the start?"

"Safe. Right. As if we'd met again after a long time apart."

"Bingo."

\* \* \* \*

Poppy placed the half-and-half for her coffee into the small refrigerator she and Bianca had carried up the narrow staircase to the upper-level apartment above the boutique. It wasn't much smaller than her apartment in New York, and cost a hell of a lot less. It was her temporary home until she made enough to move out to a regular house.

*Call Brandon.* The thought had become a mantra since the coffee with Sonja.

She wanted to, but couldn't. Couldn't put herself at the mercy of a man again.

Poppy wanted a full-fledged life partner. Someone who wanted to fly next to her, not push her, not drag her, but stay afloat together. She wanted Brandon. He was the man who walked side by side with her. Supported her and allowed her to support him. She threw back a large gulp of coffee, stinging her throat. What a mess she'd made of things. She was going to have to convince Brandon that she wanted him, bankrupt and all.

The chime of the boutique front door echoed over the wireless speaker on her tiny table. She and Bianca had figured out a way to allow her to keep track of the shop while upstairs. Since Bianca had stepped out for lunch as Poppy came back from her grocery run, Poppy needed to get downstairs ASAP.

The sound of the desk bell dinging reached her as she reached the last few steps, and she mentally prepared herself to be bright and sunny for her first client of the day.

"Hey! What can I do for you?" She spoke as she cleared the threshold and walked into the main retail space. Her resolve to appear professional and give out only the most positive, I-can-help-you-get-your-life-back vibes shattered when she recognized the man standing next to the pastel display of spring scarves. It wasn't fair that he looked so vibrant, his tan in deep contrast to the fair colors, the breadth of his frame maddeningly masculine amidst the feminine decor. His smile was relaxed and her gaze could have, should have stopped on his lips. Lips that her skin started to beg for in tiny tremors as she stared at him. But her gaze was inevitably drawn to his, and the second she looked into his blue eyes all the logic for not calling him blew apart.

"Welcome back, Yankee girl."

\* \* \* \*

Poppy froze in place except for the ends of her wavy locks that caught the air from the ceiling fan. They danced around her face, making her appear particularly angelic. Brandon only had to drop his gaze to the swell of her perfect breasts under the pale pink top she wore to remind himself his angel could do more than fly. God, he'd missed her.

"Brandon."

"That's me, Poppy. Is this a good time?"

"Of course." Her gaze flicked to the door and he soaked up her shock as she realized the "open" sign had been turned around to "closed." He'd locked the door, too. Bianca had been most helpful when he'd talked to her about his idea yesterday.

"Um, I have to keep the shop open, Brandon."

He walked around the counter, noting that she held her ground. His stubborn, smart, irreplaceable Poppy. "Turns out Bianca had a planned closure this morning for inventory purposes." He presented her with the bouquet of winter poppies he'd had behind his back. "I haven't been able to get you out of my mind, Yankee girl."

\* \* \* \*

Poppy stared at the fuchsia, persimmon, and rouge poppies Brandon held out to her. "How on earth did you find these?" A thrill of delight skipped across her heart.

"You're back in NOLA, Poppy. Anything is possible."

She blinked back tears and brushed one off her cheek. "I've been meaning to tell you I'm back in town."

"Uh huh." His hands moved to her shoulders after she accepted the bouquet. "I've never pegged you as gun-shy, Poppy."

"I'm not. But it had to be right. I couldn't just show up at your door and ask if the guest room's still available, could I?"

"Sure you could. But it's not." He kissed her forehead. "Available."

Her knees quivered and her belly swooped in time to the reverberation his touch set off. "It's not?"

"Nope. Turns out, only the master bedroom is open for new residents." He traced her cheek with his finger, his eyes half-lidded.

"What's the asking rent?"

"Depends." He gently removed the flowers from her grasp and placed them on the counter. His fingers accidentally hit the service bell and Poppy realized they were in full view of the storefront window.

"Brandon, anyone can see us."

"Take me up to your place, Poppy."

She led the way to the stairs that were just off her studio office, out of sight of any errant sightseers.

"Poppy, hang on." Brandon turned her around to face him.

"Yes?" She could barely think straight, her body hummed so loudly with want for him. With need.

With love.

"Before we go up there, you need to know something. This isn't picking up where we left off. It's the start of something new for both of us. I can't guarantee it's all going to be Southern charm, but it will be us. We are the most important thing to me. Not my boatbuilding, not your styling. Us. I love you, Poppy." He'd beaten her to it, and she loved him even more for it. It was never going to be completely "even" with Brandon. It was going to be hot and cold, rough and serene, sexy and comforting. It was going to be everything. Poppy didn't try to keep her tears back. Trusting someone meant you could show it all to them.

"I love you, Brandon. And you need to know that I'm not agreeing to anything just because we're both in the same place. And while you're the most important person in my life, and always will be, I came back for me, first. I'm at home here, more than I've ever been anywhere else."

"So you agree we could work on making it our home, together?"

Her breath hitched, preventing her from answering immediately. Instead she threw her arms around his neck, hanging on for sheer love. "Oh, Brandon, yes, yes, yes!"

He pushed her away only enough to see her face. She loved how his eyes soaked her in as if she were the only woman in the world that mattered. "I play for keeps, Poppy." His gruff declaration made her smile.

"Good thing, as you've got me for a good long while." She kissed him with all the love that poured out of her heart for him. She'd come home. To New Orleans, to herself. To Brandon.

He kissed her back and within seconds the kiss went from a declaration of their commitment to the hot need they were familiar with.

Brandon never did see Poppy's loft apartment until later that morning.

*The End*

Begging for more Bayou Bachelors?

Keep an eye out for more from Geri Krotow

Coming Soon from

Lyrical Caress!

# About the Author

**Geri Krotow** is the award-winning author of more than thirteen contemporary and romantic suspense novels (with a couple of WWII subplots thrown in!). While still unpublished, Geri received the Daphne du Maurier Award for Romantic Suspense in Category Romance Fiction. Her 2007 Harlequin Everlasting debut *A Rendezvous to Remember,* earned several awards, including the Yellow Rose of Texas Award for Excellence.

Prior to writing, Geri served for nine years as a Naval Intelligence Officer. Geri served as the Aviation/Anti-Submarine Warfare Intelligence officer for a P-3C squadron during which time she deployed to South America, Europe, and Greenland. She was the first female Intel officer on the East Coast to earn Naval Aviation Observer Wings. Geri also did a tour in the war on drugs, working with several different government and law enforcement agencies. Geri is grateful to be settled in south central Pennsylvania with her husband.

Printed in the United States
by Baker & Taylor Publisher Services